# SWORD-DANCE, DEATH-DANCE!

The circle was drawn in the sand. The swords lay in the center. A two-handed Southron sword, with gold hilt and blued-steel blade. A two-handed Northern sword: silver-hilted, rune-bladed, singing its siren song of ice and death.

A woman, standing near the circle. Waiting. White hair shining. Blue eyes calm. Gilded limbs relaxed. Waiting.

A man: sun-bronzed, dark-haired, green-eyed. Tall. Powerfully built. Except that even as he stood there, waiting to start the dance, his body changed. Lost weight. Substance. Strength. It melted off him until he was a skeleton with a bit of brown hide stretched over the bones.

He put a hand out toward the woman. The woman who sang his deathsong. . . .

# Jennifer Roberson
## in DAW editions:

*forthcoming from DAW Books

# Sword-Dancer

## Jennifer Roberson

# DAW BOOKS, INC.

**DONALD A. WOLLHEIM, FOUNDER**

375 Hudson Street, New York, NY 10014

**ELIZABETH R. WOLLHEIM
SHEILA E. GILBERT
PUBLISHERS**

DAW Book Collectors No. 684.

First Printing, September 1986

9   10   11   12   13   14   15   16   17

DAW TRADEMARK REGISTERED
U.S. PAT. OFF. AND FOREIGN COUNTRIES
—MARCA REGISTRADA,
HECHO EN U.S.A.

PRINTED IN THE U.S.A.

*For Russ Galen of the
Scott Meredith Literary Agency,
because too often authors forget
to acknowledge their agents.*

Harquahal

Cantina .

.Cistern

.Oasis

Hanjii

.Sun Sacrifice

Salzet

.Elamain's caravan

.Sasqaat

the PUNYA

.Rusali

.Julah    .Oasis

.Vashni

Aladar's mine.

# One

In my line of work, I've seen all kinds of women. Some beautiful. Some ugly. Some just plain in between. And— being neither senile nor a man with aspirations to sainthood— whenever the opportunity presented itself (with or without my encouragement), I bedded the beautiful ones (although sometimes they bedded *me*), passed on the ugly ones altogether (not being a greedy man), but allowed myself discourse with the in-betweeners on a fairly regular basis, not being one to look the other way when such things as discourse and other entertainments are freely offered. So the in-betweeners made out all right, too.

But when *she* walked into the hot, dusty cantina and slipped the hood of her white burnous, I knew nothing I'd ever seen could touch her. Certainly Ruth and Numa couldn't, though they were the best the cantina had to offer. I was so impressed with the new girl I tried to swallow my aqivi the wrong way and wound up choking so badly Ruth got off my left knee and Numa slid off my right. Ruth commenced pounding on my back awhile and Numa—well-meaning as ever—poured more aqivi and tried to tip it down a throat already afire from the stuff.

By the time I managed to extricate myself from both of them (no mean feat), the vision in the white burnous had looked away from me and was searching through the rest of the cantina with eyes as blue as Northern lakes.

Now it so happens I haven't ever *seen* any Northern lakes, being a Southroner myself, but I knew perfectly well those two pools she used for eyes matched the tales I'd heard of the natural wonders of the North.

The slipping of the hood bared a headful of thick, long hair yellow as the sun and a face pale as snow. Now I haven't seen snow either, being as the South has the monopoly on sand, but it was the only way to describe the complexion of a woman who was so obviously not a native Southroner. I am, and *my* skin is burned dark as a copper piece. Oh, I suppose once upon a time I might have been lighter—must've been, actually, judging by the paler portions of my anatomy not exposed to daylight—but my work keeps me outdoors in the sun and the heat and the sandstorms, so somewhere along the way my skin got dark and tough and—in all the necessary places—callused.

Oddly enough, the stuffiness of the cantina faded. It almost seemed cooler, more comfortable. But then it might have had more to do with shock than anything else. Gods of valhail, gods of hoolies, but what a breath of fresh air the woman was!

What she was *doing* in this little dragtail cantina I have no idea, but I didn't question the benevolent, generous fate that brought her within range. I simply blessed it and decided then and there that no matter who it was she was looking for, I'd take his place.

I watched in appreciation (sighing just a bit) as she turned to look over the room. So did every other male in the place. It isn't often you get to look on beauty so fresh and unspoiled, not when you're stuck in a dragtail town like . . . *Hoolies*, I couldn't even remember its name.

Ruth and Numa watched her too, but their appreciation was tempered by another emotion entirely—called jealousy.

Numa tapped me on one side of the face, trying to get my attention. At first I shook her off, still watching the blonde, but when Numa started to dig in her nails, I gave her my second-best sandtiger glare. It usually works and

8

saves me the trouble of using my *best* sandtiger glare, which I save for special (generally deadly) occasions. I learned very early in my career that my green eyes—the same color as those in a sandtiger's head—often intimidate those of a weaker constitution. No man scoffs at a weapon so close to hand; *I* certainly don't. And so I refined the technique until I had it perfected, and I usually got a kick out of the reactions to it.

Numa whimpered a little; Ruth smiled. Basically, the two girls are the best of enemies. Being the only women in the cantina, quite often they fight over new blood—dusty and dirty and stinking of the Punja, more often than not, but still *new*. That was unique enough in the stuffy adobe cantina whose walls had once boasted murals of crimson, carnelian, and lime. The colors—like the girls—had faded after years of abuse and nightly coatings of spewed or spilled wine, ale, aqivi . . . and all the other poisons.

*My* blood was the newest in town (newly bathed, too), but rather than sentence them to a catfight I'd taken on both of them. They seemed content enough with sharing me, and this way I kept peace in a very tiny cantina. A man does not make enemies of any woman when he is stuck in a boring, suffocating town that has nothing to offer except two cantina girls who nightly (and daily) sell their virtue. Hoolies, there isn't anything *else* to do. For them *or* me.

Having put Numa in her place (and wondering if I could still keep the peace between the two of them), I became aware of the presence newly arrived at my table. I glanced up and found those two blue eyes fixed on me in a direct, attentive stare that convinced me instantly I should change the errors of my ways, whatever they might be. I'd even make some up, just so I could change them. (Hoolies, what man *wouldn't* with *her* looking at him?)

Even as she halted at my table, some of the men in the cantina murmured suggestions (hardly questions) as to the status of her virtue. I wasn't much surprised, since she lacked a modesty veil and the sweet-faced reticence of most of the Southron women (unless, of course, they were cantina girls, like Ruth and Numa, or free-wives, who married outlanders and gave up Southron customs.)

This one didn't strike me as a cantina girl. She didn't strike me as a free-wife either, being a bit too independent even for one of them. She didn't strike me as much of anything except a beautiful woman. But she sure seemed bent on something, and that something was more than a simple assignation.

"Sandtiger?" Her voice was husky, low-pitched; the accent was definitely Northern. (And oh-so-cool in the stuffy warmth of the cantina.) "Are you Tiger?"

Hoolies, she *was* looking for me!

After losing a moment to inward astonishment and wonder, I bared my teeth at her in a friendly, lazy smile. It wouldn't do to show her how much she impressed me, not when it was my place to impress *her*. "At your service, bascha."

A faint line appeared between winged blond brows and I realized she didn't understand the compliment. In Southron lingo, the word means *lovely*.

But the line smoothed out as she looked at Ruth and Numa, and I saw a slight glint of humor enter those glacial eyes. I perceived the faintest of twitches at the left corner of her mouth. "I have business, if you please."

I pleased. I accommodated her business immediately by tipping both girls off my knees (giving them pats of mutual and measured fondness on firm, round rumps), and promised substantial tips if they lost themselves for a while. They glared at me in return, then glared at her. But they left.

I kicked a stool from under the table and toed it in the blonde's general direction. She looked at it without comment a long moment, then sat down. The burnous gaped open at her throat and I stared at it, longing for it to fall open entirely. If the rest of her matched her face and hair, it was well worth alienating *all* the Ruths and Numas in the world.

"Business." The tone was slightly clipped, as if to forestall any familiarity in our discussion.

"Aqivi?" I poured myself a cup. A shake of her head stirred the hair like a silken curtain, and my mouth went dry. "Do you mind if *I* drink?"

"Why not?" She shrugged a little, rippling white silk. "You have already begun."

Her face and voice were perfectly bland, but the glint in her eyes remained. The temperature took a decidedly downward dip. I considered not drinking at all, then decided it was stupid to play games and swallowed a hefty dose of aqivi. This one went down a lot smoother than the last one.

Over the rim of my cup, I looked at her. Not much more than twenty, I thought; younger than I'd judged on first sighting. Too young for the South; the desert would suck the fluids from her soft, pale body and leave behind a dried out, powdery husk.

But gods, she was lovely. There wasn't much of softness in her. Just the hint of a proud, firm body beneath the white burnous and a proud, firm jaw beneath the Northern skin. And eyes. Blue eyes, fixed on me levelly; waiting quietly, without seductiveness or innuendo.

*Business indeed*, but then there are degrees in all business confrontations.

Instinctively, I straightened on my stool. Past dealings with women had made me aware how easily impressed they are by my big shoulders and broad chest. (And my smile, but I'm sparing with that at first. It helps build up the mystique).

Unfortunately, this one didn't appear to be impressed much one way or another, mystique or no. She just looked at me squarely, without coyness or coquetry. "I was told you know Osmoon the Trader," she said in her husky Northern voice.

"Old Moon?" I didn't bother to hide my surprise,

wondering what this beauty wanted with an old relic like him. "What do you want with an old relic like him?"

Her cool eyes were hooded. "Business."

She had all the looks, but she wasn't great shakes at conversation. I shifted on my stool and let my own burnous fall open at the throat, intending the string of claws I wear around my neck to remind her I was a man of some consequence. (I don't know what *kind* of consequence, exactly, but at least I had some.)

"Moon doesn't talk to strangers." I suggested. "He only talks to his friends."

"I've heard *you* are his friend."

After a moment, I nodded consideringly. "Moon and I go back a ways."

For only an instant she smiled. "And are you a slaver, too?"

I was glad I'd already swallowed the aqivi. If this lady knew Moon was involved in the slave trade, she knew a lot more than most Northerners.

I looked at her more sharply, though I didn't give away my attentiveness. She waited. Calmly, collectedly, as if she had done this many times, and all the while her youth and sex disclaimed the possibility.

I shivered. Suddenly, all the smoky interior candlelight and exterior sunlight didn't seem quite enough to ward off an uncommon frosty chill. Almost as if the Northern girl had brought the North wind with her.

But of course, *that* wasn't possible. There may be magic in the world, but what's there is made for simpletons and fools who need a crutch.

I scowled a little. "I'm a sword-dancer. I deal in wars, rescues, escort duty, skirmishes, a little healthy hired revenge now and then . . . anything that concerns making a living with a sword." I tapped the gold hilt of Singlestroke, poking up behind my left shoulder in easy reach. "I'm a sword-dancer. Not a slaver."

"But you know Osmoon." Bland, guileless eyes, eloquently innocent.

"A lot of people know Osmoon," I pointed out. "*You* know Osmoon."

"I know *of* him." Delicate distinction. "But I would like to meet him."

I appraised her openly, letting her see clearly what I did. It brought a rosy flush to her fair face and her eyes glittered angrily. But before she could open her mouth to protest, I leaned across the table. "You'll get worse than *that* if you go near Old Moon. He'd give his gold teeth for a bascha like you, and you'd never see the light of day again. You'd be sold off to some tanzeer's harem so fast you couldn't even wish him to hoolies."

She stared at me. I thought maybe I'd shocked her with my bluntness. I meant to. But I saw no comprehension in her eyes. "Tanzeer?" she asked blankly. "Hoolies?"

So much for scaring her off with the facts of Southron life. I sighed. "A Northerner might say prince instead of tanzeer. I have no idea what the translation is for hoolies. It's the place the priests say most of us are bound for, once we leave this life. Mothers like to threaten their children with it when they misbehave." Mine hadn't, because as far as I know she died right after dropping me into some hole in the desert.

Or simply walked away.

"Oh." She considered it. "Is there no way I could see the trader *neutrally*?"

The white burnous opened a little wider. I was lost. Prevarication fell out of my mind entirely. "No." I didn't bother to explain that if Moon got his hands on her, I'd do my best to buy her for myself.

I have gold," she suggested.

All that and money too. A genuine windfall. Benignly, I nodded. "And if you go flashing any of it out here in the desert, my naive little Northern bascha, you'll be robbed *and* kidnapped.'' I swallowed down more aqivi, keeping my tone idle. ''What do you want to see Moon for?''

Her face closed up at once. ''Business; I have said.''

I scowled and cursed into my cup and saw she didn't understand that either. Just as well. Sometimes I get surly and my language isn't the best. Not much opportunity to learn refinement in my line of work. ''Look bascha—I'm willing to take you to Moon and make sure he doesn't fiddle with the goods, but you'll have to tell me what you want to see him for. I don't work in the dark.''

One fingernail tapped against the scarred wood of the liquor-stained table. The nail was filed short, as if it—and the others—weren't meant to be a facet of feminine vanity. No. Not in this woman. ''I have no wish to hire a sword-dancer,'' she said coolly. ''I just want you to tell me where I can find Osmoon the Trader.''

I glared at her in exasperation. ''I just *told* you what will happen if you see him alone.''

The nail tapped again. There was the faintest trace of a smile, as if she knew something I didn't. ''I'll take the chance.''

What the hoolies, if that's the way she wanted it. I told her where to find him, and how, and what she should say to him when she did.

She stared at me, blonde brows running together as she frowned. ''I should tell him 'the Sandtiger plays for keeps'?''

''That's it.'' I smiled and lifted my cup.

She nodded after a moment, slowly, but her eyes narrowed in consideration. ''Why?''

''Suspicious?'' I smiled my lazy smile. ''Old Moon owes me one. That's all.''

She stared at me a moment longer, studying me. Then she rose. Her hands, pressed against the table, were long-fingered and slender, but lacked delicacy. Sinews moved beneath the fair skin. Strong hands. Strong fingers. For a woman, very strong.

''I'll tell him,'' she agreed.

She turned and walked away, heading for the curtained doorway of the cantina. My mouth watered as I stared at all that yellow hair spilling down the folds of the white burnous.

*Hoolies*, what a woman!

But she was gone, along with the illusion of coolness, and fantasizing about a woman never does much good besides stirring up desires that can't always be gratified (at least, not right away), so I ordered another jug of aqivi, called for Ruth and Numa to come back, and passed the evening in convivial discourse with two desert girls who were not part of any man's fantasy, perhaps, but were warm, willing, and generous nonetheless.

That'll do nicely, thank you.

# Two

Osmoon the Trader was not happy to see me. He glared at me from his little black pig-eyes and didn't even offer me a drink, which told me precisely how angry he was. I waved away the smoke of sandalwood incense drifting between us (wishing he'd widen the vent in the poled top of his saffron-colored hyort), and outwaited him.

Breath hissed between his gold teeth. "You send me a bascha like that, Tiger, and then say to keep her for *you*? Why did you bother to send her to me in the first place if you wanted her for yourself?"

I smiled at him placatingly. It doesn't do to rile past and potential allies, even if you are the Sandtiger. "This one requires special handling."

He swore to the god of slavers; an improbable series of names for a deity I'd never had the necessity of calling on, myself. Frankly, I think Old Moon made it up. "Special handling!" he spat out. "Special *taming*, you mean. Do you know what she did?"

Since there was no way I could know, short of having him tell me, I waited again. And he told me.

"She nearly sliced off what remains of the manhood of my best eunuch!" Moon's affronted stare invited abject apologies; I merely continued waiting, promising nothing. "The poor thing ran screaming out of the hyort and I

16

couldn't pry him from the neck of his boy-lover until I promised to beat the girl.''

That deserved a response. I glared at him. "You *beat* her?''

Moon stared at me in some alarm and smiled weakly, showing the wealth of gold shining in his mouth. I realized my hand had crept to the knife at my belt. I decided to leave it there, if only for effect.

"I didn't beat her.'' Moon eyed my knife. He knows how deadly I can be with it, and how fast, even though it isn't my best weapon. That sort of reputation comes in handy. "I couldn't—I mean, she's a Northerner. You know what those women are. Those—those *Northern women*.''

I ignored the latter part of the explanation. "What *did* you do to her?'' I looked at him sharply. "You *do* still have her—''

"Yes!'' His teeth glinted. "Ai, Tiger, do you think I am a forgetful man, to lose such things?'' Offended again, he scowled. "Yes, I have her. I had to tie her up like a sacrificial goat, but I have her. You may take her off my hands, Tiger. The sooner the better.''

I was mildly concerned by his willingness to lose so valuable a commodity. "Is she hurt? Is that why you don't want her?'' I glared at him. "I know you, Moon. You'd try a doublecross if the stakes were high enough. Even on *me*.'' I glared harder. "What have you done to her?''

He waved be-ringed hands in denial. "Nothing! Nothing! Ai, Tiger, the woman is unblemished.'' The hands stopped waving and the voice altered. "Wellll . . . *almost* unblemished. I had to knock her on the head. It was the only way I could keep her from slicing *my* manhood off—or casting some spell at me.''

"Who was stupid enough to let her get her hands on a knife?'' I was unimpressed by Moon's avowals of her witchcraft *or* the picture of the slaver losing the portion of his anatomy he so willingly ordered removed from his property, to improve temperament and price. "And anyway, a

**17**

knife in the hands of a woman shouldn't pose much of a threat to Osmoon the Trader.''

"Knife!" he cried, enraged. "*Knife*? The woman had a sword as long as yours!"

That stopped me cold. "*Sword*?"

"Sword." Moon glared back at me. "It's very sharp, Tiger, and it's bewitched . . . and she knows how to use it."

I sighed. "Where is it?"

Moon grumbled to himself and got up, shuffling across layered rugs to a wooden chest bound with brass. He lives well but not ostentatiously, not wishing to call excess attention to himself. The local tanzeers know all about his business, and because they get a healthy cut of the profits, they don't bother him much. But then they don't know just how healthy the business is. If they knew, undoubtedly they'd all demand a bigger cut. Possibly even his head.

Moon lifted back the lid of his chest and stood over it, hands on hips. He stared down into the contents, but didn't reach down to pick anything out. He just stared, and then I saw how his hands rubbed themselves on the the fabric of his burnous, brown palms against heavy yellow silk, until I got impatient and told him to hurry it up.

He turned to face me. "It's—it's in here."

I waited.

He gestured. "Here. Do you want it?"

"I said I did."

One plump hand waved fingers at the chest. "Well— here it is. You can come get it."

"*Moon* . . . hoolies, man, will you bring me the woman's sword? What's so hard about that?"

He was decidedly unhappy. But after a moment he muttered a prayer to some other unpronounceable god and plunged his hands into the chest.

He came up with a scabbarded sword. Quickly he turned and rushed back across the hyort, then dumped the sheathed sword down in front of me as if relieved to let go of it. I stared up at him in surprise. And again, brown palms rubbed against yellow silk.

"There," he said breathlessly, "*there*."

I frowned. Moon is a sharp, shrewd man, born of the South and all of its ways. His "trading" network reaches into all portions of the Punja, and I'd never known him to exhibit anything akin to fear. . . unless, of course, circumstances warranted a performance including the emotion. But this was no act. This was insecurity and apprehension and nervousness, all tied up into one big ball of blatant fear.

"What's your problem?" I inquired mildly.

Moon opened his mouth, closed it, and opened it again. "She's a *Northerner*," he muttered. "So's *that* thing."

He pointed to the scabbarded sword, and at last I understood. "Ah. You think the sword's been bewitched. Northern witch, Northern sorcery." I nodded benignly. "Moon—*how* many times have I told you magic is something used by tricksters who want to con other people? Half the time I don't think there *is* any magic—but what there is, is little more than a game for gullible fools."

His clenched jaw challenged me. On this subject, Moon was never an ally.

"Trickery," I told him. "Nonsense. Mostly illusion, Moon. And those things you've heard about Northern sorcery and witches are just a bunch of tales made up by Southron mothers to tell their children at bedtime. Do you *really* think this woman is a witch?"

He was patently convinced she was. "Call me a fool, Tiger. But I say *you* are one for being so blind to the truth." One hand stabbed out to indicate the sword he'd dumped in my lap. "Look at *that*, Tiger. Touch *it*, Tiger. Look at those runes and shapes, and *tell* me it isn't the weapon of a witch."

I scowled at him, but for once he was neither intimidated or impressed. He just went back to his carpet on the other side of the incense brazier and settled his rump upon it, lower lip pushed out in indignation. Moon was offended: I doubted him. Only an apology would restore his good will. (Except I don't see much sense in offering an apology for something that *makes* no sense.)

I touched the sheath, running appreciative fingers over the hard leather. Plain, unadorned leather, similar to my own; a harness, not a swordbelt, which surprised me a little. But then, hearing Moon name this sword the girl's weapon surprised me even more.

The hilt was silver, chased by skilled hands into twisted knotwork and bizarre, fluid shapes. Staring at those shapes, I tried to make them out; tried to make sense of the design. But it all melted together into a single twisted line that tangled the eyes and turned them inward upon themselves.

I blinked, squinting a little, and put my hand on the hilt to slide the blade free of the sheath—

—and felt the cold, burning tingle run across my palms to settle into my wrists.

I let go of the hilt at once.

Moon's grunt, eloquent in its simplicity, was one of smug satisfaction.

I scowled at him, then at the sword. And this time when I put my hand on the hilt, I did it quickly, gritting my teeth. I jerked the blade from the sheath.

My right hand, curled around the silver hilt, spasmed. Almost convulsively, it closed more tightly on the hilt. I thought for a moment my flesh had fused itself to the metal, was made one with the twisting shapes, but almost immediately my skin leaped back. As my fingers unlocked and jerked away from the hilt, I felt the old, cold breath of death put a finger on my soul.

Tap. Tap. Nail against soul. *Tiger, are you there?*

Hoolies, *yes*! I was there. And intended to remain there, alive and well, regardless of that touch; that imperious, questioning tone.

But almost at once I let go of the hilt altogether, and the sword—now free—fell across my lap.

*Cold, cold blade, searing the flesh of my thighs.*

I pushed it out of my lap to the rug at once. I wanted to scramble away from it entirely, leaping up to put even more room between the sword and my flesh—

And then I thought about how stupid it would be—*am I not a sword-dancer, who deals with death every time I enter the circle?*—and didn't. I just sat there, defying the unexpected response of my own body and glaring down at the sword. I felt the coldness of its flesh as if it still touched mine. Ignored it, when I could.

A Northern sword. And the North is a place of snow and ice.

The first shock had worn off. My skin, acclimated to the nearness of the alien metal, no longer shrank upon my bones. I took a deep breath to settle the galloping in my guts, then took a closer look at the sword. But I didn't touch it.

The blade was a pale, pearly salmon-pink with a tinge of blued steel—except it didn't look much like steel. Iridescent runes spilled down from the gnarled crosspiece. Runes I couldn't read.

I resorted to my profession in order to restore my equilibrium. I jerked a dark brown hair from my head and dragged it across the edge. The hair separated without a snag. The edge of the odd-colored blade was at least as sharp as Singlestroke's plain blued-steel, which didn't please me much.

I gave myself no time for considereation. Gritting my teeth, I plucked the sword off the rug and slid it back into its scabbard with numb, tingling hands—and felt the coldness melt away.

For a moment, I just stared at the sword. Sheathed, it was a sword. Just—a sword.

After a moment. I looked at Moon. "How good is she?"

The question surprised him a little; it surprised me a lot. Her skill might have impressed Moon (who is more accustomed to women throwing themselves at his chubby feet and begging for release, rather than trying to slice into his fat flesh), but I know better than to think of a sword in a woman's hands. Women don't use swords in the South; as far as I know, they don't use them in the North, either. The sword is a man's weapon.

Moon scowled at me sourly. "Good enough to give *you* a second thought. She unleashed that thing in here and it was all I could do to get a rope on her."

"How *did* you catch her, then?" I asked suspiciously.

He picked briefly at gold teeth with a red-lacquered fingernail and shrugged. "I hit her on the head." Sighed as I scowled at him. "I waited until she was busy trying to eviscerate the eunuch. But even *then*, she nearly stuck me through the belly." One spread hand guarded a portion of the soft belly swathed in silk. "I was lucky she didn't kill me."

I grunted absently and rose, holding the Northern sword by its plain leather scabbard. "Which hyort is she in?"

"The red one," he said immediately. My, but he *did* want to get rid of her, which suited me just fine. "And you ought to thank me for keeping her, Tiger. Someone else came looking for her."

I stopped short of the doorflap. "Someone *else*?"

He picked at his teeth again. "A man. He didn't give his name. Tall, dark-haired—very much like you. Sounded like a Northerner, but he spoke good Desert." Moon shrugged. "He said he was hunting a Northern girl . . . one who wore a sword."

I frowned. "You didn't give her away—?"

Offended again, Moon drew himself up. "You sent her with your words, and I honored those words."

"Sorry." Absently, I scowled at the slaver. "He went on?"

"He spent a night and rode on. He never saw the girl."

I grunted. Then I went out of the hyort.

Moon was right: he'd trussed her up like a sacrificial

goat, wrists tied to ankles so that she bowed in half, but at least he'd made certain her back bent the proper way. He doesn't, always.

She was conscious. I didn't exactly approve of Moon's methods (or his business, when it came down to it), but at least he still had her. He might have given her over to whoever it was who was hunting her.

"The Sandtiger plays for keeps," I said lightly, and she twisted her head so she could look at me.

All her glorious hair was spread about her shoulders and the blue rug on which she lay. Osmoon had stripped the white burnous from her (wanting to see what he wouldn't get, I suppose) but hadn't removed the thigh-length, belted leather tunic she wore under it. It left her arms and most of her legs bare, and I saw that every inch of her was smooth and tautly muscled. Sinews slid and twisted beneath that pale skin as she shifted on the rug, and I realized the sword probably *did* belong to her after all, improbable as it seemed. She had the body and the hands for it.

"Is it because of *you* I'm being held like this?" she demanded.

Sunlight burned its way through the crimson fabric of the hyort. It bathed her in an eerie carnelian glow and purpled the blue rug into the color of darkest wine; the color of ancient blood.

"It's because of me you're being held like this," I agreed, "because otherwise Moon would've sold you off by now." I bent down, sliding my knife free, and sliced her bonds. She winced as stiffened muscles protested, so I set down her sword and massaged the long, firm calves and shoulders subtly corded with toughened muscle.

"You have my sword!" In her surprise, she ignored my hands altogether.

I thought about allowing those hands to drift a little southward of her shoulders, then decided against it. She might be stiff after a few days of captivity, but if she had the reflexes I thought she did, I'd be asking for trouble. No sense pushing my luck so soon.

"If it *is* your sword," I said.

"It's mine." She pushed my hands away and rose, stifling a groan. The leather tunic hit her mid-thigh and I saw the odd runic glyphs stitching a border around the hem and neck in blue thread that matched her eyes. "Did you unsheathe it?" she demanded, and there was something in her tone that gave me pause.

"No." I said, after a moment of heavy silence.

Visibly, she relaxed. Her hand caressed the odd silver hilt without showing any indication she felt the same icy numbness I'd experienced. She almost touched it as a lover welcoming back a long-missed sweetheart.

"Who are you?" I asked suddenly, assailed by a rather odd sensation. Runes on the sword blade, runes on the tunic. Those twisted, dizzying shapes worked into the hilt. The sensation of death when I touched it. What if she were some sort of familiar sent by the gods to determine if my time had come, and whether I was worthy of valhail or hoolies for a place of eternal rest—or torment?

And then I felt disgustingly ludicrous, which was just as well, because I'd never thought much about my end before. Sword-dancers simply fight until someone kills them; we don't spend our time worrying over trivial details like our ultimate destination. *I* certainly don't.

She wore sandals like mine, cross-gartered to her knees. The laces were gold-colored and only emphasized the length of her legs, which almost put her on a level with me. I stared at her in astonishment as she rose, for her head came to my chin, and very few *men* reach that high.

She frowned a little. "I thought Southroners were short."

"Most are. I'm not. But then—I'm not your average Southroner." Blandly, I smiled.

She raised pale brows. "And do *average* Southroners send women into a trap?"

"To keep you out of a greater one, I sent you into a

small one." I grinned. "It was a trick, I agree, and maybe a trifle uncomfortable, but it kept you out of the clutches of a lustful tanzeer, didn't it? When you told Moon 'the Sandtiger plays for keeps,' he knew enough to hang onto you until I got here, instead of selling you to the highest bidder. Since you were so insistent on seeing him without my personal assistance, I had to do something."

A momentary glint in her eyes. Appraisal. "Then it was for my—*protection*."

"In a backhanded sort of way."

She slanted a sharp, considering glance at me, then smiled a little. She got busy slipping her arms into the sword harness, buckling it and arranging it so the hilt reared over the top of her left shoulder, just as Singlestroke rode mine. Her movements were quick and lithe, and I didn't doubt for a moment she *could* nearly emasculate a eunuch who had very little left to lose anyway.

My palms tingled as I recalled the visceral response of my body to the touch of the Northern sword. "Why don't you tell me what business it is you have with Old Moon, and maybe I can help," I said abruptly, wanting to banish the sensation and recollection.

"You can't help." One hand tucked hair behind an ear as she settled the leather harness.

"Why not?"

"You just can't." She swung out of the hyort and marched across the sand to Moon's tent.

I caught up. But before I could stop her she had drawn the silver-hilted sword and sliced the doorflap clear off his hyort. Then she was inside, and as I jumped in behind her I saw her put the deadly tip of the shining blade into the hollow of Moon's brown throat.

"In my land I could kill you for what you did to me." But she said it coolly, without heat; an impartial observation, lacking passion, and yet somehow it made her threat a lot more real. "In my land, if I didn't kill you, I'd be named coward. Not *an-ishtoya*, or even a plain *ishtoya*.

But I'm a stranger here and without knowledge of your customs, so I'll let you live." A trickle of blood crept from beneath the tip pressing into Moon's flesh. "You are a foolish little man. It's hard to believe you had a part in disposing of my brother."

Poor old Moon. His pig-eyes popped and he sweated so much I was surprised the sword didn't slide from his neck. "Your brother?" he squeaked.

Cornsilk hair hung over her shoulders. "Five years ago my brother was stolen from across the Northern border. He was ten, slaver . . . *ten years old*." A hint of emotion crept into her tone. "But we know how much you prize our yellow hair and blue eyes and pale skin, slaver. In a land of dark-skinned, dark-haired men it could be no other way." The tip dug in a little deeper. "You stole my brother, slaver, and *I want him back*."

"*I* stole him!" Outraged, Moon gulped against the bite of the sword. "I don't deal in boys, bascha, I deal in women!"

"Liar." She was very calm. For a woman holding a sword against a man, very calm indeed. "I know what perversions there are in the South. I know how high a price a Northern boy goes for on the slaveblock. I've had five years to learn the trade, *trader*, so don't lie to me." Her sandalled foot stretched out to prod his abundant belly. "A yellow-haired, blue-eyed, pale-skinned boy, slaver. A lot like me."

Moon's eyes flicked to me quickly, begging silently. On the one hand, he wanted me to do something; on the other, he knew a movement on my part might trip her into plunging the blade into his throat. So I did the smart thing, and waited.

"Five years ago?" He sweated through his burnous, patching the yellow silk with ocher-brown. "Bascha, I know nothing. Five years is a long time. Northern children are indeed popular, and I see them all the time. How can I know if he was your brother?"

She said nothing aloud, but I saw her mouth move. It formed a word. And then, though the sword bit into Moon's throat no deeper, the bright blood turned raisin-black and glittered against his throat.

Moon exhaled in shock. His breath hissed in the air, and I saw it form a puff of cloudy frost. Instantly he answered. "There—was a boy. Perhaps it was five years ago, perhaps more. It was in the Punja, as I traveled through." A shrug. "I saw a small boy on the block in Julah, but I can't say if he was your brother. There are many Northern boys in Julah."

"Julah," she echoed. "Where is that?"

"South of here," I told her. "Dangerous country."

"Danger is irrelevant." She prodded Moon's belly once more. "Give me a name, slaver."

"Omar," he said miserably. "My brother."

"Slaver, too?"

Osmoon shut his eyes. "It's a family business."

She pulled the sword away and slid it home without feeling for the scabbard. That takes practice. Then she brushed by me without a word, leaving me to face the shaking, sweating, moaning Moon.

He put trembling fingers to the sword slit in his neck. "Cold," he said. "So—*cold*."

"So are a lot of women." I went after the Northern girl.

# Three

I caught up with her at the horses. She already had one saddled and packed with waterskins, a little dun-colored gelding tied not far from my own bay stud. The white burnous had disappeared somewhere in one of Moon's hyorts, so she was bare except for her suede tunic. It left a lot of pale skin exposed to the sunlight, and I knew she'd be bright red and in serious discomfort before nightfall.

She ignored me, although I knew she knew I was there. I leaned a shoulder against the rough bark of a palm tree and watched as she threw the tassled amber reins over the dun's head, looping one arm through as she tended the saddle. The silver hilt of her sword flashed in the sunlight and her hair burned yellow-white as it fell down her tunicked back.

My mouth got dry again. "You headed to Julah?"

She slanted me a glance as she tightened the buckles of the girth. "*You* heard the slaver."

I shrugged the shoulder that wasn't pressed against the tree. "Ever been there?"

"No." Girth snugged, she hooked fingers in the cropped, spiky mane and swung up easily, throwing a long leg over the shallow saddle covered with a coarse woven blanket. Vermilion, ocher and brown, bled into one another by the sun. As she hooked her feet into the leather-wrapped brass stirrups, the tunic rucked up against her thighs.

28

I swallowed, then managed a casual tone. "You might need some help getting to Julah."

Those blue eyes were guileless. "I might."

I waited. So did she. Inwardly, I grimaced; conversation wasn't her strong point. But then, conversation in a woman is not necessarily a virtue.

We stared at one another: she on a fidgety dun gelding layered with a coating of saffron dust and me on foot (layered with identical dust, since I'd come straight from the cantina), leaning nonchalantly against a palm tree. Dry, frazzled fronds offered little shade; I squinted up at the woman atop the horse. Waiting still.

She smiled. It was an intensely personal smile, but not particularly meant for me—as if she laughed inwardly. "Is that an offer, Sandtiger?"

I shrugged again. "You've got to cross the Punja to reach Julah. Ever been *there* before?"

She shook back her hair. "I've never been South at all before . . . but I got this far all right." The subsequent pause was significant. "By myself."

I grunted and scratched idly at the scars creasing my right cheek. "You got to that dragtail cantina all right. *I* got you *this* far."

The little dun pawed, raising dust that floated briefly in the warm air, then fell back to mingle once again with the sand. Her hands on the braided horsehair-and-cotton reins were eloquently competent; her wrists showed subtlety and strength as she controlled the horse easily. He wasn't placid with a rider on his back. But she hardly seemed to notice his bad behavior. "I said it before—I don't need to hire a sword-dancer."

"The Punja is my country," I pointed out pleasantly. "I've spent most of my life there. And if you don't know the wells or the oases, you'll never make it." I thrust out a hand to indicate the south. Heat waves shimmered. "See that?"

She looked. The miles and the desert stretched on forever. And we weren't even to the Punja yet.

I thought she might turn me down again. After all, she was a woman; sometimes their pride gets all tangled up with stupidity when they want to prove they're able to get along on their own.

She stared out at the desert. Even the skies were bleached at the horizon, offering only a rim of brassy blue merging with dusty gray-beige.

She shivered. She *shivered*, as if she were cold.

"Who made it this way?" she asked abruptly. "What mad god turned good land into useless desert?"

I shrugged. "There's a legend that says once the South was cool and green and fruitful. And then two sorcerers— brothers—went to war to decide who would lay claim to all the world." She turned her head to look down at me, and I saw the clear, direct gaze. "Supposedly they killed one another. But not before they halved the world perfectly: North and South, and both about as different as man and woman." I smiled in a beguiling fashion. "Wouldn't you agree?"

She settled herself more comfortably in the saddle. "I don't need you, sword-dancer. I don't need *you*—I don't need your sword."

I knew, looking at her, she was not referring to Singlestroke. A woman alone in the world, beautiful or not, learns quickly what most men want. I was no different. But I hadn't expected such forthrightness from her.

I shrugged again. "Just trying to lend a hand, bascha." But I'd lend a sword—*both* swords—if she gave me half a chance.

I saw the twitch at the corner of her mouth. "Are you broke? Is that why a sword-dancer of your reputation would offer his services as a *guide*?"

The assumption stung my pride. I scowled. "I visit Julah at least once a year. Time I went again."

"How much do you want?"

My eyes drifted the length of a well-shaped leg. So pale; too pale. I opened my mouth to answer, but she forestalled what I was more than prepared to name as my price by saying, distinctly, "In *gold*."

I laughed at her, buoyed by her awareness of her value to me as a woman. It makes the game a little more enjoyable. "Why don't we decide that when we get to Julah?" I suggested. "I always set a fair price based on the degree of difficulty and danger. If I save your life more than once, the price goes up accordingly."

I didn't mention I knew a man was hunting her. If she knew him and *wanted* to be found, she'd say so. Her behavior said she didn't. And if that was so, the price just might go up sooner than she thought.

Her mouth twisted but I saw the glint in her eyes. "Do you conduct *all* your business this way?"

"Depends." I went over to my own horse and dug through my leather pouches. Finally I tossed a bright scarlet burnous at her. "Here. Wear it, or you'll be fried by noon."

The burnous is a little gaudy. I hate to wear it, but every now and then it comes in handy. Like when one of the local tanzeers desires my company at a meal to discuss business. A few gold tassels depended here and there from sleeves and hood. I'd cut a slit in the left shoulder seam so Singlestroke's hilt poked through unimpeded; ease of unsheathing is exceedingly important when you're in a business like mine.

She held up the burnous. "A little too subtle for you." She dragged it on over her head, arranged the folds so her own sword hilt was freed, and shoved the hood back. It was much too big for her, falling into shadowed ripples and folds that only hinted at her shape, but she wore it better than I do. "How soon can we reach Julah?"

I untied the stud, patted his left shoulder once warningly, then jumped up into my blanketed saddle. "Depends. We might make it in three weeks . . . might take us three months.''

"Three months!''

"There's the Punja to cross,'' I shook the bleached tassels of my vermilion reins into place. Out here, nothing retains its original color for long. Eventually, brown swallows everything. In all its shades and variations.

She frowned a little. ''Then let's not waste any more time.''

I watched as she wheeled the little dun gelding around and headed south. At least she knew her directions.

The burnous rippled in her wind like a crimson banner of a desert tanzeer. The hilt of her Northern sword was a silver beacon, flashing in the sunlight. And all that hair, so soft and silky yellow . . . well, she'd be easy to keep track of. I clucked to my stud and rode after her.

We rode neck and neck for a while at a reasonable pace. My bay stud wasn't too thrilled to match gaits with the little dun gelding, preferring a faster, more dramatic gait (often enough, that's a full gallop spiced with intermittent attempts to remove me from his back), but after a brief "discussion," we decided on a compromise. I'd do the directing and he'd do the walking.

Until he saw another chance.

She watched me handle the stud's brief mutiny, but I couldn't tell if she appreciated my skill or not. The stud is one nobody else willingly climbs aboard, being a sullen, snuffy sort, and I've won wagers on him when betting men thought he might be the winner of the regular morning hostilities. But he and I have worked out a deal whereby he provides all the fireworks and I make it look good; whenever I come out ahead with a few coins jingling in my belt-pouch, he gets an extra ration of grain. It works out pretty well.

She didn't say a word when the stud finally settled

down, snorting dust from his nostrils, but I caught her watching me with that blue-eyed sideways appraisal.

"That's not a Northern horse you're riding," I pointed out conversationally. "He's a Southron, like me. What kind of horses do you have up North?"

"Bigger ones."

I waited. She didn't add anything more. I tried again. "Fast?"

"Fast enough."

I scowled. "Look, it's a long journey. We might as well make it shorter with good conversation." I paused. "Even bad conversation."

She smiled. She tried to hide it behind that curtain of hair, but I saw it. "I thought sword-dancers were generally a surly lot," she said idly, "living only for the blood they can spill."

I slapped one spread hand against my chest. "Me? No. I'm a peaceful man, at heart."

"Ah." With all the wisdom of the world contained in the single syllable.

I sighed. "Have you got a name? Or will *Blondie* do?"

She didn't answer. I waited, picking sandburs out of the clipped mane of my stud.

"Delilah," she said finally, mouth twisted a bit. "Call me Del."

"Del." It didn't suit her, somehow, being too harsh and abrupt—and too masculine—for a young woman of her grace and beauty. "Are you really chasing your brother?"

She slanted me a glance. "Do you think I made up that story I told to the slaver?"

"Maybe." I shrugged. "My job is not to pass moral judgment on my employer, just to get her to Julah."

She nearly smiled. "I'm *looking* for my brother. That's not chasing."

True. "Do you really have any idea where he might be or what might have happened to him?"

Her fingers combed the dun's upstanding mane. "Like I

told the slaver, he was stolen five years ago. I've traced him here—now to Julah.'' She looked at me directly. "Any more questions?"

"Yes." I smiled blandly. "What in hoolies is a girl like you doing chasing down a lost brother? Why isn't your father handling this?"

"He's dead."

"Uncle?"

"He's dead."

"*Other* brothers?"

"They're *all* dead, sword-dancer."

I looked at her. Her tone was even, but I've learned to listen to what people *don't* say more than what they do. "What happened?"

Her shoulders moved under the scarlet burnous. "Raiders. They came north about the same time we headed south, into the borderlands. They crossed over and attacked our caravan."

"Stealing your brother—" I didn't wait for her to answer "—and killing all the rest."

"Everyone but me."

I pulled up and reached over to grab her tasseled reins. Ocher tassels, and orange, no longer bright. "How in hoolies," I demanded, "did the raiders miss *you*?"

For a moment the blue eyes were shuttered behind lowered lids. Then she looked at me straight on. "I didn't say they did."

I said nothing at all for a minute. Through my mind flashed a vision of Southron raiders with their hands on a lovely Northern girl, and there was nothing pleasant about it. But the lovely Northern girl looked right back at me as if she knew precisely what I was thinking and had come to terms with it completely, neither humiliated nor embarrassed by my knowledge. It was merely a fact of life.

I wondered, briefly, if the man Moon had mentioned tracking her was one of the raiders. But—she'd said five years. Too long for a man to chase a woman.

But not for a woman to hunt a brother.

I let go of her reins. "So now you've come south on some lengthy cumfa hunt, searching for a brother who could very well be dead."

"He wasn't dead five years ago," she said coolly. "He wasn't dead when Osmoon saw him."

"*If* he saw him," I pointed out. "Do you think he'd tell you the truth while you held a sword at his throat? He told you exactly what you wanted to hear." I scowled. "Five years makes it nearly impossible, bascha. If you're so determined to find your brother, what took you so long to begin?"

She didn't smile or otherwise indicate my irritation bothered her. "There was a matter of learning a trade," she told me calmly. "A matter of altering tradition."

I looked at the silver hilt rearing above her shoulder. A woman bearing a sword—yes, that would definitely alter tradition. North *or* South. But my suspicions about the trade she referred to couldn't possibly be right.

I grunted. "Waste of time, bascha. After so long in the South—I'm sure he's probably dead."

"Perhaps," she agreed. "But I'll know for sure when I get to Julah."

"Ah, hoolies," I said in disgust. "I've got nothing better to do." I glared at her crimson back as she proceeded on ahead of me. Then I tapped heels against the stud's slick sides and fell in next to her again.

We camped out under the stars and made a meal of dried cumfa meat. It isn't what you'd call a delicacy, but it is filling. The best thing about it is it isn't prepared with salt as a preservative. In the Punja, the *last* thing you want is salted meat, except for a trace of it to keep yourself alive. Cumfa is rather bland and tasteless, but it's dressed with an oil that softens and makes it palatable, and it's the best thing for a desert crossing. A little goes a long way, and it's light, so it doesn't weigh down the horses. I've become quite accustomed to it.

Del, however, wasn't too certain she thought much of it, though she was too polite to mention her dislike. She gnawed on it like a dog with a slightly distasteful bone; not liking it, but knowing it was expected of her. I smiled to myself and chewed on my own ration, washing it down with a few swallows of water.

"No cumfa up North?" I inquired when she'd finally choked down the last strip.

She put one hand over her mouth. "No."

"Takes some getting used to."

"Ummm."

I held out the leather bota. "Here. This will help."

She gulped noisily, then replugged the bota and handed it back. She looked a little green around the edges.

I busied myself with rewrapping the meat I'd unpacked. "Know what cumfa is?"

Her glance was eloquent.

"Reptile," I told her. "Comes out of the Punja. Mean. The adults can grow to twenty feet and they're tough as old boot leather—about this big around." I held up my circled hands, thumbs and fingers not quite touching. "But catch and dress out a youngster and you've got a meal on your hands. I've got two pouches full of it, and that ought to more than get us across the Punja."

"Is this *all* you have to eat?"

I shrugged. "There are caravans we can trade with. And we can stop at a couple of settlements. But this will be our main diet." I smiled. "Doesn't spoil."

"Ummm."

"You'll get used to it." I stretched luxuriously and leaned back against my saddle, content. Here I was, alone in the desert with a beautiful woman. I had a full belly and the sunset promised a cool night. The stars made it ideal. Once we reached the Punja things would change, but for now I was happy enough. Some good aqivi would make it better, but when I'd left the cantina to go after Del, I hadn't had the coin to buy a bota of it.

"How far to the Punja?" she asked.

I glanced at her and saw her twisting her hair into a single braid. Seemed a shame to bind up all that glorious hair, but I could see where it might be a bit of a bother on the sand. "We'll reach it tomorrow." I shifted against my saddle. "Well, now that we're comfortable, how about you telling me how it was you knew to ask for me in the cantina?"

She tied off the braid with a strip of leather. "At Harquhal I learned Osmoon the Trader was the likeliest source of information. But finding Osmoon promised to be difficult, so I asked for the next best thing: someone who knew him." She shrugged. "Three different people said some big sword-dancer calling himself Tiger knew him, and I should look for *him* instead of Osmoon."

Harquhal is a town near the border. It's a rough place, and if she'd gotten such information out of people I knew to be close-mouthed without the right encouragement, she was better than I thought.

I eyed her assessively. She didn't look all that tough, but something in her eyes made a man take notice of more than just her body.

'So you came into the cantina looking for me." I fingered the scars on my jaw. "Guess I'm easy to find, sometimes."

She shrugged. "They described you. They said you were tough as old cumfa meat, only then I didn't know what they meant." She grimaced. "And they mentioned the scars on your face."

I knew she wanted to ask about them. Everybody does, especially the women. The scars are a part of the legend, and I don't mind talking about them.

"Sandtiger," I told her, and saw her blank look. "Like the cumfa, they live in the Punja. Vicious, deadly beasts, who don't mind the taste of people if they're accommodating enough to walk into a sandtiger's lair."

"You were?"

I laughed. "I walked into the lair purposely. I went in to kill a big male who was terrorizing the encampment. He took a few chunks out of my hide and raked me a good one across the face—as you see—but I beat him." I tapped the string of claws hanging around my neck on black cord. The claws are black, too, and wickedly curved; my face bears good testament to that. "These are all that's left of him; the hide went to my hyort." That blank look again. "Tent."

"So now they call you the Tiger."

"Sandtiger—Tiger for short." I shrugged. "One name is as good as another." I watched her a moment and decided it wouldn't hurt my reputation—or my chances—to let her in on the story. "I remember very clearly the day it happened," I said expansively, settling in for the tale. "That sandtiger had been stealing children who wandered too far from the wagons. No one had been able to track it down and put it out of business. Two of the men were killed outright. The shukar tried his magic spells, but they failed—as magic often will. So then he said we'd angered the gods somehow, and this was our punishment, but that the man who could kill the beast would reap the rewards of the tribe's gratitude." I shrugged. "So I took my knife and went into the lair, and when I came out, I was alive and the sandtiger was dead."

"And did you reap the rewards of your tribe's gratitude?"

I grinned at her. "They were *so* grateful, all the young, marriageable women fell on their faces and begged me to take them as wives—one at a time, of course. And the men feasted me and gave me all sorts of things to mark my greatness. For the Salset, that's reward enough."

"How many wives did you take?" she asked gravely.

I scratched at the scars on my face. "Actually—I didn't settle on any of them. I just made myself available from time to time." I shrugged. "I wasn't ready for *one* wife then, let alone several. Still not."

"What made you leave the tribe?"

I closed one eye and squinted up at the brightest star. "I just got restless. Even a nomadic tribe like the Salset can get confining. So I went off on my own and apprenticed to a sword-dancer, until I achieved the seventh level and became one myself."

"Does it pay well in the South?"

"I'm a very rich man, Del."

She smiled. "I see."

"And I'll be even richer when we're done with this chase."

She tightened the strip of leather that bound her hair into its shining braid. "But you don't really think we'll find him, do you?"

I sighed. "Five years is a long time, Del. Anything might've happened to him. Especially if he wound up with slavers."

"I have no intention of giving up," she said clearly.

"No. I didn't figure you did."

She tugged the burnous over her head and then carefully folded it, settling it next to her saddle. She'd been shrouded in it all day; suddenly seeing all that pale, smooth flesh again reminded me—vociferously—how much I wanted her. And for an ecstatic moment my hopes surged up as she glanced at me.

Her face was perfectly blank. I waited for the invitation, but she said nothing. She merely slid her sword free of its sheath and set it down in the sand next to her. With a rather long, enigmatic look at me, she lay down and turned her back on me, one hip thrust skyward.

The blade gleamed salmon-silver in the starlight; the runes were iridescent.

Chilled, I shivered. And for the first time in many a night I didn't strip off my burnous. Instead, I flattened myself on my rug and stared at the stars while I willed myself to go to sleep.

*Hoolies*, what a way to spend a night—

# Four

To the inexperienced eye, the border between the desert and its older, deadlier brother is almost invisible. But to someone like me, who has spent thirty-odd years riding the shifting sands, the border between the desert and the Punja is plain as day and twice as bright.

Del reined in as I did and glanced around at me curiously. Her braid hung over her left shoulder, the end just tickling the mound of her breast beneath the crimson silk. Her nose was pink with sunburn, and I knew the rest of her face would follow soon enough if she didn't pull up the hood of the burnous.

I did so with my own, though needing it less; after a moment she followed my lead. I pointed. "That, my Northern bascha, is the Punja."

She stared out across the distances. The horizon merged with the dunes into a single mass of dusty beige. Out here even the sky is sucked dry of all color. It is a smudge of pale taupe, paler topaz; a trace of blued-steel, met by the blade of the horizon. To the south, east and west there was nothing, miles and miles of nothing. Hoolies, we sometimes call the place.

Del glanced back the way we had come. It was dry and dusty also, yet there is a promise in the land, telling you it will end. The Punja promises too, but it sings a song of death.

Her face was puzzled. "It looks no different."

I pointed down at the sand in front of the horse's hooves. "The sand. Look at the sand. See the difference?"

"Sand is sand." But before I could reprimand her for such a stupid statement, she dropped off the dusty dun gelding and knelt. One hand scooped up a fistful of sand.

She let it run through her fingers until her hand was empty, except for the glitter of translucent silver crystals. They are the deadly secret of the Punja: the crystals catch and keep the sun's heat, reinforcing it, reflecting it, multiplying its brightness and heat one thousandfold, until everything on the sand burns up.

Del's fingers curled up against her palm. "I see the difference." She rose and stared out at the endless Punja. "How many miles?"

"Who can say? The Punja is an untamed beast, bascha, it knows no fences, no picket ropes, no boundaries. It goes where it will, with the wind, freer than any nomad." I shrugged. "One day it might be miles from a settlement; within two days it may swallow down every last goat and baby. It's why a guide is so necessary. If you haven't crossed it before, you don't know the markers. You don't know the waterholes." I waved a hand southward. "Out there, bascha, death is the overlord." I saw her twisted mouth. "I'm not being overly dramatic. I'm not exaggerating. The Punja allows neither."

"But it *can* be crossed." She looked at me and wiped her hand free of dust against the crimson, tasseled burnous. "You've crossed it."

"I've crossed it," I agreed. "But before you step over the invisible border onto the silver sands, you'd best be aware of the dangers."

The little dun nosed at her, asking for attention. Del put one hand on his muzzle, the other beneath his wide, rounded jaw, scratching the firm layers of muscle. But her eyes and her attention were on me. "Then you'd better say what they are."

She wasn't afraid. I thought she might be dissembling so I wouldn't think her a weak, silly woman trying to behave like a man, but she wasn't. She *was* strong. And, more importantly, she was ready to listen.

The stud snorted, clearing dust from his nostrils. In the still, warm air I heard the clatter of bit and shanks; the rattle of weighted tassels against brass ornamentations. An insect whined by, making for one tufted, twitching bay ear. The stud shook his head violently, ridding himself of the pest, and stomped in the sand. It raised dust, more dust, and he snorted again. In the desert, everything is a cycle. A wheel, endlessly turning in the soft harshness of the environment.

"Mirages," I told Del. "Deadly mirages. You think you see an oasis at last, yet when you reach it, you discover it's been swallowed up by sand and sky, blurring in the air. Do it one time too many and you've left yourself too far from a real oasis, a real well. You are dead."

Silently, she waited, still scratching her little dun horse.

"There are simooms," I said, "siroccos. Sandstorms, you might call them. And the sandstorms of the Punja will wail and screech and howl while they strip the flesh from your bones. And there are cumfa. And there are sandtigers."

"But sandtigers can be overcome." She said it blandly, so blandly, while I scowled at her and tried to discern if she were serious or merely teasing me about my name and reputation.

"There are borjuni," I went on finally. "Thieves who are little better than scavengers of the desert. They prey on unwary travelers and caravans. They steal everything, including the burnous right off your back, and then they kill you."

"And?" she said, as I paused.

I sighed. With her, when was enough, enough? "There are always the tribes. Some of them are friendly, like the Salset and the Tularain, but many of them aren't. The

Hanjii and Vashni are good examples. Both of them are warrior tribes who believe in human sacrifice. But their rituals differ." I paused. "The Vashni believe in vivisection. The Hanjii are cannibals."

After a moment, she nodded once. "Anything else?"

"Isn't that enough?"

"Maybe it is," she said at last. "Maybe it's more than enough. But maybe you're not telling me everything."

"What do you want to hear?" I asked curtly. "Or do you think I'm telling tall tales to occupy a child?"

"No." She shaded her eyes with one hand and stared southward, across the shimmering sands. "But you mention nothing of sorcery."

For a moment I looked at her sharply. Then I snorted inelegantly. "All the magic *I* need is that which resides in the circle."

The sunlight beat off the bright crimson of her hood and set the gold tassels to glowing. "Sword-dancer," she said softly, "you would do better not to belittle that which holds such power."

I swore. "Hoolies, bascha, you sound like a shukar, trying to make me think you're full of mystery and magic. Look, I won't say magic doesn't exist, because it does. But it's what you make of it, and so far about all I've ever seen are fools tricked out of their money or their water. It's mostly a con game, bascha. Until it's proved otherwise."

Del looked at me squarely a moment, as if she judged. And then she nodded a little. "A skeptic," she observed. "Maybe even a fool. But then—it's your choice. And I'm not a priest to try and convince you otherwise." She turned and walked away.

Automatically, I reached out and caught the reins of the little dun gelding as he tried to follow her. "Where in hoolies are you going?"

She stopped. She stood on the invisible border. She didn't answer me. She merely drew her gleaming sword and drove it into the sand as if she spitted a man, and then she let go of the hilt. It stood up from the sand, rune-scribed blade half buried. And then she sat down, cross-legged, and closed her eyes. Her hands hung loosely in her lap.

The heat beat at me. Moving, it isn't so bad. I can forget about it and concentrate on where I'm going. But sitting still on horseback with the deadly sands but a dismount away, I could feel only the heat . . . and a strange wonder, stirred by the woman's actions.

Eyes closed. Head bent. Silent. A shape in scarlet silk, cross-legged on the sand. And the Northern sword, made of alien steel (or something), hilt thrust against the fabric of the air.

I felt the sweat spring up. It rose on brow, on belly, in the pockets of flesh beneath my arms. The silk of my burnous melted against my skin and stuck there. I could smell an acrid tang.

I looked at the sword. I thought I saw the shapes twist in the metal. But that would take magic, a powerful personal magic, and there is so little in the world.

Except in the sword-dancer's circle.

Del rose at last, jerking the sword free of the sand. She slid it home over her shoulder and walked back to the dun, slipped tasseled reins over his flicking ears.

I scowled. "What was that all about?"

She mounted quickly. "I asked permission to continue. It's customary in the North, when undertaking a dangerous journey."

"Asked *who*?" I scowled. "The sword?"

"The gods," she said seriously. "But then, if you don't much believe in magic, you won't much belive in gods."

I smiled. "Bang on the head, bascha. Now, if the gods—or that sword—have given you permission, we may as well continue." I gestured. "Southward, bascha. Just ride south."

\*　　\*　　\*

The Southron sun is hard on anyone. It hangs in the sky like a baleful god of hoolies, staring down with a single cyclopean eye. A burnous is good for protecting the flesh, but it doesn't dissipate the heat entirely. The fabric of the silk, over-heated, produces heat itself, burning against the skin until you shift within the folds, seeking cooler areas.

After a while, your eyes ache from squinting against the brightness and, if you shut them, all you see are crimson lids as the sun bakes through. The sands of the Punja glitter blindingly; at first it seems a lovely sort of taupe-and-amber velvet stretching across the miles, crusted with colorless gemstones. But the gemstones burn and the velvet has no softness.

There is the silence, so oppressive, save for the slough-ing of hooves threshing through the sand and the occa-sional creak of saddle leather beneath the muffling blanket. Southron horses are bred for the heat and brightness; long forelocks guard their eyes and form a sort of insulation against the heat, and their hides are slick as silk without excess hair. Many times I'd wished *I* was as adaptable as a good desert pony, and as uncomplaining.

The air shimmers. You look out across the sand and you see the flat horizon, flat sky, flat color. You can feel it sucking the life from you, leaching your skin of moisture until you feel like a dry husk ready to blow into millions of particles on the first desert breeze. But the breeze never comes, and you pray it doesn't; if it does, it brings with it the wind, and the simoom, and the deadly sand sharp as cumfa teeth as it slices into your flesh.

I looked at Del and recalled the freshness of her pale skin and knew I didn't ever want to see it burned or scarred or shredded.

We drank sparingly, but the water levels in my botas went down amazingly fast. After a while you find yourself hyperaware of the liquid, even though you ration it care-fully. Knowing you have it within reach is almost worse than knowing you have none. Having it, you want it, knowing you can have it instantly. It's a true test of willpower and a lot of people discover they don't have that in their psychological makeup. Del did. But the water still went down.

"There's a well," I said at last. "Ahead."

She turned her head as I caught up to her. "Where?"

I pointed. "See that dark line? That's a ridge of rocks marking the cistern. The water isn't the best—it's a little brackish—but it's wet. It'll do."

"I still have water in my botas."

"So do I, but out here you don't ever pass up a well. There's no such thing as an embarrassment of riches in the Punja. Even if you've just filled up your botas, you stop. Sometimes a swim can make all the difference in the world." I paused. "How's your nose?"

She touched it and made a rueful face. "Sore."

"If we find an alla plant, I'll mix a salve. It'll leach some of the pain, and the paste keeps the sun off delicate extremities." I grinned. "No use in denying it, bascha—your tender Northern flesh just isn't up to the heat of the Punja."

A twist of her mouth. "And yours is."

I laughed. "Mine's tough as cumfa leather, remember? The Punja is my home, Del . . . as much as any place is." I stared out across the blazing sands. "If there is such a thing as home when you're a sword-dancer."

I don't know why I said it. Least of all to her. Women sometimes use such things as weapons, fighting with words instead of blades.

But Del had a sword. And it seemed she never spoke a frivolous word.

"There is," she said softly. "Oh, there is. There is always a home in the circle."

I looked at her sharply. "What do *you* know about circles, bascha?"

Del smiled slowly. "Do you think I carry a sword for mere effect?"

Well, it *was* successful. Even if she couldn't use the thing. "I saw you terrorize Old Moon with it," I admitted grudgingly. "Yes, you're handy with it. But in the circle?" I shook my head. "Bascha, I don't think you understand what a circle really is."

Her smile didn't diminish. But neither did her silence.

The bay stud picked his way down through dark umber-colored stone. After the cushioning of the sand it sounded odd to hear hoof on stone again. Del's dun followed me down and both horses picked up the pace as they smelled water.

I swung off the bay and turned him loose, knowing he wouldn't wander with water so close at hand. Del dropped off the dun, waiting silently as I searched for the proper spot. Finally I found my bearings in the huddled rocks, paced out the distance, then knelt and dug out the iron handle. It was twisted and corroded, but my hand slid into it easily enough. I gritted my teeth and yanked, grunting with effort as I dragged the heavy iron lid from the cistern.

Del came forward with alacrity, tugging the dun behind her. That's what gave me the first clue; that, and when the bay refused to drink. Del spoke to her horse, coaxing him softly in her Northern dialect, then sent me a puzzled glance. I scooped up some water, smelled it, then touched the tip of my tongue to the liquid in my palm.

I spat it out. "Fouled."

"But—" She stopped herself. There was nothing left to say.

I shoved the lid back over the cistern and dug a hunk of charred wood out of one of my pouches. Del watched silently as I drew a black X on the metal. The sand would cover it soon enough, scouring the mark away, but at least I'd done what I could to warn other travelers. Not everyone would be as we were; I've known men who drank bad water because they couldn't help themselves, even knowing it was fouled. It's a painful, ugly death.

I took one of my botas and poured good water into my cupped hand, holding it to the bay's muzzle. He slurped at it, not getting much, but enough to dampen his throat. After a moment Del did the same for the dun, using water from her last bota. We hadn't ridden hard, taking our time without pushing the horses, but now they'd have a long spell before they could water properly.

I tossed Del my last bota as the dun emptied hers. "Swallow some."

"I'm all right."

"You're burning up." I smiled at her. "It's all right. It has nothing to do with you being a woman. It's that Northern skin. A disadvantage out here, much as I admire it." I paused, noting the downward twisting of her mouth. "Drink, bascha."

Finally she did, and I could see the difference it made. There hadn't been a single complaint out of her or even a question as to how far to the next water. I appreciated that kind of fortitude, especially in a woman.

She tossed the bota back. "You?"

I started to tell her I was tough and could handle the extra miles with no water; I didn't, because she deserved better. So I drank a couple of swallows and hung the bota onto my saddle again.

I gestured, south as always. "We have enough water to reach an oasis I know. We'll fill up there. Then we'll head directly for the next well, but if that one's fouled too, we'll have to turn back."

"Turn *back*." She jerked her head around to look at me. "You mean—not go on to Julah?"

"That's what I mean."

She shook her head. "I won't turn back."

"You'll have to," I told her flatly. "If you go much farther into the Punja without knowing precisely where your next water is, you'll never make it." I shook my head. "I'll guide you to the oasis, bascha. Then we'll decide."

"*You* decide nothing." Color stood in her cheeks.

"Del—"

"I *can't* turn back," she said. "Don't you understand? I have to find my brother."

I sighed, trying to keep the exasperation out of my voice. "Bascha, if you go in without water, you'll be as dead as the rest of your family and of no use to your brother."

Loosened strands of hair framed her face. Her nose was red, and her cheeks; her eyes, so blue, were intent upon my face. She studied me so intensely I felt like a horse under inspection by a potential buyer not certain of my wind, my legs, my heart. She studied me like a sworddancer seeking weaknesses in my defense, so as to cut me down an instant later.

Briefly, a muscle ticked in her jaw. "You don't have a family. Or else—you don't care a whit about them." There was no room for inquiry in her tone. She was utterly convinced.

"No family." I agreed, divulging nothing more.

Contempt flickered at the edges of her tone. Not quite pronounced enough to offer insult, but plain enough to me. "Maybe if you did, you'd understand." It was tightly said, clipped off; she turned and swung up into her saddle and settled the reins into place. "Don't judge—don't *devalue*—what you can't understand, Sandtiger. A sworddancer should know better."

My hand shot out and caught one of her reins, holding the dun in place. "Bascha, I *do* know better. And I know better than to devalue *you*." That much, I gave her. "But I also know when a woman's being a fool to give herself over to emotionalism when she would do better to rely on a man's proven experience."

"*Would* I?" she demanded. Both hands clenched on the reins. For just a moment I thought she might swear at me some vile Northern oath, but she didn't. She simply withdrew into silence long enough to collect her thoughts, and then she sighed a little. "In the North, kinship ties are the strongest in existence. Those ties are power and strength and continuation, like the birth of sons and daughters to each man and woman. It's bad enough when a single life is lost—boy or girl, ancient one or infant—because it means the line is broken. Each life is precious to us, and we grieve. But also we rebuild, replant, replace." The dun shook his head violently, rattling bit and shanks. Automatically she soothed him with a hand against his neck. "My whole family was killed, Tiger. Only my brother and I survived, and Jamail they took. I am a daughter of the North and of my family, and I will do what I must to return my brother home." Her eyes were steady; her tone more so, even in its quietness. "I will go on regardless."

I looked up at her, so magnificent in her pride and femininity. And yet there was more than femininity. There was also strength of will and a perfect comprehension of what she intended to do.

"Then let's go," I said curtly. "We're wasting time standing out here in the heat jawing about it."

Del smiled a little, but she knew better than to rub it in.

Besides, it was only a battle. Not the entire war.

# Five

"**L**ook!" Del cried. "Trees!"

I looked beyond her pointing arm and saw the trees she indicated. Tall, spindly palms with droopy lime-colored fronds and spiky cinnamon trunks.

"Water," I said in satisfaction. "See how the fronds are green and upright? When they're brown and burned and sagging, you know there isn't any."

"Did you doubt it?" Her tone was startled. "You brought me here, knowing there might not be any water?"

She didn't sound angry, just amazed. I didn't smile. "In the Punja, water is never guaranteed. And yes, I brought you here knowing there might not be any water, because you took care to impress upon me how dedicated you are to finding your brother."

Del nodded. "You think I'm a fool. A silly, witless woman." Not really a challenge. A statement.

I didn't look away. "Does it really matter what I think?"

After a moment, she smiled. "No. No more than it matters what I think of *you*." And she rode onward toward the oasis.

This time the water was clear and sweet. We watered the horses after testing it, then filled all the botas. Del expressed surprise at finding such luxury in the Punja: the trees offered some shade and there was grass, thick Punja-grass; hummocky, pale green, linked together by a net-

51

work of tangled junctions. The sand was finer here, and cool; as always, I marveled at the many faces of the Punja. Such a strange place. It beckons you. It sucks you in and fools you with its countless chameleon qualities. And then it kills you.

The oasis was big, ringed by a low manmade rock wall built to provide shelter against simooms. Palm trees paraded across the latticework of grass. The oasis was big enough to support a couple of small tribes and maybe a caravan or two for a couple of weeks at at a time, provided the animals weren't given free rein to overgraze. Overgrazing can destroy an oasis entirely, and in the Punja not many people are willing to cut off another supply of food and water, even for their animals. What happens generally is that the nomads pitch camp for a week or two, then move on across the sands toward another oasis. That way the oasis recovers itself in time to succor other travelers, although occasionally one is destroyed by thoughtless caravans.

The cistern wasn't really a cistern, more like a waterhole. It was formed by an underground spring, bubbling up from a deep cleft in the ground. A second manmade ring of stones formed a deep pool more than a man-length across from lip to lip; a larger gods-made ring of craggy, tumbled stone jutted out of the sand like a wedge-shaped wall forming a haphazard semi-circle. It was within this larger ring the best grazing grew, tough, fibrous grass, lacking the sweet juice of mountain grass, but nourishing nonetheless.

Some seasons I've seen the spring merely a trickle, hardly filling the pool to the lip of the ring of stones. And during those seasons I approach it with sword drawn, because occasionally other travelers grow incredibly attached to the oasis, desiring no others to intrude upon it. There have been times I've had to fight just to get a swallow. Once I killed a man, so I could water my horse.

This time of year the spring runs high and fills the pool, lapping against the greenish rocks. And so Del and I, having unsaddled and watered our horses, shed our burnouses and sat in the thin shade of palms and rock ring and relaxed, enjoying the needed respite.

She tipped back her head, baring her face to the sunlight. Eyes closed. "The South is so different from the North. It's like you said—they're as different in appearance and temperament as a man and woman." She smiled. "I love the North, with its snow and ice and blizzards. But the South has its own crude beauty."

I grunted. "Most people never see it."

Del shrugged. "My father taught his children to look at all places—and at all people—with openness and compassion, and willingness to understand another's ways. You should not judge by appearances, he said, until you understand what lies beneath the clothing *or* the skin. And even, perhaps, the sex of the individual." A trace of wry humor threaded her tone. "That one's more difficult, I think, judging by Southron customs. Anyway, I don't pretend to understand the South yet, but I can appreciate its appearance."

I slapped at an insect attempting to burrow its way beneath the flesh of my thigh now bared by the absence of the burnous. I was mostly naked, clad only in the suede dhoti most sword-dancers wear; physical freedom is important in the circle. "Most people don't call the Punja a *pretty* place."

Del shook her head, and the blonde braid snaked against her shoulder as a lizard ran across the rocks behind her. "It *isn't* a pretty place. It's desolate and dangerous and angry, like the snow lions in the mountains of the North. And, like them, it walks alone, trusting to its confidence and strength. The snow lion kills without compunction, but that doesn't make it less alive." She sighed, eyes still shuttered behind her lids with their pale yellow lashes. "Its ferocity is a part of it. Without it, a lion wouldn't be a lion."

A good description of the Punja. I looked at her—head

tipped back to worship the blazing sun—and wondered how so young a girl could already have such wisdom. That sort of knowledge take years of experience.

And then, looking at her, I didn't think about wisdom anymore. Just her.

I got up. I walked over to her. She didn't open her eyes, so I bent and scooped her up, carried her to the pool and dumped her in.

She came up sputtering, spitting water, startled and angry. Wet fingers gripped the rock circle and hung on as she glared at me, hair slicked back against her head.

I waited. And after a moment I saw the lines of tension wash from her face and the rigidity from her shoulders. She sighed and closed her eyes, reveling in the water.

"Soak it up," I told her. "You need to saturate the skin before we start on the next part of the journey."

She answered me by sliding under the water entirely. I watched the bubbles a moment, then turned away to my saddle to dig some cumfa meat out of my pouches.

I heard the growl before I saw the beast. When it had come out of its lair in the rocks I have no idea, but it crouched against the grass and sand with all its black claws bared and stub tail barely twitching. Long fangs curved down from the roof of its mouth and embraced the powerful lower jaw. Green eyes glowed in its wedge-shaped, sand-colored head.

A male. Full-fleshed and muscled. Sandtigers don't grow to mammoth sizes; they don't need to. They are, quite simply, small bundles of menace: short-legged, stub-tailed, practically earless. Their eyes are large and oddly unfocused before an attack, as if their minds are somewhere else entirely. But they never are. And the disarmingly weak glare—a prelude to the razor-sharp attack stare—can prove deadly, if you fall victim to it. Sandtigers, regardless of size, pack more power in hindquarters and haunches than a full-grown horse, and their jaws can break a man's arm in a single bite.

Seeing the tiger evoked enough memories to drown a man. Images flashed inside my skull. Another cat. Another male. Prepared to rake my guts from my abdomen. Or tear the flesh from my throat.

It had been a long, long time since I had seen a sandtiger. They aren't as common anymore. It's one of the reasons my name is perfect for my profession—a sandtiger is considered by some to be a mythical beast, a figment of stories and imagination. But there's nothing mythical about a tiger. There was nothing mythical about this one.

Only about me.

Singlestroke lay in harness, dumped on the ground with my saddle. I cursed my own stupidity in being so concerned about water I neglected personal protection. Carelessness such as that could prove deadly.

I stood my ground, knowing that to move now merely invited attack. The tiger would attack regardless, no matter what I did, but I didn't want to encourage it.

*Hoolies*, but I didn't want that. Not again.

My hand slipped to my knife, closing around the hilt. Sweat made it slippery. I felt the knot tying itself in my belly.

Gods, not *now*

The slitted green eyes stared with the telltale dreamy, unfocused cast. But I saw the stare begin to change.

I heard the slop of water behind me. "Stay in the water, Del."

She called something back in a questioning tone, but the tiger leaped, and I never did hear what she asked me.

The knife was out of my sheath in an instant, jabbing toward the cat, but he was smarter than I expected. Instead of leaping for my throat, coming down on my shoulders and chest with all his compact weight, this one landed on my gut and expelled all my air.

I felt the hind legs bunch up, claws spreading and opening as I went down under the impact. My knife dug in through toughened fur and hide, and I heard the tiger's unnerving scream of pain and rage.

My left hand was at the cat's throat, straining to push its gaping mouth away from my vulnerable belly. My knife hand was slippery with feline blood. I smelled the stench of dead, rotted meat on the tiger's breath and heard his snarls and tiny screams as he fought to sink elongated fangs into me. I fought just as hard to sink my knife deeper, into something vital.

One of the powerful hind legs kicked out, raking claws along my thigh. It scared me. But it also made me angrier. I already have enough sandtiger scars to show. I don't need any more.

Then I heard the cry of a female and realized Del and I had stumbled onto a cub-lair. A sandtiger is dangerous enough on its own, but a male with a mate is worse, and a female with cubs is the worst of all.

And there was Del—

I managed to roll over, forcing myself on top of the male. The position was unnatural to him and made him fight harder, but I plunged the knife in deeper and heard the horrible scream of a cat in mortal agony. It gave me no pleasure; it never does, but I had no time for recriminations. I thrust myself to my feet and turned to go after the female—

—but Del already stood there, Northern sword gripped in both hands.

Light ran down the rune-kissed blade. She stood poised before the female like a living sculpture, water running down arms and legs, hair slicked back, teeth bared in a challenge as feral as the cat's. Had I not seen the rise and fall of her breasts to indicate she breathed, I might have thought she was a statue.

Then I quit admiring her and moved.

"No!" Del shouted. "This one is mine!"

"Don't be a fool!" I snapped. "A female is far more deadly than a male."

"Yes," she agreed, and after a moment—looking at her—I understood the meaning of her smile.

The female, in slow fits and starts, crept out of the black hole in the dark-green rocks. She was smaller than her mate but much more desperate. Somewhere back in the rocks were her cubs, and she would go to any lengths to keep them safe. Del would go down before her like a piece of fluff in the blast of a simoom.

The cat pushed off the sand and leaped straight up, hind legs coiling to rake out at Del. I didn't waste a second wondering if I could do it, I just did it. I launched myself as quickly as the cat and thrust a shoulder into her ribcage as we met in midair.

I heard Del's curse and knew she'd had to hold her swordstroke, that or risk lopping off my head. The cat went down with a cough and a grunt, the wind knocked out of her, then grunted again as I came down on top of her. I pushed my left forearm beneath her jaw, dragging her head up from the sand, and severed her throat with one stroke of my knife.

My thigh hurt. I glanced down at it as I sat hunched over the dead female and realized the male had striped me good. More scars. Then I glanced up at Del and saw her blazing more brightly than any sun.

"She was *mine*!" she cried. "Mine!"

I sighed, shoving a forearm across my sweaty forehead. "Let's not argue about it. She's dead. That's what counts."

"But you killed her and she was *mine*. You stole my kill."

I stared at her. She was white with anger, sword still gripped in rigid fingers. For a moment I had the odd impression she might bring down that deadly blade in a vicious killing swipe. "*Del*—"

She let out a string of Northern words I didn't understand, but didn't need to. The girl had mastered the most foul-sounding oaths I'd ever heard, and I'm rather good at it myself. I heard her out, letting her vent her anger, then pushed to my feet and faced her. The tip of the sword rested against my chest.

Almost at once I shivered. The blade was cold, *cold*, even in the blazing heat of the Southron sunlight. It put that finger into my soul and tapped.

Tapping: *Tiger, are you there?*

I took a single lurching step away. "That cat might have killed you." I said it curtly, more out of reaction to the sword than anger at her behavior. "Don't act like a fool, Del."

"Fool?" she blurted. "*You* are the fool, sword-dancer! Does a man steal another man's kill? Does a man forbid another man to kill? Does a man protect another man when he's perfectly prepared *and* willing to handle the situation himself?"

"Aren't you forgetting something?" I threw back. "You're not a man, Del. Quit trying to act like one."

"I'm just *me!*" she shouted. "Just Del! Don't interfere simply because of my sex!"

"Hoolies, woman, don't act like you've got sand in your head." I walked past her to the water.

"*You're* the one, sword-dancer," she said bitterly. "*You* are the fool if you think I'm helpless and soft and unable."

I ignored her. My thigh was afire, and reaction to the attack was setting in. I was also hungry, and anger never solves any confrontation, even in the circle. *Especially* in the circle. So I stripped off my sandals and stepped over the ring of stones into the water, blowing bubbles as I sank beneath the surface.

When I came up again, hanging onto the rocks, I saw Del twisting her way into the sandtiger lair. That got me out of the water instantly. I went dripping across the sand to her, roaring a question, but by the time I got there she was backing out again. When she was free of the crags, she shook back her damp braid and looked up at me. Clutched in her arms were two sandtiger cubs.

They squalled and bit at her, paws batting at her hands,

but the claws of sandtiger cubs don't break through a membranous bud until they're three months old. It's what makes the parents so protective and vicious; cubs have no natural defenses for far longer than most animals of the Punja. These still had their milkteeth, which meant they were only half-weaned.

I swore, dripping all over the sand. "You plan on keeping them?"

"They'll die without help."

"They'll die *with* help." I squatted down, ignoring the pain in my clawed thigh, and put out my hand to one of the cubs. I couldn't deny it—at two months they were cute as could be. And about as cuddly as a cumfa. "They'll be better off if I kill them now."

Del jerked back. "Don't you dare!"

"Bascha, they're helpless," I told her. "They're *sandtiger* cubs, for valhail's sake! We don't need any more of them inhabiting this oasis, or we'll start losing people."

"People can look after themselves. These cubs can't."

I sighed again, letting the cub grab onto a finger. "Right now they have no defenses. Their teeth are blunt and their nails are budded. But in a month they'll have fangs and claws, and they'll kill anything that moves."

The cub gnawed at my hand. It was painless. The purring growl was only the merest shadow of the angry scream I'd heard coming from his father.

Del thrust the cub into my arms and cradled the other one. "They're just babies, Tiger. They deserve a chance to live."

I scowled at her, but the cub kept gnawing on my finger until it fell asleep in my arms. She was right. I couldn't do it. Tough old Tiger, professional sword-dancer.

I lugged the cub over to my burnous, put it down, watched it sleep, and swore. "What the hoolies do you want to *do* with them?"

Del was dangling her braid at her cub's nose. It batted at

the hair, grizzling deep in its throat. "We'll take them with us."

"Across the Punja?" I asked incredulously. "Hoolies, bascha, I know it's a woman's prerogative to want to mother something, but we'll be lucky to get *ourselves* across. We don't need to be saddled by a pair of sandtiger cubs."

"We have no choice." She met my eyes steadily. "You killed their parents. You cut off the line. Now you owe them a debt."

"Hoolies!" I swore. "Trust me to pick up a crazy Northern woman with crazy Northern notions. And anyway— the last I heard *you* wanted to kill the female. Don't make me the villain."

Her eyes were incredibly blue beneath pale, sun-bleached brows. "You are what you are, sword-dancer."

I sighed, giving it up. "Look, I have to get some sleep. We'll talk about it when I wake up."

She quit dangling the braid at once. "I thought you wanted to go on once we'd watered and rested."

"I do. But I can't, not until I get some sleep." I saw the puzzled frown on her face. "Bascha, the claws of sandtigers are poisoned. If they claw you badly enough, they paralyze you—so they can enjoy a leisurely meal." I gestured toward my thigh. The water had washed the blood away initially, but more crawled sluggishly down my leg. "This isn't much, but it's best if I get some sleep. So, if you don't mind . . ." I stifled my grunt of effort and dropped down on my burnous, next to the sleeping cub. It—*he*— slept on, and in a moment I joined him in oblivion.

# Six

The circle. A simple shape drawn in sand. Dark against light; the shallowness of the circle a chasm in the silk of the glittering sand. And yet, even in silence, the circle was loud with the promise of blood. Its scent was a tangible thing.

Mutely, I slipped out of my burnous and let it fall from my flesh. Soft silk, its slide a sibilant whisper; billowing briefly, then settling in a bright-brown puddle against the sand. Umber-bronze against ivory-taupe.

I unlaced my sandals and slipped free of them, kicking them aside. Deftly, I unbuckled my harness and let it fall atop my sandals: a pile of oiled leather, stained sienna by my sweat. But even as it fell, I slid the sword from the sheath.

Singlestroke, whose name was legendary. Blued blade, gold hilt. Blinding in the sunlight.

I walked to the edge of the circle. I waited. Against my feet the sand was hot, yet from its heat I took my strength; desert-born and bred, the Southron sun was, to me, an energizing force.

My opponent faced me. Like me, she had shed sandals and burnous, clad only in a suede tunic bordered with blue runic glyphs. And the sword. The salmon-silver sword with the shapes upon it; alien, angry shapes, squirming in the metal.

*I looked at it. It touched me not, for we had yet to enter the circle, and still I felt the breath of death. Cold. So cold. Reaching out to touch my soul. In the heat of the day, I shivered.*

*And Del sang. She sang her Northern song.*

I jerked into wakefulness and realized I *had* shivered, because Del's hand was on my brow and it was cool, cool and smooth, against the heat of my flesh.

Her face loomed over me. So fair, so young, so grim. Almost flawless in its beauty, and yet there was an edge beneath the softness. The bite of cold, hard steel.

"Your fever's gone," she said, and took her hand away.

After a moment, I rolled over and hitched myself up on one elbow. "How long?"

She had moved away, kneeling by the wall of rock behind us. Her hands rested on her thighs. "Through the night. You talked a little. I cleaned the wound."

I looked into those guileless eyes and saw again the level gaze of a dedicated opponent about to enter the circle. Behind her left shoulder rode the Northern sword, sheathed, settled quietly in its harness, the glint of rune-worked silver almost white in the rain of sunlight. I thought of the dream and wondered what I'd said.

But somehow I couldn't ask her.

She wore the crimson burnous again. Her hair had been rebraided. The skin of her nose was redder than before, almost ready to burst and peel. That blonde, blonde hair and those blue, blue eyes pointed up the differences between North and South blatantly enough, yet I knew it didn't have to do only with physicalities, but culture. Environment. Quite simply: we thought differently.

And it was bound to come between us.

I assessed the tiny camp. Del knew what she was doing. Both horses were saddled and packed, waiting silently in the heat. Heads hung loosely at the end of lowered necks, eyes were half-shut against the sunlight, patches of flesh quivering as stud and gelding tried to rid themselves of bothersome insects.

I looked at Del, prepared to make a comment, and she handed me a chunk of roasted meat. But I knew it wasn't cumfa.

Tentatively, I tongued it. "Sandtiger," she said. "I thought the male might be too tough, so I cooked the female."

The first bite was in my mouth, but I didn't swallow. It sat there in my teeth, filling up my mouth even though it wasn't that big a bite; the *idea* of eating the animal I'd been named for struck me as something close to cannibalism.

Del didn't smile. "In the Punja, one eats what meat one can find." But there was a glint in her eyes.

I scowled. Chewed. Didn't answer.

"Besides, I fed the cubs on cumfa meat mixed with milk, so I had to replace it with something."

"*Milk?*"

"They're only half-weaned," she explained. "There was still milk in the female, so I put the cubs on her. No sense in wasting what was left."

"They suckled from their dead mother?"

Del shrugged a little; I got the feeling she knew how odd it sounded. "She was still warm. I knew the milk wouldn't turn for an hour or so, so I thought it was worth the try."

To give her credit, I'd never have thought of it. But then, *I* wouldn't be so concerned with cubs bound to turn vicious in a month. Trust a woman . . . "What do you intend to do with them?"

"They're packed on your horse," she told me. "I made room in your pouches because there wasn't any in mine. They'll be no trouble."

"Sandtiger cubs on *my horse?*"

"*He* didn't seem to mind," she retorted. "Why should you?"

Ah, hoolies, some women you just can't talk sense to.

So I didn't even bother. I finished the roasted tiger, which wasn't too bad, tugged the burnous over my head and stood up. My thigh still stung, but the poison had worked its way out of my system. The claw marks stretched from the edge of my dhoti to mid-thigh, but they weren't terribly deep. They'd slow me down for a couple of days, but I heal fast.

"You ready to ride?" I took a final drink and headed for the stud.

"Since dawn."

There was, I thought, the slightest hint of a reprimand in her tone. And I didn't like it. I glared at her as she mounted her little dun, and then I recalled the reason. "You're still angry about me killing the female!"

Del hooked her feet into the stirrups and settled her reins. "She was mine. You took her away from me. You had no right."

"I was trying to save your *life*," I pointed out. "Doesn't that count for anything?"

She sat atop the gelding, the crimson silk of the burnous almost shimmering in the sunlight. "It counts," she agreed. "Oh, it does, Tiger. An honorableness on your part." Her Northern accent twisted the words. "But in adding luster to your honor, you tarnished mine."

"Right," I agreed. "Next time I let you die." I turned my back on her. It's useless arguing with a woman when she has her back up, or her mind set on something. I've been in this kind of situation before, and there's *never* a simple resolution. (And while I'm the first to admit I've never embroiled myself in a conflict involving the right to kill a *sandtiger* before, for valhail's sake, the principle's the same.)

The stud sidled a little as I swung up, which made it difficult to hook my feet into my stirrups. I heard the hissing whip of his tail as he slashed it in eloquent protest of my temper. He swung his head low and brass ornamentation clashed. I heard a muted questioning mewl from one of the pouches and realized all over again I was packing two sandtiger cubs. Here I'd gotten my name from killing one, had just killed two more, and now I was hauling cubs across the desert like a besotted fool.

Or a soft-hearted woman.

"I'll take them on my horse," Del offered.

She'd already said her pouches were too full. The offer made no sense, unless it was a peace offering. Or, more likely, an implication I couldn't handle my horse.

I scowled at her, kicked the stud into a trot and headed out across the sand. The spine beneath my saddle twisted alarmingly a moment—the stud, when he protests, is fairly dramatic about it—and I waited for the bobbing head and whipping tail that signaled a blowup. It'd be just like him to wait until I had a pouch full of sandtigers, a wounded leg, and a gut full of irritation before he bucked me off. Then I'd have a craw full of crow.

But he didn't buck. He settled, a bit hump-backed to remind me of his mood, and walked quietly enough, for him. Del came up beside me on her undramatic dun and kept an eye on the pouches. But I heard no more protests out of the cubs and figured they'd gone to sleep. If they had any sense, they'd hibernate permanently. I wasn't looking forward to unpacking them.

"Well?" I asked. "What's the decision? Plan on raising them as pets?"

She shook her head. With the hood up I couldn't see her hair; her face, even shadowed by the bright silk, was pale as cream. Except for her sunburned nose. "They're wild things. I know what you say is true: in a month they'll be deadly. But—I want to give them that month. Why let them starve to death because their mother's dead? In a couple of weeks they'll be weaned, and then we can turn them loose."

A couple of weeks. She was downright crazy. "And what do you plan on feeding them in place of milk?"

"We only have cumfa meat. It'll have to do." Her

mouth quirked a little and I saw a glint in her eyes. "Surely if a human mouth can swallow it, sandtiger mouths can."

"It's not *that* bad."

"It's horrible."

Well, it is. No getting around it. But it's the best thing for crossing the Punja, where edible game is scarce and almost uniformly smarter than you are.

I squinted as the sunlight flashed off the silver hilt of her sword. So incongruous, harnessed to a woman. "Do you really know how to use one of these?" I tapped Singlestroke's hilt, rising above my shoulder. "Or is it mostly to scare off men you'd rather not deal with?"

"It didn't scare *you* off."

I didn't dignify that with an answer.

After a moment, she smiled. "Asking me that question makes as much sense as me asking it of *you*."

"Implying, I take it, a vigorous yes."

"Vigorous," she agreed. "Yes."

I squinted at her dubiously. "It's not a woman's weapon."

"*Usually* not. But that doesn't mean it *can't* be."

"Down South it does." I scowled at her. "Be serious, bascha—you know as well as I do that very few women can handle a *knife* well, let alone a sword."

"Perhaps because too often the men won't let us." She shook her head. "You judge too quickly. You deny me my skill, but expect me to honor yours."

I thrust out my arm, flexing the fingers of my hand. "Because you only have to look at me—and my size—to know no woman could go aginst me and win."

She looked at my fingers; my hand. And then she looked at me. "You are bigger, much bigger, it's true. And no doubt more experienced than I. But don't disregard me so easily. How do you know I haven't entered the circle myself?"

I let my hand slap down against my thigh. To laugh outright at her would be uncharitable and unnecessarily rude, but I couldn't quite hide the tail end of the sound that turned into a snort of amusement.

"Do you wish it proven?" she asked.

"How—by going aginst me? Bascha . . . no *man* has gone against me and won, or I wouldn't be here."

"Not to the death. In mock-battle."

I smiled. "No."

Her mouth twisted. "No, of course not. It would be unbearable for you if you discovered I'm as good as I say I am."

"A good sword-dancer *never* says how good he is. He doesn't have to."

"*You* do. By implication."

"I don't think so." I grinned. "I wouldn't say my reputation comes by *implication*. It wouldn't be fair to Singlestroke." I hunched my left shoulder and joggled the hilt a little.

Del's mouth fell open in eloquent shock. "*You named your sword.*"

I frowned at her. "Every sword has a name. Doesn't yours?"

"But—you gave it to *me*." She reined in the gelding and stared at me. "You told me the name of your sword."

"Singlestroke," I agreed. "Yes. Why?"

Her left hand rose as if to touch her own sword hilt protectively, then she stopped the motion. But her face was pale. "What did your *kaidin* teach you?" She asked it almost rhetorically, as if she couldn't believe the thoughts forming in her head. "Didn't he teach you that to make your sword's name known is to give its power to another?" I didn't answer, and she shook her head slowly. "To *share* a magic that is personal, meant only for one, is sacrilege. It goes against all teachings." Pale brows drew down. "Do you place so little trust in magic, Tiger, that you deny your own measure of it?"

"If *kaidin* is a Northern word for shodo—sword-master— then I'd have to say he taught me respect for an honorable blade," I said. "But—a sword is still a sword, Del. It takes a man to give it life. Not magic."

"No," she said. "No. That's blasphemy. In the North, the *kaidin* teach us differently."

The stud stomped in the sand as I frowned at her. "Are you maintaining you learned from a sword-master?"

She didn't appear interested in answering my questions, only in asking me hers. "If you don't believe in magic, then how did you come by your sword?" she demanded. "In whom did you quench it? What power does it claim?" Her eyes were on Singlestroke's golden hilt. "If you can tell me its name, you can tell me all of this."

"Wait," I said, "wait a minute. First of all, how I came by Singlestroke is personal. And I never said I didn't believe in magic, just doubted the quality—or *sense*—in it. But what I want to know is why you sound like you've been apprenticed."

A little of her color came back. "Because I was. I learned a little from my father and uncles and brothers, but—later, there was more. I was *ishtoya*." Her lips tightened. "Student to my sword-master."

"A woman." I couldn't hide the flat note of disbelief in my tone.

Surprisingly, she smiled. "Girl, not woman, when my father first put a sword into my hands."

"*That* sword?" A jerk of my head indicated the weapon riding her shoulder.

"This?—no. No, of course not. This is my bloodingblade. My *jivatma*." Again, her eyes were on Singlestroke. "But—aren't you afraid your sword might turn on you now that you've told me its name?"

"No. Why should it? Singlestroke and I go way back. We look after one another." I shrugged. "It doesn't matter to me who knows his name."

She shivered a little. "The South is so—different. Different than the North."

"True," I agreed, thinking it an understatement. "And if

that's your way of telling me you're a sword-dancer, it's not very convincing."

A glint came into her eyes. "I'll let my dance speak for itself if we ever meet in the circle."

I looked at her sharply, thinking of my dream; at the shrouded, hooded figure of a woman fit for a tanzeer, sharp as a blade and twice as deadly.

Sword-dancer? I doubted it. I doubted it because I had to.

Del frowned. "Tiger—is that a breeze I feel?" She pushed back her hood. "Tiger—"

We had been standing on horseback abreast of one another, facing south. I twisted in the saddle, looking back the way we had come, and saw how the sky had turned black and silver, which meant the sand was already flying.

The storm hung in the air, swallowing everything in its path. Even the heat. It's an immensely peculiar sensation, to feel the heat sucked out of the air. Your hair stands on end and your skin prickles and your mouth goes very, very dry. When the desert turns cold, so does your blood, but it's from fear, no matter how brave you are.

"Tiger—?"

"Simoom," I said harshly, wheeling around and tightening my reins as the stud began to fret. "We're only a couple of miles from the oasis. There's shelter back in the rocks. Del—*run for it*!"

She did. I caught a glimpse of the dun as Del shot by me. The gelding's ears were pinned back and his eyes were half-closed, anticipating the storm. No horse likes to face into the wind, particularly a desert-bred horse, so it spoke volumes for Del's horsemanship that she managed to outdistance the stud, even for a moment. Our tracks showed plainly in the sand and Del followed them easily, ignoring the rising wind.

It's frightening to ride *into* a deadly simoom. All your instincts scream at you to turn tail and flee in the opposite direction, so you won't have to face it. I'd never turned into the face of a simoom before and intensely disliked the feeling; it left me sweating and slightly sickened. And I wasn't the only one: a line of sweat broke out on the stud's neck and I heard his raspy breathing. He crowhopped a bit, then lined out and overtook Del's dun almost instantly.

"Faster!" I shouted at her.

She was hunched low in the saddle, hands thrusting the reins forward on the gelding's neck. The scarlet hood flapped behind her as my own flapped behind me, tassels glinting in the strange amber-green light. Everything else turned gray-brown, hanging over our heads like an executioner's sword. Only, when it dropped, it would fall so quickly we'd never see the blow.

A cold wind blew. It filled my eyes with tears and my mouth with grit, chapping and tearing at my lips. The stud faltered, snorting his alarm, fighting his own demons in the wind. I heard Del shouting and turned in my saddle in time to see her little dun rear and plunge, totally panicked. She tried to ride it out but the gelding was terrified. And the delay was costing us.

I yanked the stud around and raced back to Del. By the time I reached her she was standing on the ground, fighting the dun from there because riding him had become impossible. But now she was in danger of being trampled, and I yelled at her to let the horse go.

She shouted something back, and then the world was brown and green and gray and my eyes were filled with pain.

"Del! *Del*!"

"I can't see you!" Her shout was twisted by the storm, ripped away from her mouth and hurled into the wailing of the wind. "Tiger—I can't see *anything*!"

I dropped off the stud, slapped him on the left shoulder and felt him go down, folding up and rolling onto his side, as he'd been trained. He lay quietly, eyes closed and head tucked back into his neck, waiting for my signal to rise. I hung onto the reins and knelt next to him, shouting for Del.

"Where are you?" she called.

"Just follow my voice!" I kept yelling until she reached me. I saw a faint shape loom up before me, one hand thrust out in front of her. I grabbed the hand and pulled her to me, shoving her down by the stud. His body would shelter us against the worst of the storm, but even so we'd be buffeted and blasted senseless if the simoom lasted long.

Del's breath rasped. "I lost my horse," she panted. "Tiger—"

"Never mind." My hand was on her head, urging her down. "Just stay down. Curl up and stay next to the stud. Better yet, stay next to me." I pulled her closer and wrapped an arm around her, glad of a legitimate excuse to touch her. Finally.

"I have knife and sword," came her muffled voice. "If you'd like to keep your hands, put them where they belong."

I laughed at her and got a mouthful of sand for my trouble. Then the simoom was on us in all its fury, and I had surviving on my mind instead of seducing Del.

Well, time for that later.

# Seven

You don't count the minutes during a simoom, or even the hours. You can't. You simple lie huddled against your horse and hope and pray the storm will blow itself out before it strips your bones of flesh and spills your brains into the sand.

Your world is filled with the raging banshee howl of the wind; the scouring caress of gritty, stinging sand; the unremitting drying up of flesh and eyes and mouth until you don't dare even *think* about water, because to think about it is torture of the most exquisite kind.

The stud lay so still I thought, for a moment, he might be dead. And the thought filled me with a brief, over-whelming uprush of fear because in the Punja a man on foot is prey to many predators. Sand. Sun. Animals. Humans. And all can be equally deadly.

But it was only a brief moment of fear—not because I am incapable of the emotion (though, admittedly, I don't usually admit to it)—because I couldn't risk trying to find out; I was alive myself at the moment and worrying too much about the stud might effectively get me killed, which more or less goes against my personal philosophy.

Del was curled in a lump of twined limbs, face tucked down against her knees as she lay on her side. I'd pulled her against my chest, fitting my body around hers as an additional shield; it left some of *me* bare to the wind and sand, but I was more concerned about her Northern skin than my Southron hide, which was—as she'd said—tough as old cumfa leather. So Del lay cradled between the stud's back and my chest, blocked from most of the storm by us both.

Much of my burnous had already shredded, which left me mostly naked except for my dhoti. I felt the relentless buffeting of the wind and sand as it scoured my flesh. After a while it merged into one unending blast, which I blocked out fairly well in my mind. But at least Del didn't have to deal with it much; I had the feeling that if she lost *her* burnous, she'd wind up shedding more than crimson silk. Probably most of her skin.

Her back was against my chest, rump snugged up against my loins. Since I have never been the stalwart sort when it comes to denying myself the pleasures of the flesh—or, occasionally, the mind—it made things a little rough for me in more ways than one. But the circumstances certainly didn't encourage any intimate notions, so I restrained myself and concentrated mostly on simply breathing.

Breathing seems easy, most of the time. But it isn't when you're swallowing sand with every inhalation. I sucked air shallowly, trying to regulate my breathing, but it's not a simple thing when you want to suck in great gulps. My nose and mouth were masked with a portion of my hood, but it wasn't the most efficient filtering system. I cupped my hand over my face, stretching fingers to shield my eyes, and waited it out as patiently as I could.

But after a while, I sort of slid off the edge of the world into a cottony blankness with only the faintest of textured edges.

I woke up when the stud lunged to his feet and shook himself so hard he sent a shower of sand and dust flying in all directions. I tried to move and discovered I was so stiff and cramped I hurt in every fiber of my body. Muscle and sinew protested vociferously as I slowly straightened everything out. Stifling the groan I longed to make (it doesn't do to shake the foundations of a legend), I slowly pushed myself into a sitting position.

I spat. There was no saliva left in my mouth, but I expelled grit nonethelss. My teeth grated. I couldn't swallow. My eyes were rimmed with caked sand. Carefully I peeled the layers away, de-gumming my lashes, until I could open both eyes at once without fear of sand contamination.

I squinted. Grimaced. Nothing makes a man feel filthier inside *and* out than surviving a simoom.

On the other hand, I much prefer filth to death.

Slowly I reached out and grasped Del's shoulder. Shook it. "Bascha, it's over." Nothing much came out of my throat except a husky croak. I tried again. "Del—come on."

The stud shook again, clattering brass ornaments. A tremendous snort cleared most of the dust from clotted nostrils. I saw eyelids and lashes as gummed as my own, even beneath the brown forelock. And then he yawned prodigiously.

I pushed myself up, stretching to crack knotted sinews. Then I looked around, slowly, and felt the familiar grue slide down my spine.

The aftermath of a simoom is so quiet it is oppressive. Nothing is the same; everything *looks* the same. The sky is flat and beige and empty; the sand is flat and beige and empty. So is a man's soul. He has survived the savage sandstorm, but even the knowledge of survival is not as exciting as it might be. In the face of such strength and mindless fury—and the awesome power of an elemental force no man may hope to master—all you sense is your own mortality. Your transience. And an overwhelming fragility.

I moved to the stud and used the remains of my shredded burnous to finish clearing his nose. He snorted again, but I didn't curse him for the blast of damp sand and

74

mucus that splattered me. His head drooped dispirit-
edly; horses fear what they can't understand, trusting to
the rider to keep them safe. In a simoom, only luck keeps
you safe.

I patted him on his dusty bay face and carefully de-
gummed his eyes. By the time I was done, Del was up.

She was in better shape than the stud, but not by much.
Her lips were cracked, gray-white, even when she spat out
sand. Her face and body were one uniform color, the color
of sand; only her eyes had any true hue, and they were
made bluer by the raw, red rims.

She hawked and spat again, then looked at me. "Well,
we're alive."

"For the moment." I unsaddled the stud and set the
pouches on the sand, pulling my burnous off all the way to
wipe him down. His fear had caused him to sweat and
sand was caked on him, altering his color from dark bay to
taupe-gray. Carefully I began scrubbing it off, hoping his
flesh wasn't so abraded he'd refuse to carry us.

Del walked over to the the pouches stiffly, hissing as she
discovered how much she hurt. She knelt and unlaced one
of the big pouches and pulled forth the two sandtiger cubs.

I'd forgotten about them entirely. And I had put the stud
down on his side without even considering the results if
he'd gone down on top of the pouch they rode in. Crushed
cubs.

Del, realizing it about the same time I did, sent me an
accusatory glare. Then she winced and sat down all the
way, cradling the cubs in her lap.

From all appearances they were unharmed and equally
unsanded. Protected by the pouch, they'd slept through the
entire simoom. Now they rediscovered one another and
attacked, rolling around in her lap like kittens.

Except they weren't.

Already their green eyes had the unfocused menace of
adult sandtigers. Their tiny stub tails stuck straight up in
the air as they crouched and attacked. Watching, I thanked

valhail their claws were budded and their fangs immature. Otherwise Del would have been clawed, poisoned, paralyzed, and wide awake as they consumed her flesh.

Eventually, I unplugged one of the botas and handed it to her. Del took it in shaking hands, ignoring the cubs as they rolled and tumbled and sank buds into her legs. Some of the water trickled out of her mouth, channeling dark lines in the dusted face; she cupped a hand beneath her chin in an attempt to catch the precious drops.

Her throat moved as she swallowed. Again. Again. Then she stopped herself and handed the bota back, staring at one dampened hand. The moisture was sucked into her flesh almost instantly.

"I didn't know it would be *this* dry." She squinted through gummed lashes. "It was hot before, when I crossed over from the North. But this is—worse."

I sucked down a substantial swallow of water and plugged the bota again, tucking it into the pouch. "We can turn back."

Del stared at me, eyes unfocused like those of the cubs still scrabbling about in her lap. She was—somewhere else. And then I realized she was dealing with the experience in her own way, acknowledging her fear and therefore dissipating its power over her. I could see it move through her body, knotting her sinews until they stood up beneath her dusty skin; unknotting, passing through her body like a ripple of cumfa track in the sand.

She sighed a little. "We'll go on."

I licked at my cracked lips, wincing inwardly at the pain. "We risk another simoom, bascha. There's rarely one when there can be two. Or even three."

"We survived this one."

I looked at the set of her jaw: locked into place, it was a blade beneath her flesh, sharp-edged and honed. "Your brother means *that* much to you, even though it's possible you might die trying to find him?"

She looked back at me. In that moment her eyes mirrored her soul, and what I saw made me ashamed of my question; of myself. Of my tactless, unthinking assumption that she valued her life more than her brother's.

But I was alone in the world, as I have always been, and the realization of such familial loyalty is not very easy to deal with.

Such binding, *powerful* kinship, as alien to me as the sword she bore. And the woman herself.

Del rose, cradling the cubs by fat, tight bellies as she pushed them back into the pouch. She ignored their mewling, muted protests as she laced the leather closed. Her spine was incredibly rigid. I had offended her deeply with my question.

I resaddled silently. Done, I swung up and held my hand down to Del, who used my stiffened foot as a stirrup as she climbed up behind me.

"Half-rations," I told her. "Water and food both. And that goes for the cubs, too."

"I know."

I tapped the stud's dusty sides with my heels, hooking toes into the stirrups. I fully expected him to protest the added weight—he's more than strong enough to carry a heavier second load than Del; he just likes to make a fuss—but he didn't. I felt a hitch-and-a-half in his first step out, then something very like a shrug of surrender. He walked.

We headed south again.

Surviving a simoom sucks the strength and heart out of you. I knew we couldn't go on much longer. The stud was stumbling and weaving; I swayed in the saddle like a wine-drowned man and Del slumped against my back. The cubs were probably the most comfortable of us all. I almost envied them.

The fouled well had also fouled our course. Because we had gone to the oasis, we now no longer followed the shortest way to Julah. It meant we had to go even farther before we reached water again. I knew it. Del, I had the feeling, also knew it. But the stud didn't.

A horse can't acknowledge the need for rationing. He simply wants. *Needs*. In the Punja, with the sun burning down on a blazing carpet of crystal sand, water becomes a commodity more precious than gold, gems, food. And I have known times when I was more than willing to trade a year of my life in exchange for a drink of cold, sweet water.

Even *warm* water.

The sand had scoured us dry, leaching our flesh of moisture. Slowly, we died of thirst from the outside in. The stud wobbled and wavered and drifted in a ragged journey across the bright sands. I didn't do much better, though at least I could ride instead of walk.

I roused Del twice when I slid to the ground to pour a little water into my cupped hand for the stud, but she refused her own ration. So did I. A taste can become a gulp, a gulp a sustained swallowing, and that consumes the resource so fast you only hasten your own death.

And so the water became the stud's property, and we his parasites.

I felt her hand on my bare back. "What are these marks?"

Her voice was raspy from dryness; I almost cautioned her not to talk, but at least speaking kept us from sliding all the way into a stupor.

I shrugged, enjoying the sensation of Northern flesh against Southron. "I've been a sword-dancer more than ten years. It takes its toll."

"Then why do it?"

Another shrug. "It's a living."

"Then you would do something else, given the chance?"

I smiled, though she couldn't see it. "Sword-dancing *was* my chance."

"But you might have stayed with—who? The Salset? —and avoided swordwork altogether."

"About as much as you could turn your back on your brother."

She removed her hand from my spine.

"You claim *you're* a sword-dancer," I said. "What's the story behind that? It's not exactly the sort of life every woman carves out for herself."

I thought she wouldn't answer. Then, "A pact," she said, "with the gods, involving a woman, a sword, and all the magic in a man."

I snorted. "Of course."

"A contract," she said. "Surely you understand that much, Tiger . . . or do you not have such here in the South?"

"With the gods?" I laughed, though not—*quite*—unkindly. "*Gods.* What a crutch. And the weak, who can't rely on themselves, sure know how to use it." I shook my head. "Look, I don't want to debate religion with you— it's never accomplished anything. You believe whatever you want. You're a woman; maybe you need it."

"You don't believe in much of anything, do you?" she asked. "*Is* there anything, for you?"

"Yes," I answered readily. "A warm, willing woman . . . a sharp, clean sword . . . and a sword-dance in the circle."

Del sighed. "How profound . . . and how utterly predictable."

"Maybe," I agreed, though the jibe hurt my pride a bit. "But what about you? You claim yourself a sword-dancer, so you know what the circle involves. You know about commitment. You know about predictability."

"In the circle?" I heard a measure of surprise in her tone. "The circle is never predictable."

"Neither is a woman." I laughed. "Maybe you and the circle are well-matched after all."

"No less than a woman and a man."

I thought maybe she smiled. But I didn't turn my head to find out.

Later, Del told me the stud was tired. As he'd been stumbling and trembling for quite some time, I agreed.

"We should rest him, then," she said. "We should walk." She didn't wait for my answer. She simply slid off his dusty rump.

And landed in a tangle of arms and legs.

I reined in the stud and looked down on her, admiring the clean lines of her long legs since the burnous was caught around her hips. For a moment, only a moment, my fog evaporated, and I smiled.

Del glared up at me wearily. "You're heavier than I am. Get off."

I leaned forward in the shallow saddle and joggled my right foot enough to free it of the stirrup. Then, sloppily, I dragged the leg across the stud's rump and saddle and slithered down, scraping my bare abdomen against the left stirrup. And not caring.

Discovering a desire in my legs to collapse upon themselves, I clung to the saddle until I could lock my knees. Del remained sprawled in the sand. although she had decorously rearranged the burnous.

"Neither of us is in any shape to walk anywhere," I informed her. But I bent and caught a muscled wrist, pulling her to her feet. "Hang onto me, if you want."

We staggered across the desert in a bizarre living chain: me leading the stud and Del latched onto the harness holding Singlestroke. Though he was two legs up on us, the stud didn't do much better; he had that many more legs to coordinate. He stumbled, kicking sand against my ankles. It added to the layers already there. And even though my hide is accustomed to the heat and sunlight, I could still feel the exposed portions of my body, which was everything but the areas covered by my dhoti and harness, broiling in the blistering glare. But at least I could take it better than Del, still wrapped in scarlet silk. There were rents in the fabric and most of the gold tassels were gone, but I didn't miss such questionable majesty. At least what remained protected her somewhat.

We walked. Always southward. Horse and man and woman.

And the two sandtiger cubs, oblivious of it all.

The stud sensed it first. He stopped short, head swinging clumsily eastward, nearly knocking me over. His nostrils expanded as he blew loudly, and I saw his ears twitch forward rigidly. Eastward. Telling me precisely the direction from which the threat came.

I squinted. Stared. Shaded my eyes with one hand. And eventually made out what came riding from the east.

"Hoolies," I said flatly.

Del stood next to me, mimicking my posture with one pale hand. But her puzzlement was manifest, as was her consternation. Her Northern eyes couldn't see it. I could. Clearly.

Across the horizon rose a shadow, an ocher smudge against bleached blue sky. A fine veil of sand, floating, floating, prefacing an arrival. And when the veil dissolved into the undulating vanguard of a line of riders, Del touched my arm.

"Maybe they'll share water with us," she said.

"I don't think so." It was all I could do not to snap at her.

"But the courtesy of the traveler—"

"In the Punja there is no such thing. Out here there's one simple philosophy: fend for yourself. No one will do it for you." I didn't take my eyes off the advancing line of riders. "Del—stay behind me."

I heard the hissing whine of a sword withdrawn.

I glanced at her sharply over a shoulder and saw grim determination in her face. "Put it away!" I snapped.

"Don't *ever* bare blade in the Punja unless you understand desert customs. Bascha—*sheathe* it!"

Del looked past me to the approaching riders a long moment. I knew she was tempted to disobey me; it was in every line of her posture. But she did as I had asked. Slowly. And when I glanced back myself and saw the rippling black line shimmering in the heat like a wavering mirage, I sucked in a deep, deep breath.

"Del, *do not* say a word. Let me do the talking."

"I can speak for myself." Coolly, not defiantly; a simple declaration.

I swung around and trapped her head between my hands. Our faces were only inches apart. "Do as I say! A mouth flapping when it shouldn't can lose us our lives. Understand?"

Her eyes, looking past me, widened suddenly. "Who *are* those men?"

I let her go and turned around. The line of riders drew up before us, spreading out in a precise semicircle that effectively cut off our escape in three directions. The fourth lay open behind us in obscene invitation: we'd be dead before we mounted, if we were foolish enough to try it.

Like me, they were half naked. Like me, they were burned dark by the sun, but their arms were striped with spiraling scars dyed a permanent blue. Bare chests bore blue sunburst designs of differing complexities; each boy, upon reaching puberty, competes with his peers at designing the sunburst his mother—or closest female relative—incises into his skin in a painful scarification ritual. But there was one uniformity in all the sunbursts: each was offset by a yellow eye set in the exact center. Black hair was greased, clubbed back, laced with cords of various colors. Black eyes dwelled avidly on Del and me.

"Their *noses*—" she said in horror.

Well, they had them. But each nose was pierced by a flat enameled ring. The color of the rings, along with the cords in their hair, denote rank; colors are changed if they move upward or downward in the caste system. In this tribe, nothing is immutable except ferocity.

"Hanjii," I said briefly.

Del's indrawn breath of alarm was audible. "The *cannibals*?"

"They'll give us a bath," I told her. "Makes us taste better."

I ignored her muttered comment and turned my attention to the warrior who wore a gold ring in his nose, signifying highest rank and equivalent authority. I used the Desert dialect as I spoke to him; it passes as a universal language in the Punja.

I told him the truth. I left out nothing, except that Del had hired me to lead her across the Punja. And with good reason: to the Hanjii, women are slaves. Non-people. If I indicated that Del claimed any amount of authority over me, even in something so simple as an employer-employee relationship, I'd be considered a non-man and therefore perfectly acceptable for their cannibalistic rites. Since I didn't want to wind up in their cookfires, I took care to depreciate Del's value as an individual. No doubt it would earn me her enmity, if she knew, but then I didn't intend to tell her.

Unless, of course, I had to.

I finished my story, grandly embellished Hanjii-fashion, and waited, hoping Del would keep her mouth shut.

Gold Ring conferred with the others. They all spoke Hanjii with a few scattered slang terms in Desert, so I was able to follow well enough. The gist of the discussion was they hadn't had a feast for a while and wondered if our bones might appease their rather voracious gods. I swore inwardly and hoped my apprehension wouldn't transmit itself to Del.

Finally the Hanjii stopped discussing matters altogether and simply stared at us intently. Which was worse. And then Gold Ring rode forward to face us from a distance more conducive to intimidation.

Except I wasn't intimidated. Just tense. There's a difference.

Gold Ring had four knives stuck in his braided belt above the short leather kilt he wore. The others all carried two and three, which meant he held very high rank indeed.

He gestured toward the stud . "Now."

That needed no interpretation. I turned to Del. "We've been invited home for supper."

"Tiger—"

I shut her up with a hand pressed aginst her mouth. "Poor joke. They haven't decided anything yet. We're supposed to mount up and go with them." I sighed and patted the stud's dusty shoulder. "Sorry, old man."

Mustering what energy I had left (the Hanjii are merciless when it comes to tormenting those they believe are weak), I sprang up into the blanketed saddle and leaned down to offer a hand to Del. It took all I had not to fall out of the saddle as she swung up behind me.

Her hands, clasping my waist, were ice-cold.

For that matter, so were mine.

# Eight

Hanjii women, like Hanjii men, believe scarification enhances beauty. I've seen the results before and therefore can afford to be a bit blasé about them; Del, who hadn't, reacted much as I'd expected: in horror and disgust. But, thank valhail, also in utter silence.

The women go barebreasted to show off the designs spiraling around their breasts, each line dyed bright crimson. Like the men, they wear rings in their noses, but plain silver ones; women don't earn the colors of rank through the same system. Their rank is earned through marriage or concubinage, and it's only after they've achieved one or the other that they undergo the scarification ritual.

You can always tell a Hanjii woman who's still a virgin because her dark skin is smooth and unmarred, her nose free of silver. For a man like me, who prefers unblemished women, it's easy to overlook the older women with their scars and dye and nose-rings and look instead to the younger ones. But there is a problem: the Hanjii believe no woman should remain a virgin past the age of ten, which leaves the unblemished girls very young indeed.

And I've never thought much of bedding babies.

"I feel overdressed." Del's whisper crept over my shoulder to my ear, and I grinned. She *was*. Hanjii women wear only a brief linen kilt; Del's tunic and my borrowed burnous covered almost all of her.

Which I *preferred*, in the middle of a Hanjii camp.

"Keep your hood up," I advised, and was pleasantly surprised to hear silence in return. The girl was catching on.

We were escorted by all forty members of the warrior party through the flock of dusty sheep (sheep being the tribe's primary source of food; the second being people) to a yellow hyort at the very center of the circular encampment. The Hanjii don't call them hyorts, but I couldn't think of the proper term. There we were told to dismount, which Del and I did with alacrity.

Gold Ring hopped off his horse and disappeared inside the hyort. When he came back out he was flanked by a man whose hide was liberally scarred and dyed with colors of every desert shade: vermilion, ocher, amber, verdigris, carnelian, sienna, and many more. His nose-ring was a flat plate of gold flopping down against his upper lip; difficult to eat, drink or talk, I thought, but then you don't argue with a Hanjii who thinks he's beautiful.

Besides, this man was the shoka himself.

Before anyone could say anything, I jerked Singlestroke from the sheath and knelt, pressing callused knees against hot sand, and carefully set my sword in front of the shoka. The sunlight flashing off the blade was blinding. I squinted. But didn't move again.

A dozen or so knives came out of the closest belts, but no one moved to strike. Properly obeisant, I waited, head bowed, then—judging the homage time sufficent—I rose and walked around to the right side of the stud, unlacing the largest pouch.

I pulled the two squalling sandtiger cubs from it, carried them back to the shoka, and bent to dump them at his sandaled feet.

"A gift." I spoke in Desert. "For the shoka of the Hanjii, may the Sun shine on his head."

I heard Del suck in a shocked and outraged breath—they were *her* pets, after all—but she wisely kept her mouth shut.

I stood before the chieftain of the Hanjii and hoped her Northern gods thought highly of her, since she spoke to them so often. The whole enterprise was a risk. I'd heard others had managed to buy their way out of a festival fire with gifts, but no one could predict what might catch the eye—and therefore the clemency—of a Hanjii shoka.

The cubs rediscovered one another and began rolling around in the sand, growling and shrieking and generally doing a first-rate job of sounding fierce—if a trifle ineffective. The shoka stared down at them a long moment, as did everyone else. I watched his face instead of the cubs, holding my breath.

He was an older man, most likely an *old* man; it was impossible to gauge his age with certainty. In the Punja the youth gets baked out of a face very quickly, and I've seen thirty-year-olds who looked fifty. (Or older.) This warrior had a good thirty or forty years on me, I thought, which meant he was especially dangerous. You don't live to the age of sixty or seventy here without learning a few nasty tricks. Especially among the Hanjii.

He glared down at the cubs, dark forehead furrowed so that graying black brows knitted together over his blade of a nose. The Hanjii are not a pretty race, with all their scars and dyes and nose-rings, but they are impressive. And I was dutifully impressed.

Abruptly the shoka bent and scooped up one of the cubs, ignoring its outraged grunts and shrieks of protest. He peeled back the dark lips to examine its—*his*—forming fangs, then carefully spread each paw and felt the buds on each of the immature claws. Black eyes went to the string of claws around my neck, then to the scars on my face.

He grunted. "The shoka has heard of a dancer called the Sandtiger." Unaccented Desert, though he used the Hanjii habit of referring to himself as a third person. "Only the Sandtiger would ride in the desert with cubs in a pouch on his horse."

High praise, from a Hanjii. Grudging respect. (Grudg-

ing because the Hanjii consider themselves the toughest
tribe in the desert; while they admire courage in others,
they hate to admit others possess the attribute). I was
surprised he recognized me, but said nothing about it.
Instead, I looked back at him gravely. "He is indeed the
Sandtiger."

"The Sandtiger has given the Hanjii a great gift."

"The gift is deserved." Careful intonation: enough neg-
ligence to emphasize the reputation of the Hanjii; enough
conviction to win his approval. "The Sandtiger has heard
of the ferocity of the Hanjii and wished only to add to the
legend. Who but the shoka of the Hanjii would keep
sandtigers in his camp?"

Who but the shoka of the Hanjii would *want* to? The
cubs would prove very violent pets, but if any tribe was a
match for them the Hanjii were. I'd let the shoka worry
about it, although most likely he'd be delighted with their
ferocity.

The old man smiled, showing resin-blackened teeth.
"The shoka will share aqivi with the Sandtiger." He
shoved the cub at Gold Ring and disappeared within the
hyort.

"Reprieve," I muttered to Del; it wouldn't do to let the
others see me speaking to her, since a woman is beneath
general conversation. "Come on."

Silently, she followed me into the hyort.

The shoka turned out to be a very civil sort, generous
with aqivi and compliments. By the time we finished the
first bota we were good friends, telling one another what
marvelous warriors we were and how no man could possibly beat us. Of course it happened to be *true*; had anyone
ever beaten the shoka he'd have gone into the cooking pot,
on his journey to the Sun. As for myself, had anyone
beaten *me*, I wouldn't be sharing a Hanjii hyort with a
rainbow-scarred shoka and a blond-haired Northern woman
who was smart enough to keep her mouth shut.

By the time we finished the second bota, we were done with trying to impress one another with our battle exploits, and the talk turned to women. This necessitated the embellishment of how many conquests we had made over the years; when we had first lost our virginity—he claimed at eight, I went him better and claimed six, until I remembered I was in *his* hyort and 'admitted' I was wrong—and methods. All this made me very conscious of Del sitting so silently by my side.

After a while I tried to turn the talk to another subject, but the shoka was perfectly content to ramble on for hours about all of his wives and concubines and how tiring it was keeping so many women satisfied, yet how fortunate he was that the Sun had blessed him with endless vigor and a magnificent tool.

For a horrible moment I thought he might propose we compare, but he downed another squirt of aqivi and seemed to forget all about the subject. I breathed a deep sigh of relief that stopped short when I heard Del's muffled snicker.

It also caught the shoka's attention.

He peered at her out of black eyes that suddenly reminded me of Osmoon's: small, deep-set, piggy, and full of clever guile. He reached out and flipped back the hood, revealing bright hair, pale face, and blue, blue eyes.

It was his turn to suck in a breath. "The Sandtiger rides with a woman of the Sun!"

The sun—or Sun—is their major deity. So long as he considered Del so blessed, our safety was more or less assured. I shot her a sharp glance and saw the limpid expression in her eyes and the faint polite smile curving her lips.

"The shoka wishes to see her better."

I looked back quickly at the old man as I heard the belligerent note in his voice and saw how avidly his eyes traveled over the burnous-shrouded form.

"What do I do?" she muttered between her lips.

"He wants to see you. I think it's safe; he believes you've been blessed by the Sun. Go ahead, Del—take the burnous off."

She rose and pulled the crimson burnous over her head, dropping it at her feet in a bright pile of silk and gold tassels. She was dusty and droopy with exhaustion, but none of it hid her flawless beauty and magnificent pride.

The shoka stood up suddenly and reached out, spinning Del around before she could say a word. I was on my feet instantly, but all he did was look at the sword strapped to her shoulder.

I saw what he saw: how the alien shapes in the hilt seemed almost alive, squirming in the silver. A basket of serpents, tangled in living knots—a dragon's mouth belching flame that became the draperies of a woman; the kilt of a fighting warrior—Northern knotwork with no beginning, no middle, no end—countless, nameless things, all set into the metal.

Inwardly I shivered, recalling the touch of that sword, and how *cold*, how cold the steel felt. How it tapped at my soul, seeking something I could neither give nor comprehend.

I saw how the shoka looked at the sword and then at Del. After a moment, he looked at me. "The woman wears a sword." All friendliness was gone.

I cursed myself for forgetting to take the sword and harness from her, claiming both as my own. Flouting custom in the Punja can be deadly.

I sucked in a careful breath. "The Sun shines also in the North beyond the Punja," I said clearly. "The Sun that shines on the shoka's head also shines on hers."

"Why does she wear a sword?" he demanded.

"Because in the North, where the Sun also shines, customs are different from those of the shoka and the Sandtiger."

He grunted. I could feel tension radiating from Del. We

stood almost shoulder to shoulder, but even two against one would result in our deaths. Killing a shoka would simply buy us a more painful, lingering death in the Hanjii stewpots.

He looked at her again. All of her. He chewed on the tip of his tongue. "The shoka has never painted a woman of pale skin."

The thought of Del's fairness marred with scars and dye made me sick. But I kept it from him. I actually managed to smile at him. "The woman belongs to the Sandtiger."

His brows shot up. "Does the Sandtiger wish to fight the shoka of the Hanjii?"

Hoolies, he was asking for her. The Hanjii have an elaborate courtesy that circles around and around the issue until it finally comes close enough for you to figure out what they really mean. Inviting me to fight him for Del was his way of telling me he fully expected me to hand her over without argument, for no man willingly goes against a Hanjii warrior.

"He wants you to fight." Del had just discovered it. And very calm she was, too, considering the fight would be to the death.

"Looks like he might just get it, too. I mean—part of the deal we struck is to make sure you get to Julah, not into an old man's bed." I grinned. "Ever had two men fight over you before?"

"Yes," she said grimly, surprising me; but not surprising me at all, once I thought about it. "Tiger—tell him no."

"If I tell him I won't fight, it means I'm giving in to him," I pointed out. "It means I'm making a gift of you to him."

Del squared her shoulders and looked the shoka in the eye. Not a wise thing for a woman to do. And it got worse when she totally circumvented custom and spoke to him directly. "If the shoka wishes to fight over the Northern woman, he will have to fight the woman first."

Plainly put, the shoka was flabbergasted. So was I, to be honest. Not only had she ignored the rules of common Hanjii courtesy, but she also challenged him personally.

His nose-ring quivered against his lip. Every sinew in his body stood up beneath his sun-darkened skin. "Warriors do not fight *women*."

"I'm not a *woman*," she said dryly, "I'm a sword-dancer as is the Sandtiger. And I will fight you to prove it."

"Del," I said.

"Be quiet." She'd given up on politeness altogether. "You're not stealing *this* fight from me."

"By all the gods of valhail," I hissed, "don't be such a fool!"

"Stop calling me a fool, you stupid sand-ape!"

The shoka grunted. "Perhaps it would be better if the woman fought the Sandtiger."

Del didn't see the humor in that, especially when I laughed aloud. "I will fight," she said clearly, "anyone."

A gleam crept into the shoka's black eyes. He smiled. That effectively banished my momentary good humor and Del's irritation, and we exchanged frowning glances of consternation.

"Good," he said. "The Sandtiger and the woman will fight. If the Sandtiger wins, the woman is his . . . and then he will fight the shoka of the Hanjii to see which of us may keep her." His eyes drifted from my face to Del's. "If the woman wins—" his tone expressed eloquent disbelief as well as elaborate courtesy "—she is obligated to no man, and given her freedom."

"I have that already," Del muttered, and I waved a hand to shut her up.

Hoolies, the shoka was smart. He knew I would win, thereby obliging his wish to fight me for Del. There was no way he believed Del capable of fighting me on a warrior's terms, so he was certain of winning her in the end because

the shoka would be fresh while I was not—*and* after I'd let
him see my habits in the circle, which is an advantage
every man likes to have. It would make his victory all the
sweeter.

I looked at Del and saw the realization in her eyes. Then
I saw a tightening of her face and defiant determination—
and felt the first brush of fear.

I couldn't throw the fight. To do so would damage my
reputation; while I was certain I could survive the damage
ordinarily, the shoka would be so insulted he might forget
all about letting us live. We'd undoubtedly become dinner.

Besides, there is no way I'd deliberately lose to a woman.
There's such a thing as pride.

Del smiled. "See you in the circle."

"Ah, hoolies," I said in disgust.

Within a matter of minutes the news made the rounds of
the camp. Everyone knew the Northern woman and the
Sandtiger would meet in a circle for the sword-dancer. The
Hanjii don't have swords, but they do appreciate a good
dance. And they're masters with the knife. Once I'd de-
feated Del, I'd have to give up Singlestroke and fight the
shoka with my knife, which isn't my strongest weapon.
I'm deadly enough with it, but the sword is my magic and
I've always felt incredibly at ease with Singlestroke resting
so comfortably in my hands.

Del hadn't bothered to put the burnous back on. We
stood outside the hyort in full view of the camp, and her
fair coloring and unblemished skin were causing a lot of
comment. Me they ignored altogether.

"I can't throw the dance," I told her quietly. "You
know that. It has to be real."

She slanted me an enigmatic glance. "I admire your
modesty."

"Del—"

"I dance to win," she said evenly. "You need have no
fear of damaging your name or your pride by matching a

woman who will go down with the first stroke. The Hanjii won't be disappointed.''

"Del, I don't want to hurt you. But if I hold back too much, they'll know it.''

"So don't hold back,'' she suggested.

"I just want to apologize in advance for any cuts and bruises.''

"*Ah.*''

I scowled at her. "Del, come on—be serious about this.''

"I *am* serious. I don't think *you* are.''

"Of course I'm serious!''

She faced me squarely. "If you were truly serious, you'd stop talking and simply judge me as a dancer instead of as a woman.''

She had a point, much as I hated to admit it. Never before had I *apologized* for any injuries I might administer to an opponent. The whole thing suddenly struck me as ludicrous, so I ignored her altogether and stared grimly out at the gathering Hanjii.

Del started singing softly under her breath.

We were both tired and sunburned and sand-scoured and uncertain of the dance facing us. Del's face was unreadable, but I could see it in her eyes. For all her proud talk, I doubted she'd ever gone against a man before.

As for me, I felt helpless and exasperated. I knew she'd fight me with all her strength and skill—expecting me to do the same—yet knowing I'd be hampered by the knowledge of her sex. It was an advantage for her. And I wasn't about to give in to it.

She was still singing softly as the Hanjii warrior with the gold nose-ring led us to the circle drawn in the sand. Del unlaced her sandals and tossed them aside; I did the same. Both of us were unharnessed, having shed them in the shoka's hyort along with our burnouses. And then she unsheathed her sword.

I heard startled exclamations, indrawn breaths, astonished mutters. Well, I couldn't really blame the Hanjii. Cold, clean steel can startle anyone not accustomed to it. But then, Del's sword was not precisely clean *steel*.

But cold? Yes. Unequivocally. She unsheathed that thing in the bright sunlight of the Punja, and the day immediately altered. It wasn't just that she was a stranger from the North or a woman with a sword. It was as if the black cloud of a summer storm had shut away the face of the sun, banishing the heat.

Hot? Yes. Still was. But I felt the flesh tighten and rise on my bones, and shivered.

She stood just outside the circle. Barefoot, bare-legged, bare-armed. Waiting. With that unearthly sword held lightly in one hand.

I glanced briefly at Singlestroke. Blue-steel, glinting in the sunlight. Honed and polished and prepared, as Singlestroke always was. But—there was a difference. For all he was a formidable sword, he didn't alter the tenor of the day.

Together we stepped into the circle and walked to the center, to the blood-red rug spread precisely in the middle of the circle. We set our weapons down carefully.

Singlestroke was inches longer and certainly heavier than her nameless Northern sword. No, not nameless—just unnamed to me. I thought the weapons as unevenly matched as we were.

Perhaps that's what got the Hanjii so excited. They crowded around the circle like men wagering on a dog fight.

Del and I walked to opposite sides of the circle and stepped outside facing one another. It would be a foot race to the swords in the center, then the sword-dance proper, full of feints and slashes, footwork and flashing blades.

Her lips still moved in the song. And as I looked at her I was revisited by my dream: a Northern woman singing a Northern sword-song facing me across the circle.

I felt an unearthly tremor slide down my spine. Shook it away with effort. "Luck, Del," I called to her.

She tilted her head, considering it. She smiled, laughed——and then she was racing for her sword.

# Nine

**D**el's sword was in her hands and slashing at my face
before I got my hands on Singlestroke. I felt the breeze—
oddly, in this heat, a *cool* one—as the Northern blade
whipped over my head in a bizarre salute. By then
Singlestroke was up and facing her, and she backed off.
But the first blow had been struck, and it was hers.

I did not return it immediately. I moved away, slipping
through the sand to the edge of the circle, and watched
her. I watched how she held her sword, judging her grip;
watched how her thighs flexed, muscles rolling; watched
how she watched me.

And I watched the sword.

It was silver-hilted, the blade a pale, subtle pink; not the
pink of flowers or women, but the pink of watered blood.
There was an edge to it. Hard, honed, prepared, just as
Singlestroke was. But my blade was plain. Runes like
water ran down Del's blade from the twisted, elegant
crosspiece to the tip. In the sunlight, they glittered like
diamonds. Like ice. Hard, cold, ice.

And for just a moment, as I looked at the blade, I could
have sworn it was still sheathed; not in leather, but ice.
Ice-warded against the heat of the Southron sun.

And the skill of a Southron sword-dancer.

Del waited. Across the circle, she simply waited. There
was no tension in her body, no energy wasted in anticipa-

JENNIFER ROBERSON

tion. Patiently, unperturbedly, she waited, assessing me as
I assessed her; judging my skill with the eye of a student
taught the rituals of the dance by a shodo. Or, in her
language, a *kaidin*.

Silver. White, blinding metal tinged with salmon-pink,
intensified by the sunlight. And as she swept the sword up
to salute the beginnings of the dance, a salmon-silver line
seemed to follow the motion of the blade like a shooting
star trailing smoke and flame.

Hoolies, what *was* that sword?

But the dance was begun, and I had no more time for
questions or imagery.

Del moved around the circle in a blaze of yellow hair,
feinting and laughing and calling out encouragement in her
Northern tongue. The muscles in her calves and forearms
flexed, sinews standing up in ridges whenever she shifted
her stance. I let her do most of the dancing while I judged
her technique.

No doubt my performance disappointed the Hanjii for its
lack of fire, but I was too busy trying to discover a weak
spot in Del's defense to give it a thought.

Like her, I stayed up on the balls of my feet, weight
shifted forward, evenly distributed. I moved through the
sand smoothly, but I don't rely on the supple quickness
that appeared to be her particular strength. My dance is
one of strength and endurance and strategy. I'm too heavy
for suppleness, too muscled for that light quickness, though
far from being slow. But Del's upright posture and amazingly precise blade patterns made me look like a lumbering
behemoth.

Still, we were poorly matched. It wasn't a proper sword-
dance, because neither of us particularly wanted to dance
against the other. At least, *I* didn't want to dance against
Del. She looked fairly well pleased by it, herself.

Singlestroke beat back her every advance with ease. I
had a longer reach, longer sword; she was quicker but
couldn't get in close enough, so her advantage didn't tip

the odds in her favor. On the other hand, I was clearly hampered by not wishing to hurt her. I didn't employ my strength and experience to overcome her utterly. We danced like a coy, teasing mare and a determined, frustrated stud; neither winning, neither losing, and both of us getting wearier by the moment.

Some sword-dance. The simoom had sapped us of energy, no matter what the demands for greater exertion under these bizarre circumstances. Pride notwithstanding, neither of us had the endurance to make a proper showing. We simply followed the rituals perfunctorily, without exhibiting the skills and techniques a shodo-trained sword-dancer ordinarily exhibits.

But then Del wasn't really a sword-dancer, even if she did claim to be *kaidin*-trained. Southroner I am, but I'm also a professional sword-dancer; one of the responsibilities of the profession is keeping up to date on all sword-related customs.

And women weren't part of them, even in the North.

But she was good. Incredibly good. Even slowed by fatigue and heat, even pressed as she was, her skill was obvious. Her bladework was limited to a small area generally, pointing up the unexpected strength in her wrists and the differences in our styles. Tall as I am, my reach is much longer than that of most opponents. Singlestroke is correspondingly longer and heavier, therefore. Which gives me an advantage over many men. But not much of one over Del.

Rarely did she employ scything sweeps or thrusts that might overextend her balance; never did she exhibit the frustration that often leads men to attempt foolhardy patterns that do little more than tire them or leave them open to counterthrust. I used a few of my ploys, trying to force her into my style of fighting (which would, of course, jar her out of her own and make my victory easier), but she didn't fall for my 'suggestions'. She just danced.

Coolly, so coolly, she danced. Blocked, feinted, riposted.

Parried. Thrust, tightly and with incredible forearm/wrist control. Caught my own blade again and again, twisting it aside. Smoothly, so smoothly, she danced.

Hoolies, but how the woman could dance!

Nonetheless, fatigue began to take its toll. Del's face slowly flushed an alarming shade of red. It was already burned from the sun, and the rising color only confirmed she was on the edge of imminent collapse. The combination of sun and heat and sand would overcome her long before I could.

Especially as I was just as worn out as *she* was, and more than ready to call a halt to this farce.

Again and again Del dipped her head to scrub her brow against an arm, wiping away the sweat that threatened her vision. I was covered by it myself, aware of it trickling down my belly, my back, my brow. But I am more accustomed to it, and accustomed to ignoring it, and I didn't allow it to distract me.

I worried about her. I worried so much I forgot about the object of the sword-dance, which is victory. Del's blade twisted out from under mine and came up to nick the underside of my left forearm, spilling blood so fast it stained the taupe-gray sand vermilion.

For a moment I hesitated (which was stupid), then leveled my sword in renewed defense.

Del's teeth were gritted so hard the muscles of her jaw stood up, sculpting her face into a mask of delicate marble; silk and satin and infinitely seductive. As well as determinedly dangerous. "Fight me—" she gasped. "Don't just throw up a guard—*fight* me!"

So I did. I stepped forward, feinting a stroke that I quickly turned against her. I slapped the flat of my blade against her upper arm, smacking it hard enough to raise a welt instantly. Had I used the edge, it would have sheared off her arm at the shoulder.

The Hanjii were a blur. Part of me heard their voices muttering and mumbling, but most of me was focused on the dance, and my opponent. Breathing came hard and painful because I was hot and tired and dehydrated, yet somehow I had to conserve my strength for the second fight. If I allowed Del to tire me too much, I'd go down far too easily beneath the shoka's knife.

"I dance to *win*—" Del lunged at me across the circle.

I'll admit it, she caught me by surprise. Her sword slid easily under my guard, nicked the heel of my hand and continued along the line of my ribs.

Angrily I slapped the flat of her blade aside with my bare hand (not generally recommended, but she'd stabbed my pride with the move), caught her wrist and squeezed hard enough to drop the sword from her hand. Her red face went white with pain. Ignoring it, I hooked an ankle around her feet and jerked.

(Not precisely a move approved by the shodos, either, but then this had gone past being a ritualized dance).

Del went down. Hard. She bit her lip, which bled immediately, and sprawled so awkwardly I almost felt sorry for her. She had blooded me twice, but in a single move I'd disarmed and tripped her onto her back, leaving her throat bare to my blade. I had only to rest the tip against her neck and ask for her to yield, and the dance was done.

But not for Del. Her sword was out of reach, but not the rug. I'd forgotten about it. She hadn't. She tore it from the sand, threw it around Singlestroke to foul the blade, then scooped a handful of sand into my face.

To hoolies with the sword and the dance! I dumped it and lunged for Del, blind but not helpless. Both hands went around a slim ankle. I heard her cry out and felt her struggle, twisting, but I dragged her to me, inch by inch. Through the sand clogging my vision I saw her hand clawing out for the nearest sword—my own—but both were out of reach.

"*I* don't need the sword to win," I jeered, trying not to gasp aloud. "*I* can kill you with my bare hands. How do you want it, bascha?" I put my hands around her throat and hung over her, knees on either side of her hips. "I can strangle you, or break your neck, or just plain *sit* on you until you suffocate." I paused. "You can't do anything to me—you can't even *move*—so why don't we just end this little farce? Do you yield?"

Blood from her bitten lip was smeared across her face, mingling with the dusting of sand. Her breasts quivered as she struggled to breathe, which only made me want to forget all about winning and smother her in another fashion, with my mouth on hers.

Del twisted her hips and jammed a knee up between my spread thighs. Hard.

Once I finished making a thoroughly disgusting and humiliating spectacle of myself by throwing up into the sand, I realized the dance was decidedly over. So I just lay there trying to recover my breath and composure while over a hundred Hanjii warriors and double the number of wives and concubines looked on in silence. And astonishment.

But I thought the women looked suspiciously satisfied.

Del stood over me with her rune-worked sword grasped in one hand. "I have to ask you to yield," she pointed out. "Are you all right?"

"Are you happy now?" I croaked, refusing to give into the urge to cradle the portion of my anatomy she'd nearly destroyed. "You practically turned me into a eunuch without even using a knife."

Del's expression was suitably apologetic, but I saw something lurking in the corners of her eyes. "I'm sorry," she said. "It was a trick. It wasn't fair."

At least she *admitted* it. I just lay there on my side and stared up at her, wishing I had the strength to jerk her down into the sand again. But I knew any sort of violent—or even *non*violent—movement would renew the pain, and so I didn't. "Hoolies, woman, why do you even bother with a sword? You can beat a man with a *knee*!"

"I have to ask you to yield," she reminded me. "Or do you wish to continue the sword-dance?"

"That wasn't a dance," I retorted. "Not a *proper* one. And I don't think I can continue anything right now." I scowled up at her. "All right, bascha . . . I yield. *This* time. And I think even the shoka will be satisfied that the woman beat the Sandtiger."

She pushed loose hair back with one hand. "You're right, it wasn't proper. My *kaidin* would be outraged. But—it's a trick my brothers taught me. A woman's trick."

I sat up and wished I hadn't. "Your brothers taught you *that*?"

"They said that I needed an advantage."

"Advantage!" I said in disgust. "Hoolies, Del—you almost ruined me for life. How would you like *that* on your conscience?"

She looked at me for a long moment, shrugged a little, and turned her back on me as she marched across the circle to the shoka. By the time I was on my feet (trying to act as if I felt fine) and had Singlestroke in harness again, strapped on, the shoka himself had buckled the harness on her, though he studiously avoided touching the sword. A mark of high respect, since ordinarily the Hanjii shun anything to do with swords. (And women, too, much of the time.)

He looked at me as I joined them. "The dance was good. The woman was good. The Sandtiger was not so good."

Privately I agreed with him, but I didn't say it aloud. Somehow my pride wouldn't quite let me.

Especially in front of Del.

"The Hanjii have need of strong warriors," the shoka announced. "Hanjii women do not always breed enough. The shoka will take the Northern woman as his wife and will improve the blood of the Hanjii."

I stared at him. Del, not understanding the dialect, glanced at me sharply. "What does he say?"

I smiled. "He wants to marry you."

"*Marry* me!"

"You impressed him." I shrugged, enjoying the look of horror on her face. "He wants to get children on you— Hanjii warriors." I nodded a little. "See what you get for resorting to dirty tricks?"

"I *can't* marry him," she squeezed out between gritted teeth. "Tell him, Tiger."

"*You* tell him. You're the one who impressed him so much."

Del glared at me, looked at the shoka a minute, then back at me again. Still glaring. But also, apparently, at a loss for words.

I wasn't, but neither could I figure out a diplomatic way of refusing the man. Finally I cleared my throat and tried the only thing that came to mind: "The woman is more than the Sandtiger's woman, shoka. She is his wife, blessed by the Sun."

He stared at me out of malignant black eyes. "The Sandtiger did not tell the shoka that before."

"The shoka didn't ask."

Del frowned, watching us both.

The shoka and the Sandtiger spent endless minutes staring at one another, then at last the old man grunted, relinquishing his claim. "It was agreed: if the woman won, she was free to choose. The woman will choose."

I breathed a sigh of relief. "Pick one of us, bascha."

Del looked at me a long, silent moment, blandly weighing us both. I knew it was all for my benefit, but I couldn't say anything or risk being accused of manipulating her decision.

And she knew it.

Finally, she nodded. "The woman has a husband, shoka. The woman chooses him."

I translated.

If nothing else, the Hanjii are an honorable sort of people. The shoka had said she could choose; she had chosen.

He couldn't go back on his word, or he'd lose face in front of all his people. I felt a whole lot better.

Then the shoka looked at me with hostility in his eyes, which is a whole lot worse than malignancy. Hostility he might *do* something about.

He did. "The shoka promised nothing to the Sandtiger. He has his fate to suffer. Since the woman has freely chosen him, she will suffer it also."

"Uh, oh," I muttered.

"*What*?" Del whispered.

"We're free," I told her, "in a manner of speaking."

Del opened her mouth to ask me something, but she shut it again as the shoka gestured. A moment later Gold Ring arrived on horseback along with his thirty-nine fellow warriors. He led two horses: Del's dun gelding and my bay stud.

"You go," the shoka said, and made the sign of the blessing of the Sun. A rather definitive blessing.

I sighed. "I was afraid of that."

"*What*?" Del demanded.

"It's the Sun Sacrifice. They won't kill us or cook us—they'll just let the sun do it for us."

"Tiger—"

"Mount up, bascha. Time to go." I swung up on the stud. After a moment, she climbed up on the little dun gelding.

Gold Ring led us into the desert. We rode in circles all over for an hour or two before he motioned us to dismount, and even then I don't think Del quite understood. At least, not until two other warriors gathered the reins to our horses.

I patted the stud as he was led away. "Luck, old man. Remember all your tricks." I grinned, recalling them myself. Some I'd taught him; most he'd been born knowing, as horses sometimes are.

Del watched as her dun was taken away. And then she understood.

Neither of us said anything. We just watched the Hanjii ride out of sight into the line of the horizon, an undulating line of black against the brown. The sun beat down on our heads, reminding us of its presence, and I wished it *was* a god.

Because then we might reason with it.

Del turned to face me squarely. She waited.

I sighed. "We walk." I answered her unasked question, "and hope we're found by a caravan."

"What if we followed the Hanjii? At least we know where they are."

"We've been dedicated to the Sun," I told her. "If we go back, they'll cook us for certain."

"We'll cook out here, anyway," she said in disgust.

"That *is* the general idea."

We stared at one another. Del's pride and defiance warred with realization in her sunburned face, but the acceptance portion won. She looked at me in irritated acknowledgment. "We could die out here."

"We're not dead yet. And I'm tough as old cumfa leather, remember?"

"You're wounded." Consternation overrode the dry displeasure in her tone. "I cut you."

The cut wasn't deep, mostly just a shallow slice along my ribs. It had bled quite a bit but was dry now, starting to crust, and it wouldn't bother me much.

Recalling the rather painful trick she'd played on me in the circle, I was tempted to let her think the sword cut was worse than it really was. But I decided it would be utterly stupid in light of the situation.

"It's nothing," I told her. "Hardly more than a scratch. See for yourself."

She touched the wound with gentle fingers and saw I spoke the truth. Her mouth twisted. "I thought I cut deeper than that."

"Not dancing against *me*," I retorted. "You're lucky you got close enough even for a little cut like this."

"That wasn't a real dance. That was a travesty. And you weren't so tough," she threw back. "You went down quickly enough when I kneed you. Howled like a baby, too."

I scowled at her. "Enough, woman. Do you know how hard it was for me to ride a horse out here?"

She laughed, which didn't do much to settle my ruffled feathers. Then she recalled our circumstances and the laughter went away. "Why did they leave us our weapons?"

"We're a Sun Sacrifice. It would be blasphemy if we went to the god incomplete, and the Hanjii believe a man without his weapons is incomplete. It would lessen the sacrifice. As for *you* . . . well, I guess you proved yourself worthy in the circle."

"For whatever good it did me." She scowled. "Maybe if I'd *lost*, we wouldn't be here."

"We wouldn't," I agreed. "If you'd lost, I'd have had to fight the shoka. And if *I'd* lost, you'd have become his wife—all scarred and dyed. And that's something I wouldn't stand for."

She looked at me expressionlessly a moment. Then she walked away from me and drew her sword. Again I saw the blade plunged into the sand and her cross-legged posture on the hot sand. The hilt stood rigidly upright, a locus for the sunlight. The shapes twisted in the metal.

I shivered. Frowned. Wanted to accuse her of carrying an ensorcelled sword, which took her right out of the realm of fairness when it came to a proper sword-dance.

But Del was talking to her gods again, and this time I did some talking to my own.

# Ten

**W**ithin two hours, Del was bright red all over. The sun sought out all the portions of her skin that the burnous had hidden, and now she was on the verge of blistering. Never had I seen such color in a sunburn; such angry red flesh. Against the blonde hair and brows and blue eyes, the burn looked twice as bad.

There was nothing I could do. The skin would swell until something had to give, and the skin itself would give, forming blistered pockets of fluids that would burst, spilling badly needed moisture over other blisters. And then she would burn again as the flesh—lacking moisture—shriveled on her bones, until she was nothing more than a cracking hide stretched incredibly taut over brittle bones.

Hoolies, I hated the idea. And yet I was helpless to prevent it.

We walked. To stop would only intensify the heat, the pain, the futility of our situation. Movement gave the impression of a breeze, though nothing moved at all. I almost wished for a simoom; was glad there was none, for the wind and sand would scour the burned flesh from our bones.

For the first time in my life, I wanted to see what snow was like; to learn firsthand if it was as cool and soft and wet as people claimed. I thought of asking Del if it were true—but didn't. Why speak of something you can't have? Especially when you need it.

The Punja is filled with mystery, including the mystery of its own sands; one moment you walk on hardpack, the next you stumble into a pocket of loose, deep softness that drags at your feet, slowing you, making the effort of continuing that much harder. Poor Del was having a more difficult time than I because she didn't know and couldn't tell the subtle differences in the sand's appearance. Finally I told her to step where I did, and she fell in behind me like a lost, bewildered puppy.

When darkness fell, she threw herself down on the sand and flattened herself against it, trying to soak up the sudden, unexpected coolness. This is yet another danger of the Punja: the days are hot and blistering, yet by night—if you are unprotected—you can shiver and shake with cold. When the sun drops below the horizon, you draw in a sigh of relief: release from the heat; and then the Punja turns cold and you freeze.

Well, cold is relative. But after the blistering heat of the days, the nights seem incredibly cold.

"Worse," Del muttered. "Worse than I thought. So much *heat*." She sat on the sand with the sword unsheathed, resting across red thighs. Recalling the cold bite of the alien metal, almost I wanted to take it from her and touch my flesh with its own.

Except I recalled also the numbing tingle I'd experienced, the bone-deep pain that was unlike any pain I'd ever felt. And I didn't want to experience that again.

I saw how her hands caressed the metal. The hilt: tracing out the shapes. The blade: gently touching the runes as if they might bring her surcease. Such odd runes, worked into the metal. Iridescent in the twilight. They lighted the blade with a rosy, shimmering lambence.

"What is it?" I asked. "What is it *really*?"

Del's fingers caressed the shining sword. "My *jivatma*."

"That doesn't tell me anything, bascha."

She didn't look at me. Just stared out across the blackening desert. "A blooding-blade. A *named* blade. Full of the courage and strength and skill of an honorable fighter, and all the power of his soul."

"If it's so powerful, why doesn't it get us out of here?" I was feeling a trifle surly.

"I asked." Still she didn't look at me. "But—there is so much heat . . . so much sun. In the North, there would be no question. But *here* . . . I think its strength is diluted even as my own is." She shivered. "Cool now, but it's wrong. It's just—*contrast*. Not an honest coolness."

And yet with her skin burned so badly and her physical defenses down, Del was twice as chilled. She sheathed the sword and drew herself up into a ball of huddled misery. I shared my own measure of the discomfort: your skin is so burned it feels incredibly hot, even when the night is cool. And so you burn and freeze all at once.

I wanted to touch her, to hold her close and give her some of the fiery heat of my own burned flesh, to warm her, but she cried out at my touch, and I realized it hurt too much. The sun had seared her Northern skin, while my Southron hide was barely darkened.

We slept side by side in fits and starts, dozing and waking, only just losing ourselves in the blissful release of sleep before we would wake again, and the cycle would begin once more.

By midday the sun is so hot it burns the soles of your feet and you walk with funny, mincing steps, trying to avoid keeping each foot on the sand for very long. Your toes curl, arching back over your foot until they cramp, and then you find yourself hopping on one burning foot while you rub the cramp out of the other. When the heat is too bad and the cramp is worse, you sit down until you can stand again, and then you walk some more.

If you have tough soles, like mine, the foot stays on the sand longer and the toes do less curling; the stops are less frequent, and you keep your rump off the sand. But if your soles are like Del's—softer, thinner, whiter—each step is agony, no matter how quickly you hop onto the other foot. After a while you stumble, and then you fall, and then you do your best not to cry because your feet are burning, your skin is afire, and your eyes are so hot you can hardly see.

But you don't cry. To cry means using moisture, and by now you have none left.

Del stumbled. Nearly fell. Stopped.

"Bascha—?"

Her hair was white against the livid redness of her skin, which had formed blisters and spilled now-caking fluids down her flesh. I saw how she trembled from pain and exhaustion.

"Tiger . . ." It was little more than a breath of sound. "This is not a good way to die."

I looked down and saw how her toes curled up away from the sand; how she shifted her weight continually: foot to foot, hip to hip, until she fell into a rhythm she could focus on. I'd seen it before. Some people, with the sun beating on their brains, lose touch with their physical coordination. Del didn't look that far gone yet, but close. Too close.

I reached out and pushed some hair from her face. "*Is* there a good way to die?"

She nodded a little. "In battle, honorably. Bearing a child who will be better, stronger. When the heart and soul and body weaken after years and years of life. In the circle, following all the rituals. Those are good ways. But this—" an outthrust hand, trembling, encompassed all we could see of the Punja, "— *this* is like burning a perfectly good candle until it's all gone, leaving you with nothing . . ." Her breath rasped in her throat. "Waste—*waste*—"

I stroked her hair. "Bascha, don't rail at it so. It sucks the heart out of you."

**111**

She looked at me angrily. "I don't want to die like this!"

"Del—we're a long way from dying."

Unfortunately, we were.

In the desert, without water, your lips crack until they bleed, and you lick at the moisture with a swollen tongue. But blood tastes like salt and it makes you thirsty, and you curse the sun and the heat and the sand and the helplessness and the absolute futility of it all.

But you go on, you go on.

When you see the oasis, you don't believe in it, knowing it's a mirage; wondering if it's real. This is the edge of torture, honed sword-sharp; it slides in painlessly and then, as you stare in surprise, it opens you from guts to gullet, and what's left of your spirit spills out into the sand.

The oasis will be the saving of you; it will be the killing of you.

It moves as you move, shifting on the burning sands: first near, then far, then but inches from your feet.

Finally you cry out, and then you fall onto your blistered, weeping knees when the vision fades and leaves you with a mouthful of hot sand that clogs your throat and makes you sick.

But being sick is an impossibility because there is nothing in your belly to bring up.

Nothing.

Not even bile.

When I went down, I pulled Del down with me. But she got up again almost immediately and staggered onward. I watched her go. On hands and knees, half-delirious, I watched the Northern girl go on stumbling through the sand.

Southward. Unerringly.

"Del," I croaked. "Bascha—*wait*—"

But she didn't. And that got me up on my feet again.

"Del!"

She didn't even glance around. I felt a flicker of disbelief that she could leave me behind so easily (a man likes to think he inspires at least a *little* loyalty), but it was replaced with the hollowness of fear. It punched me full in the gut and drove me into a staggering run.

"Del!"

Still she stumbled on: bobbing, weaving, nearly falling, but continually moving southward. Toward Julah. Toward whatever news she could learn of her brother; poor, pretty boy (if he was anything like his sister), whose probable fate was the ugliest of all.

Better to die, I thought grimly.

But I wasn't about to tell his sister that.

I caught up to her easily enough; for all I was near delirium from the heat and the sand and the sun, I wasn't as bad off as Del. Not nearly as bad off.

And when she swung around to face me, I knew she was worse than that.

Del's face was swollen, crusty, seared so badly she could hardly see. Her eyelids were giant, puckered blisters, stretching the skin out of shape until they broke, sealed over, broke again, until she wept without shedding tears.

But it was what lay behind the lids that chilled my soul: the first touch of coldness I'd felt since daybreak. Her eyes, so blue, so bright an alien hue, were filled with emptiness.

"Hoolies," I croaked in despair, "you're sandsick."

She stared at me blindly. Maybe she didn't even recognize me. But as I put out a hand to touch her arm, meaning to urge her down onto the sand before she ran amok from all the pain and delirium, she tried to jerk her sword from its sheath.

There was no grace in her movement, no flexibility. Just

**113**

an awkward, ragged motion as she tried to drag the sword
from her harness.

I caught her left arm. "Bascha—no."

The other arm continued to move. I saw the futile
cross-reaching of her right hand, clawing at the silver hilt
that stood up behind her left shoulder. As always, the
sunlight flashing off the blade nearly blinded me. But
squinting hurt too much.

I caught her other arm. I felt her instant withdrawal: my
touch, lighter than normal, was still too much for her
blistered flesh. Her indrawn breath of pain hissed in the
stillness of the desert.

"Del—"

"Sword." There was no shape to the word; no recog-
nizable tone with inflections. Just—noise. A ragged, whispered word.

A plea. "Bascha—"

"Sword." Her eyes were out of focus, like the stare of
a sandtiger cub. It was eerie, and for a moment I nearly let
her go.

I sighed. "No, bascha, no sword. Sandsickness makes
you crazy—no telling what you'd do. Probably cut out my
heart." I tried to smile, but the motion cracked my lips
and made them bleed again.

"*Sword.*" Pitifully.

"No," I told her gently, and she began to cry.

"*Kaidin* said—*an-kaidin* said—" She could hardly speak
in her incoherence. "*An-kaidin* said—*sword*—"

I caught the difference at once. *An-kaidin*, not *kaidin*.
"No sword." Gently, I overrode her. "*Tiger* says no."

Tears welled up into her eyes again; the right one spilled
its weight of moisture in a single drop that rolled down her
cheek. But the tear didn't reach her chin. Her skin sucked
it up immediately.

"Bascha," I said unevenly, "you have to listen to me.
You're sandsick, and you'll have to do as I tell you."

"*Sword*," she said, and jerked both wrists from my grasp.

Seared flesh broke, leaking fluid mixed with blood. But her hands were on the hilt of her sword, closing, jerking it up and then over when she forced it to extension; a travesty of her normally supple unsheathing. But however awkward the motion, the fact remained that Del had a sword in her hands.

I'm no fool: I fell back a step. Men say I'm fearless in the circle; let them. It helps the reputation. But I wasn't in the circle now; what I faced was a woman full of sandsickness with a glittering sword in her hands.

Her grip shifted. The blade pointed downward, parallel to her body. Both hands gripped the hilt by the curving crosspiece; she lifted the sword slowly toward her face, and then she pressed the pommel against her cracked, blistered lips.

"*Sulhaya*," she whispered, and shut her eyes.

I watched her warily. I wanted to take the weapon from her, but she was too unpredictable. What skill she claimed made her doubly dangerous: no man risks himself against a blade *and* a sandsick woman. Not even against a woman without any sword-skill at all.

She whispered something to the sword. I frowned, disturbed by the note in her voice; I've seen sandsickness before, and I know how it can strip a man—or woman—of a mind, leaving nothing behind but madness. Generally it's fatal, because about the only time people *get* it is when they're stuck in the desert without water or shelter or any hope of rescue.

Just like Del and me.

"Bascha—" I began again.

She turned away from me. Awkwardly, she lowered herself and the sword to the ground, kneeling: angry red flesh against sepia sand. The suede tunic she wore was taut against her body—a sheath around a blade—and yet for once I didn't consider what the supple body could do for my own. I just watched her, feeling despair rise up within me, as the girl gave in to the imbecility of the sandsick.

Hoolies, what a waste.

She knelt, but did not crouch. Her spine was straight. Carefully she put the tip of the blade into the sand and pushed downward on the hilt, trying to seat it firmly. But she was too weak, the sand too firm; it was me, finally, who leaned on the pommel and pushed it into the ground so that the sword stood upright like a standard.

But not before I felt the pain that seared my palm. It ran up my arm to the shoulder, thrumming so hard I shook with it, and it was only as I wrenched my hand away that the eerie sensation abated.

"*Del*," I said sharply, shaking my tingling hand. "Bascha—what in hoolies *is* this sword—?"

I felt a bit of a fool for asking—a sword, after all, is a sword—but the remembered explosion of pain in my hand confirmed that, indeed, the Northern blade was more than merely a piece of steel coaxed into the shape of a lethal weapon. My palm itched; I looked at it suspiciously, rubbed it violently with my other hand, and glared at Del.

Simple tricks and nonsense, designed for gullible people. But I'm not a gullible man.

And, though I'm quick enough to scoff, I know the smell of real magic when it clogs the air I breathe.

Like now.

Del didn't answer me; I wasn't certain she had heard me. Her eyes were fixed on the hilt that was level with her face. She said something—a sentence in her Northern tongue—repeating it four times. She waited: nothing (or so it appeared to me); she repeated the sentence again.

"Del, this is ridiculous. Knock it off." I reached out to yank the sword from the sand. Didn't. My hand stopped several inches away as I recalled the sickening feeling of numb weakness, the irritating, painful *itch* that had run through my veins like ice.

Some sort of spell?

Possibly. But that would make Del a *witch* . . . or something like.

Still, I couldn't touch the hilt. I couldn't *make* myself, though nothing was preventing me. Nothing, that is, except an extreme unwillingness to experience the weirding again.

Del bent, curling her body downward toward the sand. Her hands pressed flat, fingers spread. Her brow touched the sand three times. A glance at the sword. Then the homage was repeated.

The blonde braid, now bleached white, slapped against the sand. I saw the grains adhering to the blistered flesh across her forehead; to her nose, her lips. And as she bent again in obscene obeisance to the sword, I saw how her raspy exhalations stirred the dust beneath her face.

*Puff . . . puff . . . puff—*

Dust drifted: ivory-umber.

I said nothing. She was beyond any words from a human mouth.

She knelt in complete obeisance. And then, awkwardly, she stretched out until she lay prostrate on the sand. She wrapped her hands around the shining blade just above the level of the sand. I saw how the blistered knuckles, burned red, turned white from the tension in her hands.

"*Kaidin, kaidin*, I beg you—" Half the words were in Southron, the other half in Northern. So the sense of things was lost. "*An-kaidin, an-kaidin, I beg you—*"

Her eyes were closed. Her lashes were gummed by leakage and sand. It crusted on her face, where the swelling rawness obliterated the lovely lines of her flawless bones. And I felt such a rage build up in me that I bent down, pulled her hands from the sword, and—steeling myself for the weirding—jerked the blade from its makeshift altar in the sand.

Pain ran up my arm and into my chest. Ice-cold. Sharp as a dagger though nothing cut into my skin. It was just cold, *so cold,* as if it would freeze my blood, my bones, my flesh.

I shuddered. My hand seemed fixed upon the hilt, even as I tried to let go the sword. Light filled up my head, coruscating light, all purple and blue and red. Blinded, I stared into the desert and saw nothing but the light.

I shouted something. Don't ask me what. But as I shouted it, I hurled away the sword with all the strength I had left. Which, at the moment, wasn't very much.

My hand, thank valhail, came unstuck. Several layers of flesh were peeled away in ridges, still adhering to the hilt. In my hand remained the pattern of the hilt, the twisted, alien shapes of Northern beasts and runes. Beads of moisture sprang up into the patterns seared into my hand. Dried. Cracked. Sloughed away with an additional layer of skin.

I was shaking. I gripped my right wrist with my other hand, trying to hold it still; trying to dull the ringing pain. Hot metal burned. Seared. I'd seen cautery before. But this—*this* was something different. Something more. This was *sorcery.* Ice-cold sorcery. The North personified.

"Hoolies, woman!" I shouted. "What kind of sorceress *are* you?"

Still prostrate, Del stared up at me. I saw the complete incomprehension in her eyes. Utter bewilderment. Her mouth hung open. Elbows shifted, rising; she pressed herself up from the ground, though she very nearly didn't make it. She knelt on one knee, bracing herself with a shaking hand thrust against the sand.

"The magic," she said in despair, "the magic wouldn't come . . ."

"*Magic!*" I was disgusted. "What power does that— that *thing* hold? Can it make the day cooler? Can it soothe our blistered flesh? Can it turn the sun's face from us and give us shade instead?"

"All those, yes. In the North." She swallowed and I saw the blistered flesh of her throat crack. "*Kaidin* said—"

"I don't care what your sword-master told you!" I shouted. "It's just a sword. A weapon. A blade. Meant for cutting through flesh and bone, shearing arms and legs and necks—to take the life from a man." And yet even as I denied the power I'd felt, I looked at my hand again. Branded with the devices of the North. Ice-marked by the magic.

Del wavered. I saw the trembling in her arm. For a moment there was sense in her eyes. And bitterness. "How could a *Southroner* know what power lies in a sword—"

I reached up and caught Singlestroke's heated hilt with one broad hand, ignoring the twinge in my newly-scarred hand, and jerked him free of his sheath. I presented the tip of the blade to her just inches from her nose. "The power in a sword lies in the skill of the man who wields it," I said distinctly. "There isn't anything else."

"Oh yes," she said, "there is. But I doubt you will ever know it."

And then her eyes rolled back in their sockets and she crumpled bonelessly to the sand.

"Hoolies," I said in disgust, and put Singlestroke away.

I heard the horses first. Snorts. The squeak of leather. Clattering bits and shanks. The creak of wood, and voices.

Voices!

Del and I lay sprawled on the sand like cloth dolls, too weak to go on; too strong to die. We lay an arm's-length apart. When I turned my head and looked at her, I saw the curve of hip and the spill of her sun-bleached braid; long, firm, blistered legs, with white striations across the knees.

And sand, crusted on her sun-crisped flesh.

When I could manage it, I turned my head the other way. I saw a dark-faced woman wrapped in a blue burnous, and I knew her.

"Sula." It came out on a croak that died on my swollen tongue.

I saw her black eyes widen. Her wide face expressed utter astonishment. And then it shifted to urgency.

She turned, shouting, and a moment later other wagons pulled up. People gathered around us. I heard the surprised exclamations as I was identified. My name was passed around from man to woman, woman to woman, woman to children.

My *old* name, which isn't a name at all.

Nomads like the Salset understand the desert. With very few words of instruction necessary, they wrapped Del and me in cool, wet cloths and brought the wagons closer to throw some shade upon us. Camp was established immediately. The Salset are good at that: a hyort here, one there, until there's a huddled bunch of them packed onto a tiny stretch of desert. And they call it home.

I couldn't speak, though I wanted to tell Sula and the other women to tend Del first. My tongue was too thick and heavy in my dehydrated mouth, and when I breathed it took great effort. Finally, after Sula kept shushing me, I gave in to silence and let them do the work.

When the cloths dried on my scorched body, Sula dampened them again from the wooden barrels of water lashed to the wagons. After the fifth application of wet linen, she called for alla paste and I sank into blissful numbness as the cool salve soaked crusted tissue and leached away the pain. And Sula, thank the gods of valhail, lifted my head and gave me my first drink of water in two days.

My last coherent thought was for Del, recalling how oddly she had behaved. As if the sword was more than merely a sword. As if she expected the sword to get us out of our predicament.

Singlestroke, much as I respect and admire him, is only a sword. Not a god. Not a man. Not a magical being.

A sword.

But also my deliverance.

*     *     *

I've always healed fast, but even so it took me days before I felt like a living being again. My skin was peeling off in clumps and layers that left me feeling like a cumfa in molt, but regular applications of alla paste kept the new skin underneath moist and soft until it could toughen normally. The Sandtiger, who had always been dark as a copper piece, emerged looking like some unfortunate woman had birthed a full-grown baby; I was splotchy and pink all over, except where the dhoti had covered me.

And since that's a part of my body I'm rather attached to, in more ways than one, I was significantly grateful.

Del, however, was very ill. She lay in Sula's little orange-ocher hyort, lost in sandsickness delirium and the black world of the infusion Sula poured into her several times daily. Even the alla paste couldn't entirely assuage her pain.

I stood just inside the door-slit, staring down at the shape beneath the saffron-dyed cotton coverlet. All I could see was her face. Still burned. Still blistered. Still peeling.

"She won't talk to you." Sula spoke with the Salset intonations I hadn't heard in so long. "She has no mind. The mindless don't talk."

"It'll *pass*." More wishful thinking than anything else; sandsickness is a serious thing.

"Maybe." Sula's wide face didn't give me the benefit of the doubt.

"But she's getting good care now," I reminded her. "She has water again and that stuff you're giving her. The sandsickness will go away."

Sula shrugged. "She won't talk to you."

I looked again at Del. She moaned and cried in her drugged stupor, whispering in her Northern tongue. I heard *kaidin*, over and over, but if she spoke of the sword I didn't know the word.

Resigned, I shook my head. "Foolish little bascha. You should have stayed in the North."

I wanted to sleep in the hyort at nights, but Sula—

cognizant of Salset proprieties—wouldn't allow it. I was an unmarried male and she an unmarried woman, who tended yet another. And so I slept outside curled up in a rug that smelled of goat and dog, evoking memories of many years before. Memories I preferred to forget, but couldn't.

Each day I exercised, trying to work the stiffness out of my muscles and stretch the tender new skin until it fit me better. I practiced with Singlestroke for hours, amused when all the children gathered to watch with their cunning black eyes stretched wide in astonishment, and yet I sensed a restlessness within me. Apprehension. I couldn't shake it, either. And when I walked among the hyorts and wagons, recalling my childhood with the tribe, I felt oppressed and sick and scared; *scared*: the Sandtiger. I wanted to get away—*needed* to get away—but I couldn't go. Not without Del.

I mean, I'd made a deal with her to do a job. I had to finish it or tarnish my reputation.

The shukar came and looked at me once, studied the sandtiger scars on my face and the claws hanging around my neck and went away again, saying nothing. But not before I saw the bitterness in his eyes: his recollection of the past, the present, the future. Crafty old man. Cunning old shukar. He went away from me, but not before I saw the ugly set to his mouth.

Gods, the man hated me.

But no more than I hated him.

The men refused to speak to me, which wasn't particularly surprising. They remembered, too. The matrons ignored me utterly: Salset custom doesn't allow a married woman to speak to or indicate interest in another man except for traditional courtesy; I especially was not deserving of that. At least, not from those women old enough to remember me from before.

But the young women didn't remember me at all, and the young *unmarried* women—having more freedom than their sisters—watched me with avid, shining eyes. And yet instead of making me feel tall and tough and strong, it made me feel small. And weak. And wary.

The Salset are an attractive race. They aren't as dark as the Hanjii with their spiraled, dyed flesh; the Salset are golden-brown and smooth-skinned. Hair and eyes are uniformly black. They are, for the most part, short and slender, though many of the older women—like Sula—run to fat. They are supple and quick, like Del, but they aren't a warrior race.

They are nomads. They wander. They live for each day, from dawn to dusk, and they blow with the sand; coming, going, staying. They have a tremendous sense of freedom, strong traditions, and a great love for one another that makes an outsider feel ashamed he cannot share it.

They made *me* feel ashamed, as they intended to, because I am not a Salset, though once I lived with them. I couldn't be a Salset then, or now. Not with my height, my bulk, my color; my green eyes and brown hair; my strength and natural sword-skill.

I was alien to them; then, now, forever. And for the first sixteen years of my life they had tried to beat it out of me.

# Eleven

**S**andsickness is a frightening thing. It makes a sieve of
your mind: spilling some memories, retaining others; those
it loses are replaced by dreams and visions that are so real,
so *very* real, you have to believe them, until someone tells
you no.

I told Del no, but she wasn't listening. She lay on a rug
in Sula's orange-ocher hyort and slowly healed physically,
but I wasn't certain about what she was inside her head.
Her skin was lathered generously in alla paste. Sula had
wrapped her in damp linen to keep the peeling skin moist.
She resembled not so much a living person as a dead one,
sloughing a ruined shell. But at least she breathed.

And dreamed.

I settled into a daily routine: food, general exercises,
food, sword practice, companionship to Del. I sat by her
for hours each afternoon, talking as if she could hear me,
trying to let her know someone was with her. I don't know
if she heard me. She whispered and moaned and talked,
but it was only rarely that I understood her. I don't speak
her Northern tongue.

Sometimes, neither of us spoke at all. We shared long
private silences—Sula had tribal chores—while Del slept
and I stared at the woven walls of the hyort, trying (mostly
unsuccessfully) to reconcile my presence once again among
the Salset. It had been more than sixteen years since I'd

left the tribe, thinking (hoping) never to see the Salset again. But not much had changed in the intervening years. Sula was a middle-aged widow instead of the young woman I recalled. The children all had grown to adulthood, reflecting the traditional biases and beliefs of the tribe, rearing their children as they themselves had been reared. The old shukar also was the same, oddly unchanged in his strange, ageless fashion: fierce, austere, bitter—tight as a wineskin filled to bursting with an impotent anger whenever he looked at me.

But I recalled the years it hadn't been impotent.

Sitting in Sula's hyort, I thought about how time changed all things except the Punja and everything which lived in it. How time had changed *me*.

Time, and a relentless desperation.

Sula entered silently. I paid no attention to her, accustomed to her quiet comings and goings, but this time she dropped a leather-wrapped bundle into my lap and I glanced at her in surprise.

She was swaddled in a rich, cobalt-blue; the blue of a starless Punja night. Black hair, greased back from her face, held a tracery of silver. "I kept them for you," she said. "I knew I'd see you again before I died."

I looked into her golden face and saw the sunlines clustered around her eyes, the sag at her jowls, the heaviness of hips, breasts, shoulders. But most of all, I saw the calmness in her black Salset eyes and realized Sula had accepted me for what I had made of myself and not what I had been.

Slowly, I unwrapped the bundle and freed both items. The short spear, blunted at one end and pointed at the other, painstakingly sharpened by a piece of broken stone and hands too big for the boy who used them. Now the spear was about the length of my arm; once it had been half my height.

The wood was darker than I recalled, until I realized it still bore bloodstains, blackened by the years. The lopsided, unbalanced point was scarred with claw and bite marks. Holding it in my hands again, sensing the ambiance of memory recalled, I felt all over again the emotions I'd experienced so many years before.

Wonder. Determination. Desperation. Fear, of course. And pain.

But mostly the blind, fierce defiance that had so nearly killed me.

The other item was exactly as I recalled it. A piece of bone, carved in the shape of a beast. A sandtiger, to be precise. Four stumpy legs, a nub of a tail, snarling mouth agape to show the tiny fangs. Time had weathered the bone to a creamy yellow-brown, almost the color of a real sandtiger. The incised eyes and nose were worn down almost to smoothness. But I could still see traces of the features.

My hands were bigger now. The bone tiger fit into the palm of my right hand easily. I could close my fingers over the toy and hide it from sight. But sixteen or so years before, I couldn't. And so I had stroked it every night, whispering the magical words into the tiny bone ears as the wizard had told me to do, and dreaming of a wicked beast come to eat my enemies.

Oh yes, I believe in magic. I know better than to doubt it. Although much of it is little more than tricks and sleight of hand practiced by charlatans, there are genuine magicians in the world. And genuine magic with such power as to completely alter a life in dire need of it.

But that kind of power carries its own cost.

I shut the toy in my right hand, pressing the smooth yellowed bone against the palm that bore the ice-brand of the Northern sword, and looked at Sula.

I saw the compassion in her eyes; a complete comprehension of the emotions the spear and toy recalled. And I put them both back into her hands. "Keep them for me . . . to recall the good nights we shared."

She accepted them, but her mouth tightened. "I'm surprised you can say there were good nights, after the bad days—"

I cut her off. "I choose to put away the days. I'm the Sandtiger now. The days before are forgotten."

She was unsmiling. "The days before are *not* forgotten. They can't be. Shouldn't be. Not by the shukar, not by me, not by the tribe . . . not by you. The days before are what *made* you the Sandtiger."

I made the sharp gesture of negation. "A shodo made me the Sandtiger. Not the Salset." Inwardly, I knew better. And chose to deny it. "No one here tells me what to remember, to think, to speak . . . to wish for." I scowled at her fiercely. "*Not— any—more.*"

Untroubled by exaggerated distinctness, Sula smiled. In her face was the serenity I had always associated with her. But in her eyes was a bittersweet knowledge. "The Sandtiger no longer walks alone?"

She meant Del. I looked at the linen-draped, sunburned Northern girl and opened my mouth to tell Sula the Sandtiger—human or animal—*always* walks alone (being an exceedingly solitary beast); then I recalled, oddly, how I had killed a male sandtiger attempting to protect his mate, his cubs.

I smiled. "*This* one only temporarily walks with the Northern woman."

Sula, kneeling, wrapped spear and bone in the leather binding again. She tilted her head assessively as she studied Del. "She's very ill. But she's also strong; others less burned and not so ill have died, while she hasn't. I think she'll recover." Sula glanced at me. "You had sand in your head to bring a Northern woman into the Punja."

"Her decision." I shrugged. "She offered me gold to lead her across to Julah. A sword-dancer never says no to gold—especially when he's been out of work for a while."

"Neither does a chula say no to gold—*or* to a danger-

ous, tragic endeavor—if it buys him the freedom he craves.''
Sula rose and ducked out of the hyort before I could
summon an answer.

I felt the faintest breath of a touch on my leg and
glanced down in surprise to find Del's eyes open and
locked on my face. ''What does she mean?''

''Bascha! Del—don't talk—''

''My voice isn't burned.'' She formed the words carefully, a little awkwardly; her lips were still blistered, still
cracked. No smile—she couldn't manage it—but I saw it
in her eyes.

Blue eyes, bluer than I recalled; lashes and hair bleached
whiter by the sun. New skin, vividly pink, showed in the
rents of peeling flesh.

I scowled. ''Concentrate on resting. Not talking.''

''I *will* survive, Tiger—even if it means you have sand
in your head for bringing me into the Punja.''

''You heard Sula.'' Accusation.

''I heard it all,'' she answered. ''I haven't been asleep
the *whole* time.'' And suddenly there were tears in her
eyes; embarrassed, she tried to hide them from me.

''It's all right,'' I told her. ''I don't think you're weak—at
least, not *weak* weak. Just tired from your bout with
sandsickness.''

Her throat moved as she swallowed heavily. Old skin
cracked. ''Even when I was lost and wandering, I knew
you were here. And—something told me you'd be here
even when I found myself again.''

I shrugged, discomfited. ''Yes, well . . . I owed you
that much. I mean, you're paying me to get you to Julah. I
can hardly go off and leave you; it plays hoolies with the
reputation.''

''And a sword-dancer never says no to gold.'' Irony; a
little.

I grinned at her, feeling better than I had in days. ''You
realize I'll have to raise my price, don't you? I told you I

charge based on how many times I have to save your life."

"This is only once."

"*Three* times."

"Three!"

I ticked them off on my fingers. "Sandtiger. Hanjii. Now this rescue."

She glared as much as she was able to. "You got us lost in the *first* place."

"That was the Hanjii. Not my fault."

"You had nothing to do with the Salset finding us," she pointed out. "That was the will of the gods." She paused. "*Mine.*"

I scowled. "We'll argue about it when we reach Julah. And besides, I may have to save you a few more times—in which case my price climbs even higher."

"Aren't you forgetting something? The Hanjii took all my gold." Her eyes glinted. "I can't pay you any more."

"Well then, we'll just have to work out another arrangement." I gave her a slow, suggestive smile.

She hissed something at me in her unintelligible Northern tongue. Then, weakly, she laughed. "Perhaps we *will* have to make another arrangement. Some day."

Anticipating it, I nodded consideringly. Smiling.

Del sighed. "Northern, Southron—you're all alike."

"Who is?"

"*Men.*"

"That's sandsickness talking."

"That's *experience* talking," she retorted. Then, more softly, "Will you tell me about it?"

"Tell you about what?"

Her eyes didn't move from my face. "Your life with the Salset."

I felt like I'd been kicked in the gut. Talking with Sula about my past was one thing—she'd been a part of it—but telling it to a stranger was something I had no intention of doing. Even Sula skirted the edges of the topic, knowing how delicate it was. But with Del's blue eyes fixed on me in calm expectation (and knowing she'd just lived through her own sort of hoolies), I thought perhaps I *should* tell her.

I opened my mouth. I shut it almost immediately.

"Personal," I muttered.

"She said the past had made you what you are. I *know* what you are. I want to know what you *were*."

Tension gripped my body. Muscles knotted. Belly churned. Sweat broke out on my new skin. "I *can't*."

Her eyes drifted closed, lids too heavy to keep raised. "I've trusted my life to you. You've honored that trust. I *know* what you want from me, Tiger—what you're hoping for—because you mask your face but not your eyes. Most men don't even bother." The corners of her mouth moved a little, as if she wanted to smile wryly. "Tell me who you were so I can know who you are."

"Hoolies, Del—it's not the sort of thing that makes for polite conversation."

"Whoever said you were polite?" A definite smile, though somewhat tentative. "These are your people, Tiger. Aren't you happy to see them again?"

I recalled how close Northern kinship circles were. It's what had brought her here, against odds most would never face, man *or* woman. "I'm not a Salset," I told her flatly, figuring I owed her that much. "Nobody knows *what* I am."

"Well—the Salset raised you. Doesn't that matter?"

"It matters. *It matters*." It spilled out of my mouth unexpectedly, a flood of virulent bitterness. "Yes, the Salset raised me . . . *in hoolies*, Del. As a chula." I wanted to spit out the word so I'd never know its foul taste again. "It means slave, Del. *I didn't even have a name*."

Her eyes snapped open. "*Slave!*"

I looked at her shocked, pitiful face and saw a horror as eloquent as my own. But not disgust (in the Punja slavery is a stigma you escape only in death). Empathy, instead; honest, open empathy, as well as astonishment.

Maybe in the north they don't believe in slavery (or else they don't consider it a horrible fate), but slavery in the South—especially the Punja—guarantees a lifetime of utter misery. Complete humiliation. A slave is unclean. Tainted. Locked into a life that is less than a life. In the South, a slave is a pack-animal. A slave is a beast of burden forced to withstand beatings, curses, degradation. It is a bondage of the spirit as well as the body. A slave is not a person. A slave is not a man. He is less than a dog. Less than a horse. Less than a goat.

A slave develops self-hatred.

In the South, a slave is a simply a *thing*.

A pile of dung upon the ground.

Which is where I had learned to sleep, when I could sleep at all.

I heard the indrawn hissing of Del's sucked-in breath and realized I had said the words aloud. And I wanted to take them back, grinding them up between my teeth and swallowing them back down my throat where they could remain hidden away, not vomited out like foul, malodorous bile.

But it was too late. I'd said them. They couldn't be unsaid.

I shut my eyes and felt the stark desolation fill up my soul again, as it had so often in childhood. And the anger. Frustration. The rage. All the insane fear that gave a boy the courage to face a full-grown male sandtiger with only a crude wooden spear.

No. Not courage. Desperation. Because that boy knew he could win his freedom if he killed the beast.

Or if he let the beast kill him.

"And so you killed it."

I looked at Del. "I did more than kill it, bascha . . . I *conjured* the tiger."

Del's lips parted. I saw her start to form a question, and then she didn't. As if she had begun to comprehend.

I drew in a deep breath. And for the first time in my life, I told a woman the story of how I had won my freedom.

"There was a man. A wizard. And the Salset honored him, as they honored anyone with power." I shrugged a little. "For me, he was more than that. He was a god come to life before me because he promised me absolute freedom." I recalled his voice very well: calm, smooth, soothing—telling me I could be free. "He said a man always knows his freedom in what he can make for himself, in how he conjures dreams and turns them into reality; that if I believed in myself hard enough, I could become anything I desired; that magic such as his was known only to a few, but the kind *I* needed was available to anyone." I drew in a deep breath, remembering all he had told me. "And so when I took to following him around, even though I was beaten for it, he knew my misery, and did what he could to ease it. He gave me a toy."

"A *toy*?"

"A sandtiger carved out of bone." I shrugged. "A trinket. He said a toy can give a child freedom in mind, and freedom in mind is freedom in body. The next day he was gone."

Del said nothing. Silently, she waited.

I looked down at the palm that bore the brand of the Northern sword. And I thought it likely Del could comprehend the magnitude of the power I had summoned, having her own measure of it.

"I took the toy, and I talked to it. I named it. I gave it a history. I gave it a family. And I gave it a great and terrible hunger." I recalled the echoes of my whispers again, hissing into the ivory ears. "I begged for deliverance in such a way as to convince even the shukar I

**132**

deserved my freedom. I asked for the tiger to come to me so I could kill it.''

Del waited, locked in silence.

I recalled the smooth satin finish of the bone beneath my fingers. How I had stroked it, whispering; how I had shut out the stink of dung and goat, the pain of a whip-laced back, the emotional anguish of a boy reduced to a beast of burden when he needed to be a man.

How I had shut out everything, dreaming of my tiger, and the freedom he would bring.

"He came," I said. "The tiger came to the Salset. At first word I rejoiced: *I would win my freedom*—but then I saw what the cost of that freedom would be.'' I felt the familiar sickened twisting of my gut. "My tiger came because I conjured him. A live sandtiger, big and fierce as I could wish for, filled with a great and terrible hunger. And to diminish that hunger, he began to eat whatever prey he could catch.'' I didn't look away from Del's direct gaze. "Children, bascha. He began to eat the children.''

A soft, quiet breath of comprehension issued from her lips.

I swallowed heavily, cold in the warmth of the hyort. "The Salset have no understanding of weapons and killing, being a tribe who raises goats for food, and trading. When the sandtiger began stealing children, the elders had no idea of how to stalk and kill it. They *tried*—two men tracked it to its lair and tried to kill it with knives, but it killed them. And so the shukar—after all his magic failed—told us it was a punishment for unknown transgressions, and that to break the beast's power would make its killer permanently blessed by all the tribal gods.'' I remembered his speech so clearly; the old, angry man, who had never thought a *chula* might be responsible for the beast. "It was mine to do. And so I made my spear in secret because the tribe would never countenance a chula considering such a thing; and when I could, I went after the tiger myself.''

Her hand was on my clenched fist. "Your face—''

I grimaced, scraping a broken fingernail across the marks. "Part of the price. You've seen sandtigers, Del. You know how quick, how deadly they are. I went after my conjured tiger with only my spear—somehow I hadn't provided for genuine ferocity while I did my conjuring. I'm lucky these scars are all he gave me." I sighed. "Still, he'd eaten four children and killed three men. It was more than worth the risk, after what I'd done."

Something blazed up in her eyes. "You don't *know* you conjured it! It might have been coincidence. That old wizard told you what *anyone* could tell you: believe in something hard enough and often you will get it. Sandtigers are common in the Punja—you told me so yourself. Don't blame yourself for something you may have had nothing to do with."

After a moment, I smiled. "You're a sorceress, bascha. You know how sorcery works. It's twisted. It's edged. It gives you what you want if you request it properly and then it demands its price."

Her jaw tightened. "What makes you say I'm a sorceress?"

"That sword, bascha. That uncanny, weirding sword with all the rune-signs in the metal." I lifted my hand and displayed the ice-marked palm to her for the first time. "I've felt its kiss, Del . . . I've felt a measure of its power. Don't try to deny the truth to a man who knows sorcery when he smells it . . . or when he *feels* it. That sword *stinks* of Northern sorcery."

Del turned her head from me and stared steadfastly at the woven wall of the hyort. I saw the gulping of her throat. "It stinks of more than that," she said unevenly. "It stinks of guilt and blood-debt, as much as *I* do. And I too will pay the price." But even as I opened my mouth to question her, she was telling me to finish what I had begun.

I sighed. "I crawled into the lair in the heat of the day, when the tiger slept. He was full of the child he had eaten earlier. I took him in the throat with the spear and pinned him against the wall, but when—thinking he was dead—I crawled closer to admire my handiwork, he came to life again and caught me here.'' I touched the scars again; the badges of my freedom. "But my poison was stronger than his because he died and I didn't.''

Del smiled a little. "And so you won your conjured freedom.''

I looked at her grimly, remembering. "There was no freedom. I crawled away from the lair—sick from the cat's poison—and nearly died in the rocks. I was there for three days: half-dead, too weak to call for help . . . and when the shukar and the elders came hunting the cat and discovered it dead—with no one claiming the kill—the old man said his magic had worked at last.'' It hurt to swallow. My throat was filled up with bitterness and remembered pain. "I didn't come back. They assumed I'd been eaten, too.''

"But—*someone* must have found you.''

"Yes.'' I smiled a little. "She was young then, and beautiful. And unmarried.'' The smile faded. I masked my face to Del. "Not everyone treated me as a chula. I was big for my age—at sixteen, the size of a man—and some of the women took advantage of that. A chula can't refuse. But—I didn't want to. It was the only kindness I knew . . . in the women's tents . . . at night.''

"Sula?'' she asked softly.

"Sula. She took me into her hyort and healed me, and then she called the shukar to me and told him he couldn't hope to deny that I had killed the tiger. Not with the marks on my face. My *proof*.'' I shook my head, remembering. "Before the entire tribe he had to name me a man. He had to give me the gift of freedom. And when the words were said, Sula—who had cut off the sandtiger's claws—gave this necklace to me.'' I tangled my fingers in the cord. "I've worn them ever since.''

"The death of the boy, the birth of the man.'' She seemed to understand.

"I walked away from the tribe the day I put on the claws. I never saw the Salset again—until the day they found us."

"The cat who walks alone." Del smiled a little. "Are you so certain you're tough enough for that?"

"The Sandtiger is tough enough for *anything*."

Her eyes challenged me briefly, then closed. "Poor Tiger. I have your secret. Now I should tell you mine."

But she didn't.

# Twelve

Del healed slowly. She was, she claimed, like an old woman: crippled, stiffened, withered. First she shed linen wrappings, then alla paste, but Sula frequently applied an oil also made out of the alla plant so the new skin wouldn't tear and crack from unaccustomed movement. Finally some of the vivid pinkness faded and she looked more like the Del who had walked into the cantina in search of a sword-dancer called the Sandtiger.

With my long-buried feelings about the Salset dredged up and vocalized, I felt a little as if the hounds of hoolies had been exorcised from my soul. Though undoubtedly I remained alien to most of the tribe, *I* didn't consider myself an outsider anymore. I was still different, but differences are tolerable. No longer was I the nameless boy whose only past, present and future was that which faced a chula.

Now, when the young women looked at me, I looked back.

And when the shukar, in passing one day, muttered an insult beneath his breath, I stepped into his path and confronted him.

"The chula is gone," I told him. "There is only the Sandtiger now—a shodo-trained, seventh-level sword-dancer—and such a man is due common Salset courtesy."

Sixteen years with the Salset had embedded certain

137

behavior codes within me. Sixteen years *away* from the Salset hadn't quite erased them, I discovered. Even as I challenged him, I felt the old feelings of insignificance and futility rousing themselves from the corners of my being. It was difficult to look him in the face; to meet his eyes, because for too many years I had been permitted only to look at his feet.

A shukar must always be respected, revered. He is different from everyone else; more than a man. He has magic. He is sacred. Touched by the gods; the touch was evidenced by the deep, wine-red splotch on the old man's sallow face, stretching from chin to left ear. The Salset have no kings, no chiefs, no war-leaders. They rely on the voice of the gods (shukar means *voice*, in Salset speech), and the voice tells them what to do and where to go. He is the pattern of the days, forever, until the gods choose another.

To confront this old man before the rest of the tribe was my first genuine act of freedom and independence. Even as a newly-freed chula, I'd been unable to face the man. I had simply walked away from him; from the others; from the memory of my conjured tiger.

Age had swallowed the golden pigmentation of his skin. He wore a saffron-colored burnous freighted with copper stitching around the hem. His hair, once black, was now completely gray. I smelled the acrid tang of the oil he used to slick it back from his face, meaning for all the world to see the wine-purple mark of the gods on his face; showing the mark, he showed his rank. His authority. And his black eyes, fixed on my face, hadn't lost one degree of their hatred for me.

Deliberately, he drew back lips from teeth like a dog showing his dominance and spat on the ground next to my right foot. "I have no courtesy for you."

Well, I hadn't really expected any different. But the denial of common courtesy (the highest order of insult in Salset customs) still rankled.

"Shukar, you are the voice of the gods," I said. "Surely they have told you the Sandtiger walks where he will—*regardless* of what the cub once was." I had his attention now; he glared back as I met his eyes directly. "You gave me no courtesy when I killed that cat so many years ago," I pointed out, reminding him of his failure to conduct himself as a proper shukar. "I'm claiming it now, before the entire tribe. Will you shirk your duty? Will you bring disgrace upon the Salset?"

I left him no choice. In front of so many people (many of whom knew me *only* as the Sandtiger), even a bitter old man knows how to bow to necessity. I hadn't claimed the courtesy due me when I killed the sandtiger, thereby releasing the shukar from a very distasteful duty; now I claimed it with every right and justification. He had to honor the request.

"Two horses," I said. "Water and food for two weeks. When I ask for them."

His mouth worked. I saw how yellowed his teeth had become from chewing beza nut, a mild narcotic. A common habit in the Punja; supposedly it enhances magic, provided one has it already. "We have given you life again," he said curtly. "We reclaimed you and the woman from the sand."

I folded my arms. "Yes. But that's something the Salset must do for anyone. The tribe has my gratitude for the reclaiming, but *you* must honor my request for courtesy." Idly I ran a finger along the black cord around my neck, rattling the claws. Reminding him how I had won my freedom.

Reminding him he had absolutely no choice.

"When you ask for them," he said bitterly, and turned his back on me.

I watched him walk away. I knew satisfaction in the victory, but it wasn't as sweet as I'd expected. When a man is grudgingly given what he is due anyway, there is no pleasure in it.

\*   \*   \*

Del was on her feet before I expected it, moving slowly
with the aid of a staff. At first I protested until she rattled
off something in her Northern tongue that sounded angry,
frustrated and impatient, all at once, and I *knew* she was
almost back to normal.

I breathed a sigh of relief. We had shared a brief, odd
closeness in the hyort as she lay trapped in sandsickness.
While it had been special, it also proved discomfiting for
me. Staying with the Salset upset the hardwon equilibrium
I'd so carefully built in the years since I'd left. It left me
vulnerable to things, feelings I'd left behind. The Sandtiger
had lowered his guard, even if only briefly, and it was
something I simply couldn't afford. I was a professional
sword-dancer, earning my living by doing dangerous, demanding work few others were willing to tackle. There
was no time, no room for sentimentality or emotions other
than those necessary to survival, if I were to continue.

Del came out as I lounged in the shade of an awning
outside Sula's hyort. She had put on her belted tunic once
again (Sula had cleaned and brushed it), and the blue runic
embroidery glowed brightly against the brown suede. Most
of the pink new flesh had toughened, weathering to a more
normal color (though a little darker); she was a smooth,
pale gold all over. Sunbleached hair was tied back with
blue cord, sharpening the lines of her jaw and cheekbones.
She was thinner, slower, but she still moved with the grace
and poise I admired.

I admired it so much I felt my mouth dry up. If I hadn't
been so sure she was still weak and easily tired, I might
have pulled her down beside me to investigate the possibility of payment in something other than gold coin.

Then I realized she was in harness and carried that
sword in her hand.

"Del—"

"Dance with me, Tiger."

"Bascha—you know better."

"I have to." There was no room for argument. "I'll be no good if I don't dance. *You* know that."

Still sprawled nonchalantly, I glared up at her. But there was nothing nonchalant about my tone of voice. "Hoolies, woman, you almost died. You still might, if I join you in a circle." I looked at her bared sword, scowling, and saw how the patterns of the designs seemed to move in the metal, confusing my eyes. I blinked.

"You're not *that* good."

I quit looking at the sword and looked instead at her. "I am," I explained with dignity, "the best sword-dancer in the Punja. *Possibly* even the South." (I thought it likely I *was* the best sword-dancer in the South, but a man has to maintain some sense of modesty.)

"No," she said. "We haven't tested each other properly."

I sighed. "You're good with a sword—I saw that when we danced before the Hanjii—but you're no sword-dancer, bascha. Not a *proper* one."

"I apprenticed," she said, "very much as you did. Before that, my father, uncles and brothers taught me."

"*You* apprenticed?" I asked. "*Formally*?"

"With all attendant ritual."

I studied her. I could grant that she had trained with father, brothers and uncles, because she *was* good—for a woman—but formal apprenticeship? Even in the North, I doubted a woman would be admitted into the sort of relationship I had known with my shodo.

"Formal, huh?" I asked. "Well—you *are* quick. You're supple. You're better than I expected. But you haven't got the strength, the endurance or the coldness."

Del smiled a little. "I am a Northerner—a *sorceress*, he claims—and he says I am not cold."

I raised an eyebrow. "You know what I mean. The *edge*."

"Edge," she echoed, exploring the word.

"A sword-dancer is more than just a master of the blade, bascha," I explained. "More than someone who

141

ॱ

understands the rituals of the dance. A sword-dancer is also a killer. Someone who kills without compunction, when he has to. I don't mean I kill without good reason, just for the hoolies of it—I'm not a borjuni—but if the coin and the circumstances are right, I'll unsheathe Singlestroke and plant him in the nearest belly requiring it."

Del looked down on me; I hadn't bothered to get up. "Try to plant him in mine," she suggested.

"Hoolies, woman, you've got sand in your head," I said in disgust.

She glared at me as I made no movement to rise. After a moment the expression altered. She smiled. I knew enough to be wary of her, now. "I'll make a deal with you, Tiger."

I grunted.

"Dance with me," she said. "Dance with me—and when we catch up to my brother, I'll pay you in something other than gold. Something—*better*."

I won't say it was easy to show no change of expression. "We may never *find* your brother; what kind of a deal is that?"

"*We'll find him.*" The flesh of her face was taut. "Dance with me now, Tiger. I need it. And if we get to Julah and can't find any traces of him, none at all . . . I'll still honor the deal." She shrugged a little. "I don't have any gold. I don't even have any copper."

I looked at her. I didn't let my eyes roam over her body; I'm not *entirely* insensitive. Besides, I already knew what she had to offer.

"Deal, bascha."

The sword glittered in the sunlight. "Dance with me, Tiger."

I looked at her weapon. "Against *that*? No. Against another sword."

The flesh of her face stiffened. "*This* is my sword."

Slowly I shook my head. "No more secrets, bascha.

That sword is more than a sword, and you have someone hunting you.''

She went white, so white I thought she might faint. But she didn't. She recovered her composure. I saw only the briefest clenching of her jaw. "That is private business."

"You didn't even know," I accused. "What's private about something *I* have to tell you?"

"I have expected it," she said briefly. "It comes as no surprise. It is—blood-debt. I owe many *ishtoya*. If this is one, I will accept the responsibility." She stood rigidly before me. "But this has nothing to do with what I ask *you* to do."

"You've invited me into the circle," I said blandly. "And you ask me to dance against an ensorcelled sword."

"It's not—ensorcelled," she said flatly. "Not exactly. I don't deny there is power in this sword . . . but it must be *summoned*—much as your tiger had to be conjured." Indirectly, she challenged me. "In this circle, against the Sandtiger, my sword will be a sword."

I looked down at my palm. Closed it to shut away the brand. But it didn't shut away the memory of the pain or the power I had felt.

My harness was at my right side. I pulled Singlestroke free of the sheath and pushed myself to my feet. "The circle will be small," I said flatly. "The dance will be short and slow. I will not contribute to your death."

Del showed her teeth in a feral little smile. "*Kaidin* Sandtiger, you honor your *ishtoya*."

"No I don't," I assured her blandly, "I'm just *humoring* her."

Within weeks she was sleek and supple again, swift as a cat, though not swift as *this* cat. I held back in the circle, teasing her along because I didn't want to overextend her; she knew it, I knew it, but there was little she could do about it. A couple of times she tried to push me, dancing faster, darting the shining sword at me in a barrage of

intricate patterns and parries, but I beat her back with the
strategies I had learned long ago. It wasn't difficult. It
would take time for her to regain her rhythm and strength.

Our styles were incredibly different. It was to be expected of a man and woman, matched, but Del's blade
patterns were quicker and shorter, confined in a much
smaller space. It took great strength and flexibility in the
wrists themselves, as well as the arms and shoulders, and
it proved she had indeed been properly trained. But by a
shodo—or, in her tongue, *kaidin*? I doubted it. For one,
she employed no ritual in her practice dance. She simply
moved, moving well, except I could see no formal patterns. No signature. Nothing that indicated a formal apprenticeship. Nothing that exhibited the hallmark of a true
*master*, no signature pattern that identified a sword-dancer
as a former student of this shodo or that one.

Still, with her yellow-white hair darkened by sweat and
her long, supple limbs moving so smoothly in the circle, it
was easy to imagine she had been taught by *someone*. And
someone very good.

But not good enough to dance against the Sandtiger.

For real, that is.

After a few short weeks spent walking, running, dancing, Del's quickness and strength were restored. Sula's
alla oil kept her skin from tearing; natural health and
vitality did the rest. Five weeks after our rescue from the
sands, Del and I mounted the horses I claimed from the
shukar and rode away from the Salset.

As we headed south, Del studied me in blandness and
unsettling candor. "The woman cares for you."

"Sula? She's a good woman. Better than the rest."

"She must have loved you very much when you were
with the tribe."

I shrugged. "Sula looked after me. She taught me a
lot." I recalled some of the lessons in the darkness and
privacy of her hyort. Thinking of the heavy, aging woman
now made me wonder how I could have desired her, but

the flicker of disbelief faded quickly into comprehension. Even had Sula not been young and beautiful when I killed the sandtiger, her kindness and warmth would have made her special. And she had made me a man, in more ways than one.

"I had nothing to give her," Del said. "To thank her."

"Sula didn't do it for *thanks*." But then I saw the genuine regret in Del's face, and subsequently regretted my curtness.

"I feel wrong," she said quietly. "She was deserving of a guest-gift. Something to acknowledge her kindness and generosity." She sighed. "In the North, I would be considered a rude, thoughtless person, unworthy of courtesy."

"You're in the South. You're not rude, thoughtless *or* unworthy," I pointed out. Then I grinned. "When do you plan on thanking *me*?"

Del looked at me consideringly. "I think I liked you better when you thought I might die of sandsickness. You were nicer."

"I'm never nice."

She reconsidered. "No. Probably not."

I brought my horse up next to hers so we rode side by side. I'd been pleasantly surprised by the choice the shukar had made for us: both geldings were good ones, small, desert-bred ponies. I had a buckskin with a clipped black mane and tail; Del rode a very dark sorrel marked by a strip of white running from ears to muzzle. The vermilion blankets over our shallow saddles were a bit threadbare; the quality of the animals *under* the saddles and blankets was more important. But someone had cut the tassels off the braided yellow reins.

"What do you plan on doing when we get to Julah?" I asked. "It's been five years since your brother was stolen. That's a long time, down here."

Del pulled at the azure burnous Sula had given her, settling it around her harness. Sula had given me one also, cream-colored, silk edged with brown stitching. Both Del and I had immediately cut slits in the shoulders for our swords. "Osmoon said his brother Omar was the trader who'd be able to tell me about Jamail going on the slaveblock."

"How do you know Omar is still in Julah?" I asked. "Slavers move around a lot. And how do you know he'll be willing to tell you anything even if he *is* still in Julah?"

Del shook her head. "I *can't* know . . . not until we get there. But I have planned for certain instances."

My buckskin reached out to nibble on the cropped, upstanding mane of Del's sorrel. I kicked free my right foot from the stirrup, stretched my leg between the horses, and banged a heel against the buckskin's nose. He quit nibbling. "I don't think you'll make much progress, bascha."

"Why not?" She popped her reins a bit and rattled shanks against bit rings, suggesting to her sorrel he not seek redress from the buckskin.

I sighed. "Isn't it obvious—even to *you*? It's true that here Northern boys are prized by tanzeers and wealthy merchants who have a taste for such things. But that isn't the rule. Usually it's Northern *girls* who are so highly prized." I looked at her steadily. "How in hoolies do you think you'll find anything out when every slave trader in Julah is going to be trying to steal *you*?"

I saw the realization move through her face and eyes, tightening her skin minutely. A muscle ticked in her jaw. Then she shrugged. "I'll dye my hair dark. Stain my skin. Walk with a limp."

"Are you going to be mute, too?" I grinned. "Your accent is Northern, bascha."

She glared at me. "I suppose you've already worked out a solution."

"As a matter of fact . . ." I shrugged. "Let *me* do the looking. It'll be safer and probably quicker."

"You don't know Jamail."

"Tell me what to look for. Besides, there can't be that

many Northern boys in Julah who are—what, fifteen? I don't think it'll be hard to track him down, provided he's still alive.''

"He's alive.'' Her conviction was absolute.

For her sake, I hoped he was.

"Dust,'' Del said sharply, pointing eastward. "Is it another simoom?''

I saw the billows of sand rising in the east. "No. Looks like a caravan.'' I woke up my buckskin with heels planted into his flanks; his bobbing head indicated he was half-asleep. Hoolies, but I missed the stud. "Let's go take a look.''

"Isn't that asking for trouble? After the Hanjii—''

"Those aren't Hanjii. Come on, bascha.''

When we got within clear sight of the caravan, we discovered it *was* under attack, as Del had feared. But the attackers weren't Hanjii, they were borjuni; although the desert bandits are extremely dangerous, they're also generally very slow about killing their prey. They like to play with you first.

I glanced at Del. "Stay here.''

"You're going in?''

"We need gold if we're to buy information in Julah. One way of getting it is to aid a caravan under attack; the leader is always incredibly grateful and usually very generous.''

"Only if you're alive to collect the reward.'' Del arranged her reins in one hand—her left. "I'm going in with you.''

"Have you got sand in your head?'' I demanded. "Don't be such a fool—''

She drew her sword with her right hand. "I really wish you'd stop calling me a fool, Tiger.'' Then she slapped her Salset horse with the flat of the rune-worked blade and galloped straight toward the shouting borjuni.

"God of hoolies, *why* did you saddle me with this woman?'' And I went after her.

147

Originally the caravan had been guarded by outriders. Most of these were dead or wounded, although a few of them still tried to put up a defense. The borjuni weren't incredibly numerous, but then they don't need to be. They ride quick, knee-trained horses that allow them to strike, wheel and leap away, wheeling back to finish what they have started. Never do borjuni stand and fight when they can slash and ride.

I let loose with a bloodcurdling yell and rode smack into the middle of everything, counting on catching the borjuni off-guard. I did, but unfortunately the caravan outriders *also* were caught off-guard; instead of attacking while the borjuni were momentarily surprised, they stood and stared.

Then Del shouted from the other side of the wagons and the melee broke out afresh. I caught glimpses of her streaking by on the sorrel horse, burnous snapping and rippling, sword blade flashing silver-white until it turned red and wet. For a moment I was astonished by her willingness to shed blood. The next moment I was too busy to worry about it.

I wounded two, killed three, then came face to face with the borjuni leader. He wore shiny silver earrings and a string of human finger bones around his neck. His sword was the curved blade of the Vashni. It's unusual to find a Vashni out of his tribe; they are fiercely loyal to one another, but occasionally a warrior leaves to make his own way.

Unless, of course, he's been exiled, which makes him doubly dangerous. He has something to prove to the world.

The Vashni's teeth were white and bared in a red-brown face as he came at me on his little Punja horse, curved blade slung behind his shoulder so he could unleash a sweeping slash at my neck, thereby severing skull from shoulders instantly. I ducked, but heard the whistling hiss as the blade swept over my head. Singlestroke was there when the Vashni swung back around to try again, and the warrior tumbled slowly from his horse in a tangle of arms and legs. Minus *his* head.

I looked around for my next opponent and discovered there were none; the ones who remained were all dead, or nearly so. And then I saw Del, still engaging her final opponent.

She was off her Salset horse. The sword was bloody in her hands as she stood her ground and waited. I saw the mounted borjuni come running, right hand filled with sword, left hand filled with knife. One way or another, he'd kill the woman on the ground.

Except Del was unmoved by his ululating cry or the steadiness of his horse. She waited, and as he flashed by and lowered the sword in a scything sweep, she ducked it. Ducking, she cut at the horse's legs and severed connective tendons.

The horse fell out from under the borjuni. But the man was on his feet before he hit the ground, knife flying from his hand in Del's direction. I saw her sword flash up, strike, knock the knife aside. And as he came at her, running on foot, the sword flashed up again.

Borjuni steel and Northern blade never engaged one another. Calmly, Del dropped flat below his thrust, allowed him to overextend, rolled, came up with her blade at an angle and took him through the belly.

It was only after the body fell that I knew I'd been holding my breath. I sucked air, then slowly rode over to Del. She wiped her sword on the clothing of the borjuni who lay dead in the sand and slid the blade home in its sheath.

"You've done this before," I observed.

"This? No. I've never rescued a caravan."

"I mean: you've fought and killed men before."

She tucked loosened hair behind her ears. "Yes," she agreed evenly.

I sighed and nodded. "Seems like I've underestimated you all the way around . . . sorceress."

She shook her head. "No sorcery. Just simple sword-work."

The *hoolies* it was! But I let it go at that because a voice was shouting for our attention. "We're being summoned. Shall we go?"

"You go. I need to catch my horse. I'll join you in a moment."

I rode over to the lead wagon and saluted a fat, high-voiced eunuch clad in jewels and silken robes.

"Sword-dancer!" he cried. "By all the gods of valhail, a *sword-dancer*!"

I dropped off the buckskin and wiped Singlestroke's bloodied blade on the nearest corpse. I slid the sword home over my shoulder and said a brief word of greeting in Desert.

"I am Sabo," the eunuch explained, after exchanging customary courtesies. "I serve the tanzeer Hashi, may the Sun shine on him long and well."

"May it be so," I agreed gravely. I glanced around and saw how many of his outriders the borjuni had killed. Of ten, only two were still alive, and they were wounded. Then I frowned. "Are you *all* eunuchs?"

He looked away at once, avoiding my eyes; an acknowl-edgment of stupidity. "Yes, sword-dancer. Escort for my lady Elamain."

I stared at him in astonishment as Del rode up and dropped off her sorrel. "You're escorting a lady across the Punja with only a bunch of *eunuchs*?"

Sabo was shame-faced. Still he looked away from me. A gesture indicated a guilt willingly assumed; he would be held responsible, even if it hadn't been his idea. "My lord Hashi insisted. The lady is to be his bride, and he—he—" Sabo's eyes flicked briefly to my face, then away again. He shrugged. "*You* understand."

I sighed. "Yes. I think I do. He didn't want the lady's virtue compromised. Instead, he compromises her safety."

I shook my head. "It's not your fault, Sabo, but you should have known better."

He nodded, triple chins wobbling against the high, gem-crusted collar standing up beneath his wine-colored robes. He was dark-skinned and black-haired, but his eyes were a pale brown. "Yes. Of course. But what's done is done." He smiled ingeniously, dismissing the shame at once. "And now that *you're* here to help us, we need fear no longer."

Del's smile was ironic. I ignored it. Sabo was playing right into my hands. "I imagine the tanzeer would be—*pleased*—to recover his intended bride."

Sabo understood. And he had a flair for dramatics. "But of *course!*" His pale brown eyes opened wide. "My lord Hashi is a generous lord. He will reward you well for this generous service. And I'm sure the lady herself will be just as grateful."

"The lady *is* grateful," said the lady's voice.

I glanced around. She stepped out of a fabric-draped wagon, fastidiously avoiding the bodies scattered on the sand as she approached. She pulled her own draperies out of the way as she moved, and I saw small gold-tasseled blue slippers on her feet.

Following the dictates of desert custom, she wore a modesty veil over her face. It fell from the black braids piled on top of her head pinned with enameled ornaments. But the veil was colorless as water and twice as sheer; she looked at me out of a flawless, dusky face and liquid, golden eyes.

She dropped to the sand in a single practiced, graceful movement and kissed my foot, which was dusty and sweaty and no doubt incredibly rank.

"Lady—" Startled, I pulled the foot away.

She kissed the other one, then gazed up at me in an attitude of grateful worship. "How can this poor woman thank you? How can I say in words what I am feeling, to be rescued by the Sandtiger?"

By valhail, she *knew* me!

Sabo gasped in astonishment. "The Sandtiger! Gods of valhail, is it true?"

"Of course it's true," the lady snapped, but softened it with a smile. "I've heard of the sword-dancer with the scars on his face, who wears the claws that scarred him."

I raised her with a blood-stained hand. I felt dirty and smelly and unfit for such elegant duty.

"My, *my*," said Del.

I glanced at her suspiciously, scowled, then turned back to the lady and smiled. "I *am* the Sandtiger," I admitted modestly, "and I will be more than happy to escort you to the tanzeer whose good fortune it is to be engaged to a lady as lovely as you."

Del looked pretty amazed I'd managed to get my tongue around such eloquent words; so was I. But it had a nice effect on the blushing bride, for she blushed even more and turned her head away in appealing embarrassment.

"The lady Elamain," Sabo announced. "Betrothed to Lord Hashi of Sasqaat."

"Who?" asked Del, as I asked, "Where?"

"Lord Hashi," he replied patiently. "Of Sasqaat." Sabo waved a be-ringed hand. "That way." He looked at Del a moment. "Who are you?"

"Del," she said. "Just Del."

The eunuch looked a little disconcerted, perhaps expecting a little more out of a woman who rode with the Sandtiger, but she didn't say anything else and didn't appear to want to. Her eyes, I thought, looked suspiciously amused; I had the distinct impression she found all this gratitude rather funny.

Elamain put a soft, cool hand on my wrist, which had borjuni blood on it. She didn't seem to mind. "I wish you to ride with me to Sasqaat in my wagon. It will honor me."

Del's brows rose. "Difficult to protect the caravan if he's *in* the wagon, instead of outside guarding it."

Elamain flashed her a quick look of irritation out of those wide golden eyes. Next to her dark desert beauty, Del's fairness made her look washed out. White-blonde hair straggled down her back, wisping into her eyes; dust and blood streaked her face. Her burnous was torn, stained. The two of them, standing so close, looked about as much alike as queen and lowliest kitchen maid—especially to a man who had been around unwilling women far too long.

Elamain smiled at me. "Come, Tiger. Join me in my wagon."

Determined that Del wouldn't have the last word (or that anything she might say could have the slightest effect on my decision and subsequent behavior), I shot her a bland look and smiled at the lady. "I would be honored, princess."

Elamain led me to her wagon.

# Thirteen

The lady was properly grateful. In the privacy of her very private wagon, as it bumped gently across the sand, Hashi's intended showed me she was no modest virgin, but an experienced woman who saw what she wanted and went after it. For the moment it happened to be me, which was very satisfactory all the way around.

Riding with Del hadn't been easy. I'd wanted her from the moment she'd walked into the cantina, but I knew she'd likely stick her knife into me for any unexpected— and unencouraged—intimacy. The night she'd put her naked sword between us had pretty well informed me how she felt about the matter, and I've never been one to insist when all it requires is a little patience. *Then*, of course, we'd gotten picked up by the Hanjii, and all thoughts of making love to Del had rather quickly gone out of my head.

Especially after she kneed me.

Del's suggestion as to what could be considered "payment" for my services once we reached Julah had set my mind racing with anticipation and made the rest of me hot with impatience, but—once again—*patience* was what was required. Well, it runs out after awhile. Del wasn't available yet, but Elamain was.

Young, sweet, tempting, hungry Elamain. Only a fool

or a saint ignores a gorgeous, grateful woman when she's feeling amorous.

And, as I've said before, I'm neither.

We had to be quiet, of course. Hashi's bride was supposed to arrive unflawed and untouched. How she intended explaining to a new husband why she was no longer a virgin wasn't my problem, and I didn't allow it to linger in my mind very long. I had other things to think about.

A lot of women rather enjoy making the Sandtiger growl. I suppose it has to do with having the name in the first place. Occasionally, when the time and the woman are right, I don't mind, because I really can't help myself. But I told Elamain it was stupid to expect me to stay discreetly quiet and then do everything she could to make me growl like a big, tame cat.

She just smiled and bit me on the shoulder. So I bit her back.

Where Del was—or what she did—during all this, I have no idea. If she had any sense at all, she'd be making friends with Sabo, who could probably be very persuasive when it came to suggesting to his master that generous thanks might be in order. But I hadn't known Del long enough; although I thought she was probably pretty sensible, she was also a woman, and therefore unpredictable. And, probably, prone to behavior that is occasionally not so sensible.

"Who is she?" asked Elamain as we lay sweating gently into the cushions and silks.

I thought about asking who, then didn't. I didn't think Elamain was stupid, either. "She's a woman I'm guiding to Julah."

"Why?"

"She hired me to."

"Hired." Elamain looked at me. "No woman *hires* the Sandtiger. Not with gold." The tip of her tongue showed.

"Does she do this for you?" And she did something very creative with her hand.

After I recovered myself, I told her no, Del didn't; I did not tell her I had no way of knowing if Del *could*.

"What about this?"

"Elamain," I groaned, "if you want this pleasant little tryst to *remain* a secret, I think you'd better stop."

She laughed deep in her throat. "They're eunuchs," she said. "Who cares what they know? They're only wishing *they* could do it to me."

Probably. Nevertheless, I have *some* sense of decency, and I told her so.

Elamain ignored my comment. "I like you, Tiger. You're the best."

She probably said it to every man, but it still made me feel good. It always does.

"I want you to come with me, Tiger."

"I'm *going* with you—as far as Sasqaat."

"I want you to *stay* with me."

I looked at her in surprise. "In Sasqaat? But you're getting married, Elamain—"

"Marriage need not stop anything," she said testily. "It's an inconvenience, to be sure, but I have no intention of stopping just for *that*." Her smile came back, along with the invitation in her golden eyes. "Don't you want more, Tiger?"

"That question is unworthy of you."

She giggled and slid over on top of me again. "*I* want more, Tiger. I want *all* of you. I want to *keep* you."

This kind of talk makes any man nervous. Especially me. I kissed her, as she wanted, and did everything else she wanted as well, but deep in my gut I had the sickening feeling of apprehension.

"*Elamain has the Sandtiger* . . ." she whispered gleefully, licking at my ear.

For the moment, she certainly did.

\* \* \*

156

When the lowering sun set the horizon aglow with magenta and amethyst fire, I circled the perimeter of the tiny camp on my buckskin Salset gelding. Altogether there were eight wagons: Elamain's personal transport and those carrying her maids and possessions. The drivers were all eunuchs, the maids all women, and I the only normal male for miles. If Elamain hadn't been so accommodating, I might have been distracted by all the ladies. As it was, I didn't have the time—or the energy—for anyone else.

At one juncture I stopped and stared off across the purpled desert, lost in contemplation of Elamain's unexpected—and undeniable—skill, when Del came riding up. Her hair was freshly braided and tied back. She had washed the dust of the desert from her face, but I was too full of Elamain to notice the exquisitely bland expression.

"Sabo says we'll get to Sasqaat without the slightest difficulty, now that the Sandtiger leads the caravan," she said.

"We probably will."

Del snickered. "She keeping you happy, Tiger? Or—should I say—are you keeping *her* happy?"

I glared at her. "Mind your own business."

Her pale brows slid up in mock surprise. "Oh no, have I offended you? Should I get down and kiss your feet?"

"Enough, Del."

"The whole caravan knows," she said. "I hope you realize this Lord Hashi of Sasqaat is considered a rather short-tempered man. Sabo says he kills anyone who crosses him." She looked out across the darkening desert even as I did, exuding neutrality. "What's he going to say when he finds out you've been dallying with his bride?"

"He can't blame *me*," I declared. "She's not giving away anything she hasn't given away before."

Del laughed outright. "Then the *lady* is no lady. Well, I don't feel sorry for Hashi. I suppose he'll get what he's paid for."

I looked at her sharply. "What do you mean?"

"Sabo told me Elamain's father was more than happy to marry his daughter off. Apparently she's been—indiscreet with her affections. He was so thrilled to have Hashi offer for her that he reduced the bride-price. Hashi's getting a discount." She shrugged. "Used goods, after all."

"You're *jealous*." Belatedly, it dawned on me.

Del grinned. "I'm not jealous. Why should I be?"

We stared at one another: Del genuinely amused and me generally disgruntled.

"Why should Sabo tell *you* all this?" I demanded. "Hashi's his lord. How could he know so much about Elamain?"

Del shrugged. "He said everyone knows. The lady has a terrible reputation."

I frowned, shifting in the shallow saddle. "But if *Hashi* doesn't know . . ." I considered it.

"It seems likely he would," Del pointed out. "But I suppose there's no telling what a desert prince will do— I've been told often enough how acquisitive they are; how jealous and possessive. How poorly they treat their women— although that seems to be the generally accepted custom in the South." She cast me a bland glance. "How do you treat *your* women, Tiger?"

"Keep this up and *you'll* never find out."

She laughed. I rode away to circle back in the other direction, and Del laughed.

I didn't think it was funny at all.

Before long, Elamain gave up all pretense of being a circumspect, virtuous woman and openly declared her current passion by keeping herself as close to me as possible, even when I rode at the head of the caravan on the lookout for borjuni. She made one of the wounded eunuchs ride in her wagon on these occasions, taking his horse for herself. Underneath all the flowing draperies she wore the silken jodhpurs of desert tanzeers and rode astride with aplomb. Outside of the wagon she also wore the transparent veil, but everyone knew it was nothing more than hypocrisy. In all truth, Elamain had no right to wear the veil signifying virtuous womanhood, but no one had the courage to tell her what she undoubtedly knew anyway.

To my surprise, Elamain made some effort to get to know Del better, even to the point of asking Del into her wagon on more than one occasion. What they discussed I have no idea; women's talk doesn't interest me in the least. I wondered, uneasily, if Elamain wanted to discuss something she and Del had in common—me—but neither of them ever said.

I also wondered what Del's answer would be if I *were* the topic. She could do irreparable harm to my reputation if she told Elamain we hadn't been intimate; then again, Del was Del, and I couldn't expect her to lie. And, knowing Elamain, I doubted she'd believe Del even if she *did* deny that intimacy. Altogether it was very confusing, and I decided the better part of valor was to simply ignore the whole thing.

Still, I couldn't help wondering what Del thought of it all. The situation between us was odd. On one hand, she knew I wanted her. She also knew she'd promised to sleep with me when the journey to Julah was finished, so there was no need for coyness or games.

On the other hand, the businesslike demeanor of the entire situation dissipated all the anticipation, reducing it to a mere contract. I'd get her to Julah, she'd pay up. Before, when just Del and I were together, I was happy enough with the anticipation. Now, with Elamain so close at hand (and so *active*), I discovered my feelings for Del were ambivalent. There was no doubt I still wanted that fair-skinned, silk-smooth body, but the anticipation had altered from eagerness to acceptance.

It didn't occur to me that it was *because* Elamain was so demanding that I didn't have anything left over for Del.

The woman was insatiable. We gave up all pretense of a business relationship; I stayed with her in her wagon at night, and occasionally during the day we'd retire for a while. Her maids— well-trained—never said a word. The eunuchs also kept quiet. Only Sabo looked worried, but he said nothing to me or Elamain.

As for Del, she no longer even joked about it. I thought it was a bit of jealousy turning her fair skin green, but I wasn't too certain. Del didn't seem the jealous type, and all the jealous women I've known aren't capable of behaving so—*normally*. I wasn't even aware of any daggered glances when my back was turned.

Did she think so little of me, then, that an affair with another woman meant nothing? Or was it simply that she figured I wasn't worth the trouble?

I didn't like that idea. I decided it was because she thought she wasn't up to the competition. Which was stupid, because Del was up to anything. Clean *or* dirty.

Finally Sabo approached me. We rode at the head of the caravan, and in the distance lay the formless, sand-colored shape of Sasqaat, Hashi's city.

"Lord," he began.

I waved off the honorific. "Tiger will do."

He stared at me from his eloquent pale brown eyes. "Lord Tiger, may I have permission to speak? It's a situation of some delicacy."

Naturally. I'd been expecting it. "Go ahead, Sabo. You can speak freely to me."

He fiddled with braided scarlet reins, chubby fingers glittering with rings. "Lord Tiger, I must warn you that my lord is not a calm man. Neither is he precisely *cruel*, but he is jealous. He ages, and with each added year he fears to lose his manhood. Already some of his vigor fades, so he tries to hide it by keeping the largest harem in the Punja, so everyone will think he is still young and strong and vigorous." The eyes, couched in dark, fleshy folds, peered at me worriedly. "I speak of personal things, Lord Sandtiger, because I must. They also concern the lady Elamain."

"And therefore me."

"And therefore you." He moved plump shoulders in a shrug of discomfort, setting the gold stitching of his white burnous to glow in the sunlight. "It's not my place to interfere between my betters, but I must. I must warn you that my lord Hashi may be very angry that his bride is no longer virgin."

"She wasn't a virgin *before* me, Sabo."

"I know that." He made certain of the fit of each of his rings. "I'm certain my lord Hashi knows it, too . . . but he'll never admit it. Never."

"Then all he has to do is ignore the fact his bride is a little more experienced than he expected." I smiled. "He really shouldn't complain. If anyone can restore Hashi's lost vigor, *she* can."

"But—if she can't?" Sabo was openly fearful. "If she can't, and he fails with her, he will be angry. Violently angry. He will blame the lady, not himself, and he'll look for a way to punish her. But—because she is a lady of some repute, with a wealthy father—he can't kill her. So he'll search for another person on which to vent his anger and frustration, and I find it very likely he will look to the man responsible for the most recent 'deflowering' of his bride." His voice was apologetic. "Everyone in Sasqaat, I think, knows the lady's reputation. But *no one* will say so, because he is the tanzeer. He'll punish *you*, probably kill *you*, and no one will try to stop it."

I smiled, hunching my left shoulder so the sword moved a little. "Singlestroke and I have an agreement. He looks out for me, I look out for him."

"You can't bear arms into the presence of the tanzeer."

"So I won't see the tanzeer." I looked at him blandly. "Surely his faithful servant can tell him how helpful I've been, and suggest a fitting reward be given to me through *his* offices."

Sabo was astonished. "You would trust *me* to give you your reward?"

"Of course. You're an honorable man, Sabo."

His brown face lost color until he resembled a sallow, sickly child. I thought he was having some sort of seizure. "No one—" he began, stopped, began again. "*No one* has ever said that. It's Sabo *this*, Sabo *that*; run so fast your fat wobbles, eunuch. I am not a man to them. Not even to my lord Hashi, who is not really so bad a person. But the others—" He broke off, shutting up his mouth.

"They can be cruel," I said quietly. "I know. I may not be a eunuch, Sabo, but I understand. I've experienced my own sort of hoolies."

He gazed at me. "But—whatever it was—you left it. You must have left it. The Sandtiger walks freely . . . and whole."

"But the Sandtiger also remembers when he didn't walk freely." I smiled and slapped him on his flabby shoulder. "Sabo, hoolies is what you make of it. For some of us, it's to be endured because it makes us better people."

He sighed. His brows hooked together. "Perhaps. I should not complain. I have some small wealth, for my lord Hashi is generous with me." He waved his ring-weighted fingers. "I eat, I drink, I buy girls to try and rouse what manhood I have left. They are kind. They know it wasn't my choice—what was done to me as a boy. But it's not the same as freedom." He looked at me. "The freedom to take a woman like Elamain, as you do, or the yellow-haired Northern girl."

"The yellow-haired Northern girl is my employer," I declared at once. "No more than that."

He looked at me in utter disbelief; I couldn't really blame him. And then I got irritated all over again that I hadn't at least *tried* to get closer to Del. A sword on the sand never stopped the Sandtiger before!

But then it had never been a sword like Del's sword, wrought of hard, cold ice and alien runes that promised a painful death.

Still, it wasn't really the sword at all. It was Del herself, and that odd integrity and pride. Maybe it wouldn't stop another man, but it sure stopped me.

I sighed with deep disgust.

Sabo smiled. "Sometimes, a man does not have to be a eunuch," he said obliquely. I understood him well enough.

I glanced around, searching for Del, and saw her riding at the tail of the caravan. The sun burned brightly on her hair. She was smiling faintly, but the smile was directed inwardly and not at any person. Certainly not at me.

# Fourteen

**E**lamain was properly demonstrative during our final assignation in her wagon. We bumped closer to Sasqaat and to the end of our affair with each moment; she said she didn't want to miss anything I had to offer. By this time I wasn't certain I had anything *left* to offer—but I certainly tried.

"Growl for me, Sandtiger."

"Elamain."

"*I* don't care who knows. Everyone *does* know. Do you care? Growl for me, Tiger."

So I growled. But very softly.

Afterward, she sighed and slung one arm around my neck, snuggling her chin against one shoulder. "Tiger, I don't want to lose you."

"You're getting married, Elamain, and I'm going on to Julah."

"With *her*."

"Of course, with her. She hired me to take her there." I wondered how much Del had told her of our purpose, or if that had even come up during their discussions.

"Can't you stay a while in Sasqaat, Tiger?"

"Your husband might not like it."

"Oh, *he* won't care. I'll have him so exhausted he'll be glad to let me spend some time with someone else. Besides, why should you let a husband interfere with our pleasure?''

''He'll have a little more right to your favors than I will, Elamain. I think that's the way marriage works.''

She sighed and snuggled closer. Black hair tickled my nose. ''Stay with me a while. Or stay in Sasqaat, and then I'll have you called to the palace. For your reward.'' She giggled. ''Haven't *I* rewarded you enough?''

''*More* than enough.'' It was heartfelt.

''Well, I want more for you. I'll introduce you to Hashi—respectfully, of course, and properly—and I'll tell him how wonderful you were when you saved the caravan. How you struck down all those horrible borjuni single-handedly, and personally rescued me from their clutches.''

''It *wasn't* singlehandedly and you weren't *in* their clutches. Not yet, anyway.''

She made a moue of dismissal. ''So I'll lie a little. It will only win you greater reward. Don't you want a reward, Tiger?''

''I'm fond of rewards,'' I admitted. ''I've never yet turned one down.''

She laughed deep in her throat. ''What if I said I'd get you a reward far greater than you can imagine?''

I looked at her consideringly, but couldn't see much more than silky black hair and a smooth, dusky brow. Still, I had learned not to underestimate the lady. ''What did you have in mind?''

''That's *my* secret. But I promise you—you won't regret it.''

I traced the line of her nose. ''Are you sure of that?''

''You won't regret it,'' she whispered. ''Oh Tiger . . . *you won't*.''

Which meant, of course, I would.


Del and I had to wait in one of the outer rooms when we reached Hashi's palace in Sasqaat. Sabo flamboyantly escorted Elamain into the main part of the palace, leaving us cooling our heels, but promised he'd send word as soon as he could. He did, too; within an hour a swarm of servants descended upon us and ushered us into separate rooms. For baths, they said.

I needed no urging to climb into the huge sunken bath filled with hot water and sweet-scented oil. I jumped in before anyone could suggest it—although I did take off sandals, burnous, dhoti and harness. The dusty, sweat-stained garments disappeared at once, replaced by rich silks and soft leather slippers. My servants were all female, which didn't bother me in the least; I did wonder, however, if they gave Del women as well, or at least eunuchs.

Two of the servants came into the bath with me and proceeded to wash my hair and the rest of me as well. This led to giggling and half-serious suggestions of another way to enjoy a bath, so it took a little longer than I expected. By the time I climbed out, I was clean and drowsy and very, very relaxed. All I needed was a good meal.

I munched on fresh fruit as I got dressed. The grapes were marvelous, and the oranges; the melons were cool and juicy and delicious. The accompanying wine was light but slightly too sweet to provide a good complement to the fruit; it was also quietly powerful. By the time I'd put on the fresh dhoti and deep blue burnous freighted with genuine gold embroidery, my head felt muzzy and heavy.

One of the palace eunuchs came and escorted me to the huge audience hall. It was decked with silken and tasseled draperies of every color so that it almost resembled a giant hyort. The floor was tiled in dizzying patterns of mosaics that repeated themselves all the way up to the dais, on which rested a golden throne. Empty.

Additional eunuchs stood around the throne and dais, all dressed in magnificent clothing and all bearing great curving swords strapped to their chubby waists. Almost unconsciously, I hunched my left shoulder in the automatic gesture that told me Singlestroke rested safely in the scabbard.

Except that he didn't. I'd left Singlestroke in the bath chamber.

Hoolies, I'd left my sword!

I started to swing around and march back out of the chamber, but one of the eunuchs stepped into my path. "Lord Hashi comes soon. You must wait."

"I left my weapons behind. I'm going back for them." Inwardly I chafed in disgust that I could be so stupid.

"A man doesn't go armed in the presence of the tanzeer."

I glared at him. "I never go *un*armed."

"You do now," said Del from behind me. I swung around and she shrugged. "They took mine, too."

"You let them have *that* sword?"

She looked at me oddly, and I realized how I'd placed the emphasis. I saw a strange expression in her eyes a moment, a combination of possessiveness, apprehension, and acknowledgment. "Sheathed," Del answered. "But if they *un*sheathe it—" She stopped. Shrugged a little. "I can't be held accountable."

"For *what*?" I demanded. "What happens if anyone but you unsheathes that sword?"

Del smiled a little. "*You* have unsheathed it. *You* have put your hand upon the hilt. You are better able to explain what happens than I."

Instantly I recalled the searing pain in my hand, my arm, my shoulder, flooding through bones and flesh and blood. Hot and cold, all at once. I sweated. I shivered. Felt sick. No, she need have no fear that sword would fall into another man's hands. No one could use it, I knew. No one at all, save Del.

After a moment, I shook my head. "No. No, I can explain nothing. That—that *thing* is different from anything I know."

"So am I." And she smiled.

I glared. "If you were, I'd think you'd be a match for this man." I indicated the tanzeer's empty throne.

She shrugged. "Perhaps."

Then I forgot all about discussing magical swords and witchcraft and old men, because I saw what they'd done to Del. Gone was the loose-limbed Northern girl who claimed herself a sword-dancer; in her place was a woman swathed desert-fashion in translucent rose-colored silks that only served to make her fair body more tantalizing than ever. Each time she moved the veils parted, displaying more veils, or else showing a brief flash of long, pale leg. Her bright hair shone with washing and was twisted on top of her head, pinned with golden clips set with turquoise stones. But the servants had left off the modesty veil, perhaps assuming she wasn't a true lady if she rode across the Punja with a sword-dancer called the Sandtiger.

"Don't laugh at me," she said crossly. "*I* wanted to stay in my tunic, but they wouldn't let me."

"Who's laughing? I'm too busy staring."

"Don't stare." She scowled at me. "Didn't your mother teach you better manners?" Then she clapped a hand over her mouth, recalling I *had* no mother.

"Forget it," I told her. "Let's just try to brace ourselves for whatever's coming."

She frowned a little. "Why? What do you think is coming?"

I thought about what Elamain had said, *when* she had said it, and how she had phrased it. "Never mind. You wouldn't understand."

Her mouth twisted wryly. "Wouldn't I?"

But I didn't answer because I was too busy staring at the withered old man who was making his way onto the dais from a side door, with Sabo's assistance.

He was ancient. He was stooped and wrinkled and shaking with palsy, but his black eyes glittered fiercely as he took his seat on the throne. I gestured to Del and she turned also, automatically falling in beside me as we slowly approached.

"My lord Hashi, tanzeer of Sasqaat!" Sabo announced. "May the sun shine on him long and well!"

The sun had certainly shone on him *long*. He had to be close to ninety.

"Approach the throne!" Sabo shouted.

Since Del and I were engaged in doing precisely that, we simply continued.

"My lord Hashi wishes it known he is grateful for the service you have done him in rescuing his bride from certain death and bringing her safely to him. You will be rewarded." Sabo's expression held the faintest of secret smiles.

Del and I stopped before the dais. I made the traditional desert gesture of respect: spread-fingered hand placed over the heart while I inclined my head. Del said and did nothing, apparently having been warned that a woman never speaks to a tanzeer until he acknowledges her and invites conversation.

Hashi waved Sabo away. The eunuch moved five paces behind the throne and waited silently, his face perfectly blank. Then the old tanzeer leaned forward in his throne. "You are the sword-dancer they call the Sandtiger?"

"I am the Sandtiger."

"And the woman travels with you."

"I'm guiding her to Julah."

"Julah is not so nice as Sasqaat," Hashi said harshly, in the quick irritation of the elderly.

I didn't smile. Old men are unpredictable; old tanzeers are unpredictable and dangerous.

"The tanzeer in Julah is too young for his place," Hashi continued. "He knows nothing. He lets his servants run wild with no discipline, and he traffics in slaves. It's no wonder the city is a pisspot of common thieves, borjuni, sword-dancers, crooked merchants and slavers, as well as other foolhardy people." His beady black eyes were fastened on my face. "Sasqaat is a peaceful place, and much safer."

"But I need to go to Julah," Del said calmly, and I winced.

Hashi stared at her. His scrawny hands grasped the armrests of his throne. The veins stood out like bruises, crawling across his mottled skin. The healthy dark tan he once had known had grayed with age, leaving him ash-pale and sickly looking. It was no wonder he couldn't perform in bed anymore; I only wondered how Elamain had reacted to him.

"Elamain, you may enter," Hashi called.

I glanced around in surprise, saw a small side door open, and a moment later Elamain came into the hall. She was dressed similarly to Del, although her colors were subtle yellows and browns instead of the pale pinks and roses Del wore.

She came in smiling sweetly, black hair hanging loose past her rounded rump to her knees. I'd never seen it completely unbound before and I almost swallowed my tongue. Her smile grew a little as she looked at me, and instantly I looked at Hashi to see if he had noticed.

He had. His eyes glittered. "My lady Elamain has told me how kind you have been to her, and how thoughtful. How carefully you guarded her virtue." He smiled. "Although it is well-known Elamain has none."

Her smile froze. Her flawless face went very still and her eyes turned from gold to black as they dilated. I wasn't feeling so well myself.

"But I'll have her anyway," Hashi went on conversationally in his grating little voice. "I'm an old man, well past my prime, and I have nothing else left me in this life. It will bring me some pleasure to take the most beautiful woman in the Punja as my wife—and make certain she never lies with a man again." His smile was malicious, creeping out of the dark shadows of his soul. "Elamain has made a career out of bedding men. So many men, her father feared never to wed her properly. Well, I said I'd take her off his hands. I'll take her to wife. And I'll make certain she discovers *precisely* what it is to want someone so badly, knowing she'll never be able to have him."

Elamain was so pale I thought she might drop dead. But she didn't. She lowered herself to her knees on the tiled floor in front of the dais. "*My lord—*"

"*Silence*! This sword-dancer has delivered you to me, for which I am grateful, and I fully intend to reward him as you requested." He ignored her and looked at me. "Do you know what my bride suggested? Artfully, I must admit—she was magnificent." He grinned; he had lost most of his teeth. "She said it is customary for a husband and wife to exchange wedding gifts, gifts so special they become highly personal and therefore that much more prized. I agreed. I offered her whatever she would have, within my power to give." He nodded. "She said she would have *you*."

"*Me*?"

"You." His eyes bored into mine. "You must be good, to have Elamain require you for more than only a few nights. She never has before."

"My lord Hashi—" I attempted.

"Silence, sword-dancer. I'm not finished." He looked at Elamain. "She said I should give her the Sandtiger as a wedding gift because she had one equally magnificent for me." That almost-toothless grin again. "She said if I gave her the Sandtiger, she would give me a white-skinned, white-haired, blue-eyed Northern woman. For my own."

My hand flashed to my left shoulder and came up empty. Singlestroke was gone. So was my knife. I saw Del make the same futile gestures, and then she stood very still. She did not look at me.

"She *is* magnificent." Hashi stared at Del. "And I think I will take her."

I became aware that a cluster of tall, heavy eunuchs

were at my back and sides. The wicked, curving swords were naked in their hands.

I sucked in a breath. "We are free people," I told Hashi. "We are not chula, to be traded at your whim." I didn't tell him he couldn't get away with it, because he probably could.

"I'm not trading anything," Hashi said. "Elamain gives me a gift, which I accept." He smiled. "But I'm afraid I can't make her the same gesture. You, Sandtiger, have already had your pleasure on Elamain, and that's something no man will have again." He nodded; the cords of his thin neck trembled. "But I'll keep you here so she can see you, and be reminded of her foolishness. And lest you consider cuckolding me again, I will have it made impossible." He laughed. "I will have you made a eunuch."

That's the last thing I heard because I leaped for his stringy little throat and went down beneath a dozen guardsmen.

# Fifteen

**H**ashi had drugged the wine. I realized that after I woke up because I'd gone down with hardly a fight, and that's not like me at all. The odds had, of course, heavily outweighed me (and I'm not stupid); I knew the eunuchs would overpower me quickly.

But not so *easily*.

Hashi's generosity had ended dramatically. I still had my own room, but this time I wasn't in a bath chamber. I was in a tiny little cell somewhere in the bowels of the palace. And I wore iron jewelry.

I sat with my back against a cool, hard wall. My head ached dully from the aftermath of drugged wine and the thumping I'd received in the hall. My wrists were cuffed in iron and bolted to the wall sans chain, which limited movement considerably. Same with my ankles. My legs were stretched out in front of me, ankles cuffed and bolted to the floor. As long as I sat there quietly, I was fine. But I've never been real good at sitting quietly.

I shut my eyes against the pain in my head a moment, then opened them and looked at the damage done to my body. The scuffle had stripped me of the burnous so I could see the bruises rising on my skin, above and below the suede dhoti. My slippers also were missing, and I noticed that the little toe on my right foot stuck out to the side in a rather bizarre salute to the others. The rest of me, however, seemed to be in one piece, although that one piece was pretty sore. No one had used a sword or knife on me, so I had only bruises to show for my efforts, no cuts or slashes. I was grateful for that much.

The cell was a dark, close place, fouled with the stink of urine and defecation. Not my own; I wasn't that desperate yet. But it was obvious to me the former occupant(s) had been held for quite a while. You don't dissipate the stench of close confinement too quickly, even if you sluice the place from top to bottom. And no one had.

My neck was stiff. I had a pretty good idea I'd been in the cell for a while. And, from the way my belly felt, probably overnight. I was starving. I was also incredibly thirsty, but that might have more to do with the drugged wine than any natural factors. I tested my iron bonds and found them solid. No escaping them, unless someone unlocked them for me. And that didn't seem likely. The only one who'd unlock them was Del, and she was as much a prisoner as I—if in a different way.

Elamain wouldn't be any help, either; she was probably too busy trying to talk the old man around. Sabo?—I doubted it. He was the old man's servant. So—I was stuck.

And scared, because no man wants to think about losing his manhood.

Sickness knotted my belly until I wanted to spew it out into the cell, adding to the stench. I could *see* the sharp blade, *hear* Hashi's maniacal laughter, *feel* the pain as they started to cut. I clamped my teeth closed and screwed up my face as I tried to ignore the picture, shuddering so hard the cold bumps rose up on my skin. Better *death* than emasculation!

The door to the dungeon opened quietly, but I heard it. I'd have heard *anything* that heralded an approach. Why would Hashi want it done so soon? Or was it Elamain, come to beg forgiveness?

Well, no, she wouldn't do that. Not Elamain.

But it wasn't Elamain, or even Hashi and his eunuch-servants. The door to my cell clanked and creaked open, and it was Del.

I stared at her in the dimness, rigidly prepared to fight to the death the moment I was out of the iron cuffs. But now I wouldn't need to. It was *Del*.

She paused in the tiny doorway, ducking down to move into the cell. Her white-blond hair was tumbled around her silk-draped shoulders and over her breasts like she'd been in a man's bed.

Hashi's? The thought made me sick, sick and angry and—maybe— more than a little jealous.

"Are you all right?" Her whispered question hissed in the dimness.

"How did you get down here?" I demanded in astonishment, "How in *hoolies* did you manage it?"

She waited as I babbled all my half-incoherent inquiries, then displayed the large iron key dangling from her hand. Eloquent answer to all my questions.

"*Hurry up!*" I hissed. "Before they come after me!"

Del smiled. "That old tanzeer's got you scared silly, hasn't he? The Sandtiger, sword-dancer of the Punja, scared pissless of a little old man."

"You would be *too*, if you were a man and in my place." I rattled my cuffs. "Come *on*, Del. Don't dither."

She snickered and came into the cell, kneeling to unlock my ankles. I couldn't help myself—the moment my legs were free, I dragged them up to protect the part of my anatomy Hashi wanted to rearrange.

"How'd you get the key?" I demanded. The most obvious answer popped into my mind at once. "I suppose you let Hashi bed you in exchange for it."

Del paused momentarily as she reached to unlock my wrists. "And would it matter to you if I had?"

Her loose hair hung across my bare chest and face. "Hoolies *yes*, woman! What do you *think*?"

"What do I think?" She unlocked my right wrist. "I think you jump to conclusions pretty quickly, Tiger."

My impression was she was a tad angry. Maybe a little bitter. I don't know why; it wasn't *Del* stuck down here in a cell awaiting castration.

I peered at her face, trying to judge her expression. "You *did* sleep with that little Punja-mite."

She unlocked my left wrist. "I got you free, didn't I?"

I scrambled to my knees and grabbed her by the shoulders, imprisoning her in my big hands. "If you think I'm willing to keep my manhood in exchange for that kind of sacrifice and *not care*, you've got sand in your head."

"But you *would*," she said. "Any man would. As for caring? I don't know. Do you?"

"Care? Hoolies *yes*, Del. I don't want you to think I don't appreciate what you did for me."

Her smile wasn't really a smile, just a twisting of her mouth. "Tiger, a woman only loses her virtue once—right? She survives— right? . . . and learns what it is to pleasure a man. But that man—maybe a man like the *Sandtiger*— losing his manhood, might *not* survive. Right?"

Before I could answer, she twisted out of my hands and ducked out of the cell. I followed, cursing up a storm beneath my breath.

I hated the thought of Del in Hashi's bed. I hated the thought of her doing it for me, even if she *had* learned how to pleasure a man years before. But most of all I hated myself, because deep inside I was relieved. *Relieved* she had done it and saved me from the life of a eunuch, which was surely far worse and degrading than the life of a Salset chula.

But being relieved isn't the same as being *glad*.

I wasn't glad at all.

At the top of the narrow dungeon stairs waited Sabo. He threw me a dark-blue burnous and a leather pouch filled with coin. "Payment," he said. "For rescuing the lady and myself. Maybe Hashi isn't grateful, but *I* am." He smiled. "You treated me like a man, Sandtiger. The least I can do is make certain *you* remain one."

I saw Del hand him the iron key. "*You* gave her the key!"

Sabo nodded. "Yes. I drugged Hashi's wine, and when he fell asleep, I took Del from her room and brought her here."

I looked at her. "Then you *didn't*—"

"No," she agreed. "But you were certainly willing to believe I *had*." She brushed by me, by Sabo, and disappeared.

I looked at the eunuch. "I've made a horrible mistake. And a fool of myself."

Sabo smiled, creasing plump cheeks. "Everyone makes mistakes and every man is a fool at least once in his life. You, at least, have it out of the way." He touched my arm briefly. "Come this way. I have horses waiting for you."

"Singlestroke," I said, "and my knife."

"With the horses. Now, come."

Del waited in the darkness of a shadowed corridor. She had exchanged the diaphanous pink and rose veils for a simple burnous of apricot silk trimmed with white embroidery. The neck of the burnous gaped open and I saw her leather tunic underneath; like me, she lacked sword and knife.

I thought of her sword, and wondered if Sabo had experienced the same sort of sickening feeling I had known when touching the hilt. But I recalled Del's comment: sheathed, the sword was harmless.

Harmless. No. Not quite.

"Where?" she whispered to Sabo.

"Straight ahead. There is a door that opens into the back courtyard of the palace, where the stables are. I have seen to it that horses await you, and your weapons."

I reached out and grabbed his arm. "I give you heartfelt thanks, Sabo."

He smiled. "I know. But there was nothing else I *could* do."

Del leaned forward and slung her arms around his neck, kissing him soundly on one plump brown cheek. "*Sulhaya*, Sabo," she whispered. "That's Northern for 'thank you,' and anything else you want to make it."

"Go," he said. "Go. Before I wish to come with you."

"You could," I agreed. "Come with us, Sabo."

His pale brown eyes were dark in the dim corridor. "No. My place is here. I know you think little of my lord Hashi, but once he was an honorable man—I choose to remember him so. You go, and I will remain." He jerked his head toward the door. "Go now, before the stable servants grow uneasy and take away the horses."

Del and I left. But we did it with the knowledge that it was Sabo who had gotten us free, and not any of the skills we claimed.

We hastened out of the palace into the stableyard, glad of the darkness. I judged the hour somewhere around midnight. There was little moon to speak of. We found the horses and untied them immediately, swinging up without delay. I felt Singlestroke's familiar harness hanging over the short pommel, along with a knife tied to it. Gratefully I slid the harness over my head and buckled it around my ribs, then dragged on my burnous.

Del had arranged her own harness. The silver hilt of her sorcerous sword poked up behind her shoulder. "Come on, Tiger," she whispered urgently, and we went out of the gate Sabo had paid one of the guards to open.

We clattered through the narrow streets of Sasqaat, heading south. I did not consider staying the night in the city. It might be clever to find a place beneath the very nose of Hashi, but a tanzeer is *absolute* authority in a desert city-state, and he could easily order Sasqaat shut up and searched house by house. Better to get free of the place once and for all.

"Water?" Del asked.

"Saddle pouches," I said. "Sabo thought of everything."

We rode on through the streets, anticipating alarms from the palace. But no tocsin sounded. And it was as we rode out of the city gates and passed the clustered hovels forming the outer edge of Hashi's domain that we finally began to relax. For the first time in my life I was glad to see the Punja.

"How far to Julah?" Del asked.

"At least a week. More likely two. I've never gone by way of Sasqaat; I think it's a little out of our way."

"So what's our next water-stop?"

"Rusali," I said. "Bigger than Sasqaat; at least, from what I saw of Sasqaat."

"Too much," she said fervently.

Whole-heartedly, I agreed.


We rode through half the night and into the early hours of false dawn, not daring to stop in case the tanzeer sent men out after us. I doubted he'd do it; Hashi hadn't really lost anything. There was Del, but for a man like old Hashi it would be no trouble buying half a dozen girls, or more. Admittedly, none of them would be *Del*, but then he didn't know her, so he wouldn't know what he'd be missing.

As for me . . . well, he could make a eunuch out of someone else. Not me.

At true dawn we finally stopped to rest. Del slithered off her sorrel and hung onto the stirrup a moment, then set about untacking the horse. I watched her a moment, concerned about her welfare, then dismounted and unsaddled my own horse. Sabo had even managed to give us our own Salset mounts. I still missed the stud, but the buckskin was at least a little familiar.

I hobbled the gelding, gave him a ration of the grain Sabo had thoughtfully included in our pouches, then spread a rug and dropped onto it. My ankles and wrists ached from the iron cuffs. The rest of me was pretty tired, too.

Del slung a bota into my lap. "Here."

I unplugged it and drank gratefully. I felt a little more human as I replugged it and set it aside. I stretched out on my back and proceeded to stretch my arms and legs carefully, popping knotted sinews as I worked all the kinks out.

I very nearly drifted off. But I snapped back when I saw Del, sitting on her own spread blanket, unsheathe her sword and examine the rune-worked blade.

I rolled over onto my right hip, propping my head up on a bent elbow. I watched as she tilted the blade, turning it this way and that, studying the steel for marks or blemishes in the plum-bright light of the sunrise. I saw how that light ran down the blade: mauve and madder-violet, orchid-rose and ocher-gold. And through it all shone the white light of Northern steel.

Or whatever metal it was.

"All right," I said, "time for a real explanation. Just what *is* that sword?"

Del tucked sun-bleached hair behind her left ear. All I could see was her profile; the smooth curve of a flawless, angular face. "A sword."

"Don't go tight-lipped on me now," I warned. "You've spent the last few weeks dropping hints about your training as a sword-dancer, and I know from personal experience that sword has some form of magical properties. All right, I'll bite. What *is* it?"

Still she didn't look at me, continuing to examine every inch of the sword. "It's a *jivatma*. My blooding-blade. Surely you know what that is."

"No."

At last, she looked at me. "No?"

"No." I shrugged. "It's not a Southron term."

She shrugged a little, hunching one shoulder. "It's—a sword. A true sword. A named sword. One that has been— introduced." Her frown told me she couldn't find the Southron words that would express what she meant to say.

**180**

"Two strangers, introduced, are no longer strangers. They *know* one another. And, if they get to know one another *well*—they become more, even, than friends. Companions. Swordmates. Bedmates. Just—more." Her frown deepened. "A *jivatma* is paired with an *ishtoya* upon attainment of highest rank. I—*feed* my sword . . . my sword feeds me." She shook her head a little in surrender. "There are no Southron words."

I thought of Singlestroke. I'd told Del often enough he was just a sword, a weapon, a blade; he wasn't. What he *was* I couldn't articulate, any more than she could explain what her sword was. Singlestroke was power and pride and deliverance. Singlestroke was my freedom.

But I felt hers was more.

I looked at the runes on the blade. The shapes on the hilt. In the colors of the sunrise, the sword was everchanging.

"Cold," I said. "Ice. That thing is made of ice."

Del's right hand was set around the hilt. "Warm," she said. "Like flesh . . . as much as I am flesh."

The grue ran down my spine. "Don't make riddles."

"I don't." She wasn't smiling. "It isn't—alive. Not as you and I are. But neither is it—*dead*."

"Blooding-blade," I said. "I assume it has drunk its fill?"

Del looked down at the blade. The sunrise turned the salmon-silver carmine in the rubescence of the dawn. "No," she said at last. "Not until I have drunk *my* fill."

The grue returned with a vengeance. I lay back down on my rug and stared up at the break of day, wondering if I had gotten myself mixed up in something a little more serious than simple guiding duty.

I shut my eyes. I draped one arm across my lids to shut out the blinding sun. And I heard her singing a soft little song, as if she soothed the sword.

# Sixteen

**R**usali is your typical desert town, crawling with people of all tribes and races. Rich and poor, clean and dirty, sick and ill, legal and crooked. (Actually, Rusali pretty well fits the description Hashi had given Julah.)

Del didn't bother to put up her hood as we rode into the narrow, sandy streets and she drew plenty of attention. Men stopped dead in the street to stare at her, and the women who were for sale muttered loudly among themselves about Northerners trying to steal their business.

I realized then I'd made a mistake. I should have come in the front way, like any man with gold hanging on his hip. Instead, I'd come in as I usually do, seeking out the back streets and alleys like a thief myself. I've never *been* a thief, but sometimes a sword-dancer finds business better in the seamier parts of town.

"Just ignore them, Del."

"It isn't the first time, Tiger."

Well, it was the first time while riding with *me*. And I didn't like the way the men stared at her. Lewd, lascivious fools, practically drooling in the streets.

"We'll need to get rid of the horses," I said, to change the subject.

Del frowned at me. "Why? Don't we need them to get to Julah?"

"Just in case old Hashi *does* decide to send people after

182

us, we should switch mounts. Maybe it'll confuse the pursuit a bit.''

"Hashi won't come.'' She shook her head. ''He's got Elamain to keep him busy.''

"Elamain'll *kill* him!'' I couldn't help it. *Imagining* the old man in her bed was enough to make me laugh.

Del gave me a sidelong glance. ''Yes, well . . . then he won't be our problem any more.''

I smiled, thinking about it. ''We'll switch horses anyway. I'll sell these, then go elsewhere to buy others. That way no one'll get suspicious.'' I glanced around the street. ''There—an inn. We can get something to eat and drink. Hoolies, but I'm thirsty for some aqivi.'' I dropped off my buckskin and tied one of the reins to the ring in the buff-colored wall.

The place was dark and stuffy with smoke from huva weed. It formed a wispy, greenish layer up near the rooting beamwork of the adobe inn. There were no windows to speak of, just a couple of holes knocked in the mud bricks. I nearly spun around and marched back out, Del in tow.

Only she wasn't near enough to grab. She sat down on a stool at an empty table. After a moment spent scowling at her, I joined her.

"This isn't the place for you,'' I informed her.

Her brows rose a little. ''Why not?''

"It—just isn't.'' I made certain Singlestroke was loose in his sheath. ''You deserve better.''

Del stared at me a long moment. I couldn't read the expression on her face. But I thought I saw a hint of consideration in her eyes, and more than a trace of surprise.

Then she smiled. ''I take that as a compliment.''

"I don't care *how* you take it. It's a fact.'' Irritably, I looked around for the wine-girl and shouted for aqivi.

But I stopped looking when I heard Del's indrawn hiss of shock.

And then I looked at the tall, lanky, blond-haired

Northerner as he walked into the inn, and I knew why she stared.

Almost instantly, Del was on her feet. She called out to him in Northern, catching his attention.

It occurred to me the man might be her brother. But no, I knew better almost instantly. The big Northerner looked thirty. Not fifteen.

It occurred to me *then* the man might be the one who hunted her, one of the *ishtoya* she claimed she owed. And it was quite obvious that had occurred to Del as well, for she had drawn the Northern sword.

Conversation in the inn broke up almost at once as one by one the patrons became aware of the confrontation. And then, bit by bit, I heard the voices start up again. And all the comments had to do with the fact that one of the Northerners was a woman, and a woman with a sword.

My right hand itched. At first I thought it was the ice-brand in the palm, then realized it had nothing to do with that. What it had to do with was my desire to draw my *own* sword in defense of Del.

Except she didn't look like she needed any.

The inn was close, stuffy, cramped. What light there was came from the open door and the holes serving as windows. The scent of huva weed was cloying, almost stifling. The atmosphere was so thick you could cut it with a knife.

Or a sword.

Del waited. Her back was to me so she faced the open door; the Northerner, silhouetted, lacked clear features. But I could see his harness. I could see the bone-handled hilt of his own sword, poking up behind one shoulder. Conspicuously, his hands were empty.

Del asked him a question. His answer was accompanied by a shake of the head that told me he voiced a denial. Del spoke again for several minutes, rolling the strange-sounding syllables around on her tongue smoothly.

Again the Northerner shook his head. His hands remained empty. But I did understand a couple of words. One was *ishtoya*. The other was *kaidin*.

After a moment, Del nodded. I couldn't see her face. But she shot her sword home in its sheath, and I knew she was satisfied.

The Northerner's expression was speculative, then his eyes took on the warm, interested glow most males' eyes assume when they light on Del, and I saw his smile of appreciation.

He strolled over to the table and sat down as Del gestured to the remaining stool. The aqivi arrived with two cups; Del filled one and handed it to the Northerner, the other she took for herself. So I grabbed the jug and drank out of that.

The only thing I got out of their conversation was the word Alric, which I took to be his name. Alric was tall. Alric was strong. Alric looked powerful enough to knock down trees.

In contrast, his white-blond hair curled with a gentle softness around broad shoulders. He wore a burnous striped in desert tones—amber, honey and russet—and carried a big sword. A curved sword. A *Southron* sword, not a Northern one like Del's. And I recognized its origins: Vashni. A *Northerner* with a Vashni sword; tantamount to sacrilege, as far as I was concerned. Worse, he had also acquired a Southron tan. It wasn't nearly as dark as mine, but it would do in a pinch.

I drank from my jug of aqivi and discovered a predilection within myself to glower at Del's new friend.

I heard the name Jamail and realized she was telling Alric about her missing brother. He listened closely, frowning, and spat out a violent comment between his white teeth. Probably something about the Southron slave trade. I'm not exactly proud of the practice, myself, but nothing gave *him* the right to criticize my desert.

Del glanced at me. "Alric says there are slavers who deal *specifically* in Northerners."

"They make more money that way," I agreed.

Del turned back at once to Alric, chattering away so fast I doubted I'd be able to understand it even if I *did* speak her dialect.

After a while I got bored. "Del." I waited a moment. "Del, I'm going to get rid of the horses." I waited again, but she didn't seem to hear me. Finally, I cleared my throat noisily. "*Del.*"

She looked at me, startled. "What is it?"

"I'm going to sell the horses."

She nodded and turned immediately back to Alric.

I rose, scraping my stool against the adobe floor, and glared at them both a moment. Then I walked out of the inn, wishing the big lunk had never shown his face south of the border.

Outside, I untied the horses, mounted my buckskin and led Del's sorrel down the cobbled street. It was late in the afternoon, going on evening, and I was beginning to get downright hungry. But Alric the Northerner had left a bad taste in my mouth.

Why was Del so interested in him? Wasn't *I* getting her to Julah? What made her think *he* might be able to tell her anything?

She'd sure latched onto him in a hurry. Like I wasn't even there. And I hadn't missed the glow in his blue eyes as he looked at her, or the hungry expression on his face. Del has that effect on men.

Still, there was little I could do about it. She was a free Northern woman, and I already had the idea Northern women enjoyed a whole different order of freedom than Southron ones. Which left Del in a dangerous position here, because any woman with the freedom to come and go as she chooses is believed by one and all to be readily available.

I cursed as I rode down the street, threading my way through people afoot. I couldn't very well go back to the inn and tell the Northerner to get lost. After all, Del had a legitimate reason for talking to him. Two of them, as a matter of fact. Alric just might know something about her brother, although it was unlikely; he was also from her homeland. That could be enough of a link for her to forget all about me and take up with him. The curving sword he carried pretty well established him as a fighter. He might even be a sword-dancer.

In which case Del could *un*hire me and hire him instead.

By the time I found a local horse trader, I was angry and irritable and snappish. I sold the horses, pocketed the money, and went away without buying replacements after all. I could do it in the morning. So I went back to the inn to extricate Del from Alric's big, Northern hands.

She wasn't there. Our table was filled with four Southron men; Del wasn't anywhere to be seen. Neither was Alric.

I got a sick feeling in the pit of my belly. Then I got angry.

I approached the girl who'd brought the aqivi to the table. "Where'd she go?"

The girl was dark-haired, dark-eyed and flirtatious. Another time I might have appreciated it; right now I had other concerns on my mind.

"What do you want *her* for?" She smiled winsomely. "You got *me*."

"I don't want *you*," I told her rudely. "I'm looking for *her*."

The girl lost her smile. She tossed her head, sending dark ringlets tumbling around abundant breasts. "Then I guess she doesn't want *you*, because she left here with the Northerner. What do you want with a Northern girl anyway, beylo? You're a Southroner."

"Which direction did they go?"

She pouted, then jerked her head west. "That way. But I don't think she'll want you to find her. She looked real happy to go with him."

I muttered sullen thanks, flipped her a copper piece from the pouch Sabo had given me, and left.

**187**

I made my way down the crowded street, stopping every so often to ask vendors if anyone had seen a tall Northern girl with a tall Northern man dressed Southron. All of them had. (Who could forget Del?) Of course they all claimed they weren't *certain* it was her—until I jogged their memories with more of Sabo's reward. At this rate it wouldn't last long, but Rusali was little more than a sprawling rabbit warren; if I didn't buy the information, I might spend weeks combing the alleys and dead ends and dwellings.

I got hungrier as I searched, which didn't improve my temper at all. I was also tired, which wasn't surprising. When I stopped to think about it, I realized I had been through the mill in the past two months, thanks to Del. Clawed by a sandtiger, engulfed by a simoom, 'hosted' by the Hanjii, left for dead in the Punja (and baked to a dry husk), taken prisoner by Hashi of Sasqaat. (And Elamain, of course). All in a day's work, I might say, except the day was getting to be far too long and this worker was getting weary.

The shadows deepened as the sun went down, gilding the alleys and streets dark-umber and tawny-topaz. I walked more warily, anticipating almost anything. Rusali, like most desert cities, is a place of varied moods and inclinations, including desperate ones. I hated the thought of Del being in it unchaperoned.

Of course, with Alric, she wasn't precisely unchaperoned. He looked capable of protecting her, but for all *I* knew, he was a slaver himself. And Del, dropping into his hands like ripe fruit, would be too tempting. Even now she might be bound, gagged, and imprisoned in some smelly room, awaiting transportation to a wealthy tanzeer.

Or (possibly worse to my mind at the moment), would the big Northerner keep her for himself?

My teeth ground at the thought. I could just see it: two blond heads; pale arms, pale legs; supple, sleek bodies tangled together in the slack-limbed embrace of satisfaction.

(I could see Del giving to him what she wouldn't give to me, and all because he was Northern, not Southron, and therefore more entitled).

And I could see him laughing at Del's stories of our travels, ridiculing the big, dumb Southroner who called himself the Sandtiger because he had no real name, being born and deserted all at once, and raised a slave instead of a man.

By the time the dinner-plate moon rose and most of the shop-keepers latched their doors and shutters, I was ready to kill anything that *resembled* Alric the Northerner.

Which is why I beheaded a yellow melon as it rolled from its pile in front of a vendor's wagon.

I stood there feeling foolish and stupid and embarrassed as the sliced halves rolled neatly to the ground. Singlestroke dripped juice and pith.

Furtively, I glanced around. No one, *thank valhail*, had witnessed my foolishness. (Or else they weren't mentioning it). The vendor wasn't around, so I scooped up the cleanest half of the melon, wiped it off, and took it with me.

I was hungry, and it was delicious.

The thieves came out of the shadows like rats and surrounded me in the alley. Six of them, which meant they had to be very busy thieves because the cut for each of them would be correspondingly smaller. Instinctively, I sought the best footing in the sand-packed alley, braced myself, and waited.

They converged at once, not unexpectedly. I tossed the rind of my melon into one face, drew Singlestroke and spun around to attack the thieves at my back, who were expecting me to attack the thieves at my *front*; subsequently, they were somewhat surprised when I removed one head, sliced through the throat of a second man, lopped off the weaponed hand of a third—and swung around to defend myself against the first three.

The one with melon drippings in his face shouted something at the other two, ordering them to take me down; they were having nothing of it. Not now that the odds had rearranged themselves so suddenly.

The three sidled around me warily, armed with knives and Southron stickers, but they did not attack.

I waved my sword gently. Encouragingly. "Come on, men. Singlestroke is hungry."

Three pairs of eyes looked at the sword. Saw how my hands were locked around the hilt. Saw the smile on my face.

They backed off. "Sword-dancer," one of them muttered.

I smiled more widely. There are times the title comes in handy. In the South, a sword-dancer is considered the very highest level of expertise in the weapon-trade, be it common thievery, the life of a borjuni, or even a soldier. Sword-dancing is comprised of many different levels even within its own school, too numerous for me to detail. Suffice it to say that in the argot of the thieves, calling someone a sword-dancer meant, basically, he was off-limits. Untouchable.

Of course, there was another explanation. Thieves don't generally like to attack sword-dancers for three basic reasons: first, sword-dancers either have lots of money or none at all; why risk your life when your prey may be more broke than you? Second, sword-dancers are weapon-kin, relatively speaking, and you don't attack your own kind.

Third (and most importantly,) sword-dancers are invariably much better at killing than common, ordinary thieves because that's how we make our living.

I smiled. "Want to join me in a circle?"

They all turned me down (rather politely, I thought), explaining they had pressing business elsewhere. They excused themselves and disappeared into the darkness. I bid them good-night and turned to find the nearest corpse on which to clean Singlestroke—

—and discovered I had made a very costly mistake.

There were two corpses instead of three. The third man, missing his right hand, was still very much alive—in addition to being a bit perturbed because I had deprived him of a hand.

But it was the left hand that held the knife. As I swung around, he thrust himself against me and brought the knife down into my right shoulder, tearing through flesh and muscle until it caught on the leather harness and grated against bone.

He was too close for Singlestroke to prove effective. I grasped my own knife left-handed as I kneed him in the crotch. I sent swift thanks to Del for giving me the idea, then flipped the knife to my right hand and threw it, cursing the pain in my shoulder. Nonetheless, I was pleased to see the weapon fly home into his heart. He tumbled to the ground. This time he stayed there.

I staggered to the closest wall and leaned against it, cursing again as I tried to regain my shaken senses. Singlestroke lay in the alley where I'd dropped him, dulled by blood. It was no place to leave a good sword, but I was a trifle indisposed at the moment.

The ragged hole in my shoulder wasn't a mortal wound, but it bled frightfully. Also, it hurt like hoolies. I wadded handfuls of my burnous into the wound, clamping my left hand against the fabric to stop the bleeding. When I could stand it, I retrieved knife and sword. Bending over nearly finished me, but I wobbled back onto my feet, steadied myself, then departed the alley as fast as I could. Thieves might respect a sword-dancer when he's in good health, but stick a knife in him and he's fair game for anyone.

I knew if I behaved in any way like I'd been seriously wounded, I'd be asking for trouble. So I let the arm hang naturally as I walked, although I could feel the blood running freely beneath my burnous. I had no choice. I had to go back to the inn to patch myself up before I continued the hunt for Del.

My black-eyed hussy was there, and those eyes opened wide as I walked into the place. (Well—staggered). I guess I wasn't doing too well by then. She plopped me into the nearest chair, poured me a hefty portion of aqivi and guided it to my mouth. Without her help I'd have spilled it all over everything, because my right hand was useless and my left one was pretty shaky.

"I told you you'd do better with me than her," she reproved.

"Maybe so." The room was beginning to move in very odd patterns.

"Come with me to my room." She hitched her right shoulder under my left arm and lifted.

I grinned at her woozily. "I don't think you'll get much out of me tonight, bascha."

She smiled back saucily. "You don't know that, beylo. Marika knows many things that will restore a man, even one who's a little short on blood." She grunted a little. "Come on, beylo. I'll help."

She did. She got me through the beaded doorway and into a tiny closet of a room, but it had a bed. (Naturally). Probably a busy one.

I sat down on the edge, stared at her through foggy eyes and tried to summon a properly imperative tone. "I'll sleep here tonight. But in the morning I must be on my way to Julah, so don't allow me to sleep late. The tanzeer expects me."

Marika put her hands on her hips and laughed at me. "If that's your way of warning me to keep my fingers out of your coin-pouch, save your breath. I'll look after you *and* your money. I know enough not to mess with the Sand-tiger."

I peered at her blearily. "Do I know you?"

"I know *you*." She grinned. "*Everyone* knows you, beylo. You and that sword, and the claws around your neck." She bent down, displaying some of her charms, and ran a gentle hand across the right side of my face, caressing my scars. "And these," she whispered. "Nobody else has these."

I mumbled something and sort of faded back onto the bed. Aqivi on an empty belly has that effect. (Not to mention a knife wound accompanied by substantial blood loss.) If Marika expected the Sandtiger to perform with his legendary prowess, she was going to have to wait.

The last thing I recall is Marika removing my sandals, murmuring something about cleaning my wound, and examining my bent toe. Something else for the legend, I thought hazily, and fell asleep.

# Seventeen

I woke up to find two pairs of eyes staring at me fixedly. Waiting. Both of them were very blue. But one pair belonged to Del.

I sat up sharply, uttered one pained exclamation, and fell back against the cushions.

Del's hand felt my brow. "Stupid," she remarked. "Don't move around so much."

I opened my eyes again when my head stopped reeling and the pain faded down into a manageable level of intensity. Del appeared to be perfectly safe and healthy, no different than she had been the day before. She still wore the apricot-colored burnous, which gilded the tan she'd acquired to a warm, tawny-gold. Pale hair was confined in a single thick braid, falling over one shoulder.

"How'd you find out?" I asked.

She was hunched forward on the stool, elbows on knees, chin in hands. "Alric brought me back here to wait for you. You never showed. We hung around a couple of days, and finally Marika told us where you were."

I looked past Del to the big Northerner, who lounged against the wall like a huge, dangerous bear. "What did you do with her?"

The bear showed his teeth briefly. "I took her home, Southron. Isn't that what you expect me to say?"

I tried to sit up, but Del's hands pressed me back and I

was too weak to protest. I called Alric a rather impolite name in Southron dialect; he answered with an equally offensive term in the same tongue, unaccented. Stalemated for the moment, we glared at one another.

Del sighed. "Stop it. This is neither the time nor the place."

"What did he do to you?" I asked her, ignoring the darkening of the bear's looming face.

"*Noth*ing," she declared, enunciating distinctly. "Do you think *every* man wants to get me in his bed?"

"Every man who's not dead already—or gelded."

Del laughed. "I suppose I should thank you for the compliment, backhanded or otherwise. But right now I'm more concerned about you." She felt my brow again and critically examined my bandaged shoulder. "What happened?"

"I was looking for *you*."

She let that sit a moment. "Ah," she said at last. "I see. It's *my* fault."

I shrugged, then wished I hadn't. "If you'd stayed where I'd left you, I wouldn't be flat on my back with a knife wound in my shoulder." I glared briefly at Alric. "You trusted him too easily, bascha. What if *he* had been a slaver?"

"*Alric*?" Del gaped. "He's a Northerner!"

"Right," I agreed, "and we both know someone's looking for you. For that debt you owe." I scowled at her. "You know as well as *I* do you thought that's who Alric was when you first saw him. Well—he still might be."

Del shook her head. "No. That was settled. There are rituals involved in the collection of a blood-debt. If Alric were an *ishtoya* hunting me, we'd have settled it in the circle."

Alric said something to her in their twisty Northern tongue, which left me out and made me more sullen than ever. I've never much liked feeling weak and sick; my temper suffers for it. Of course, having Alric around didn't help that much, either.

Alric said something to Del that brought her up short. She said something very briefly, very clipped, but filled with a myriad of tones: disbelief, astonishment, denial and something I couldn't identify. Something like—discovery. And she looked at me sharply.

Alric repeated his sentence. Del shook her head. I opened my mouth to ask her what in hoolies they were wrangling about, but she clamped a hand over my mouth.

"You be quiet," she ordered. "You've already lost enough blood . . . complaining won't help any. So Alric and I are going to put a stop to it."

"Put a stop to *what*?—complaining or bleeding?" I asked when she removed her hand.

"Probably both," Alric remarked, and smiled contentedly.

"How?" I asked suspiciously.

His grin broadened. "With fire, of course. How else?"

"*Wait* a minute—"

"Be quiet," Del said sternly. "He's right. Marika bound up the wound but it's still bleeding. We have to do something, so we'll try Alric's suggestion."

"*His* suggestion, was it?" I shook my head. "Bascha, he'd sooner see me dead. Then he'd have you to himself."

"He doesn't *want* me!" Del glared. "He's already got a wife and two little babies."

"This is the South," I reminded her. "Men are entitled to more than one wife."

"*Entitled*?" she inquired distinctly. "Or is it they just *take* them?"

"Del—"

"He's a Northerner," she reminded me, somewhat unnecessarily. "He doesn't believe in multiple wives."

Alric grinned bearishly. "Del might persuade me to consider adopting the practice, though."

I glared at him, which only served to amuse him further.

He was big and strong and undeniably good-looking, as well as undoubtedly sure of himself.

I hate men like that.

"What are you going to do?" I demanded.

Alric gestured to a brazier on the floor. I saw a bone-hilted knife was in it already, blade heating. "*That's* what we're going to do."

I chewed on the inside of my mouth. "There isn't another way?"

"No." Del said it so promptly I began to suspect she was looking forward to it.

"Where's Marika?" I thought maybe the wine-girl would give me a little needed support.

"Marika is out plying her trade," Del said briskly. "Her *other* trade—the one you interrupted by taking over her bed."

"The knife is ready," Alric announced, in a tone that sounded amazingly like undisguised glee.

I looked at Del. "*You* do it. I don't trust him."

"I'd planned to," she agreed serenely. "Alric's going to hold you down."

"Hold me down?"

She bent and wrapped a cloth around the knife handle. "I think even the Sandtiger might find this a painful experience. He will probably yell a great deal."

"I don't yell."

Del's raised brows expressed eloquent doubt. Then Alric's big paws came down on my shoulders. His right hand was perilously close to the wound, which didn't make me any fonder of him. "Watch it, Northerner."

His face hung over mine. "I could *sit* on you—"

"Never mind."

Del handed me a cup of aqivi. "Drink."

"I don't need a drink. Just do it."

She smiled crookedly. "Foolish Tiger." Then she set the red-hot blade against the bleeding wound and I didn't care what Alric thought of me anymore (or even Del), I yelled loudly enough to bring down the whole building. I attempted one leaping lunge off the bed, but the Northerner leaned on me and I didn't go anywhere. I just lay there and cursed and sweated and felt sick, and smelled the stink of my burning flesh.

"You're enjoying this," I accused Del weakly through gritted teeth.

"No," she said. "No."

She might have said something more, but I didn't hear her. I just sort of went somewhere else for a while.

I woke up in a strange room in a strange place and in a very strange frame of mind. I felt floaty and detached, oddly numb, but I realized I wasn't in Marika's little room anymore.

"Del?" I croaked.

A woman came into the room, but she wasn't Del. She was black-haired and black-eyed, like Marika, but she wasn't her, either. She was also heavily pregnant. "Del is with the children." Her accent wasn't one at all, being familiarly Southron. She smiled. "I'm Lena. Alric's wife."

"Then—he really *is* married?"

"With two babies, and another on the way." She patted her swollen belly. "Northern men are lusty devils, aren't they?"

I scowled at her, wondering how she could be so blithely unconcerned with Del in the house providing all manner of distraction for a man she *herself* described as lusty. (Which wasn't anything I hadn't already suspected). "How am I?" I asked glumly.

Lena smiled. "Much better. Alric and Del brought you here a couple of days ago. You've slept since then, but you look much better. If the Sandtiger is the man I've heard he is, you should be up and around in no time."

The Sandtiger was feeling a little green around the edges. But he didn't tell her that.

"I'll get Del." Lena disappeared.

Del came in a moment later. There was an odd wariness in her eyes, and I asked her why.

"Because you're going to start in on Alric again, aren't you?"

"Shouldn't I?"

She glared. "You're being very stupid about this, you know. Alric offered us the hospitality of his house, which is hardly big enough for him, Lena and the babies. *You're* in the only bedroom! The rest of us share the front room."

Almost at once I felt pretty uncomfortable, which is precisely what she intended. "Then tell him we'll be on our way just as soon as I'm able."

"He knows that." Del hooked a three-legged stool over near the bed. "What happened to you, Tiger? Marika couldn't tell us."

I felt at the bandage over my right shoulder, wondering what the cauterized wound looked like. "Thieves. One of them got lucky." I paused. "Briefly."

"I'm sorry," Del said contritely, "I *should* have stayed at the inn; you wouldn't have gotten hurt. But Alric wanted to take me home to his wife and babies. He's very proud of them." She shrugged. "I'm a Northerner, and he hasn't seen anyone from his homeland for a long time."

"What's he *doing* here?"

She smiled a little. "Hunting dreams. Like everyone. He came South several years ago, hiring out his sword. Then he met Lena, and stayed."

"He could have taken her North."

"He could have. But he loves the South." She scowled a little. "You don't *have* to be born here to like the South, you know."

I sat up experimentally. For the moment I was all right. I shifted around so I could lean against the wall, settling my sore arm across my ribs. "He doesn't want to add to his collection of wives?"

The scowl disappeared as she smiled. "He only has

*one*—and I think she might object. Tiger . . . there's no reason to be jealous of Alric.''

"I'm not jealous. Just—protective. That's what you hired me for."

"I see." Del rose. "I'll get you some food. You look hungry."

I was. I didn't protest when she brought it. I munched away at bread and meat and goat's cheese. No aqivi, so I settled for water. (Tame stuff). Del waited as I ate, making certain the patient was doing well, and as she hunched on the stool Alric's babies came tumbling in. I stopped chewing and stared in amazement as both of them tried to climb simultaneously into Del's lap.

Both were girls, black-haired and dark-skinned like their mother, but claiming their father's blue eyes. An attractive combination. They couldn't be much older than two and three, both wobbly and clumsy, but—like puppies—all the cuter for it.

I watched Del with the girls. She had an easy way with them, showing affection without strangling them with it. An offhanded sort of manner, but obviously satisfactory. The girls looked serenely content.

So, for that matter, did Del. She smiled absently, smoothing curly black hair into place and, for a moment, hardly seemed aware of me in the room.

Abruptly, I broke the moment. "You'll go back North, then, when your business here is finished? Look for someone like Alric and start having Northern babies?"

"I—don't know. I mean—I haven't thought about it. I haven't really thought much at all past finding Jamail."

"What happens if you don't find him?"

"I told you once before: I haven't considered that possibility. I *will* find him."

"But if you *don't*," I persisted. "Del—be realistic. It's all well and good to go charging off on a quest of rescue and revenge . . . but you've got to consider all the angles.

Jamail *might be dead* . . . and then you'll have to take a look at your priorities."

"I'll look at them *then*."

"Del—"

"I don't know!" Astonished, I saw tears in her eyes.

I just stared in amazement at what I'd started with my question.

Del sucked in an unsteady breath. "You keep hammering at me, Tiger. You keep telling me I won't find him, that I can't *possibly* find my brother. Because a woman doesn't stand a chance of tracking down a boy stolen five years ago. But you're wrong. Don't you see?" Her eyes were fastened on my face. "My sex doesn't matter. It's the task. That's all. It's what needs to be done. And I can do it. I *have* to do it."

"Del, I didn't mean—"

"Yes you did. They all do; all the men who look at me and see a woman with a sword. Laughing inwardly—*and* outwardly—at the games of a silly woman. And humoring me. *Humoring* me because they want me in their beds, and they'll put up with just about any silliness to get me there." She shook back her braid. "Only it isn't silliness, Tiger. It's a need. A duty. I *have* to find Jamail. I *have* to spend days, weeks, even years searching for him, because if I don't—" She stopped abruptly, as if all the emotions that had propelled her through her declaration spilled out at once, leaving behind an empty shell.

But she went on regardless. "Because if I don't, I have failed my brother, myself, my kin, my *kaidin* . . . and my sword."

The food was forgotten. One after the other, the girls climbed out of Del's lap and went away, frightened by the anger and grief in her voice. Tears spilled down her face unchecked and she didn't wipe them away.

I inhaled a careful breath. "There is only so much a person can do, Del. Man or woman."

"I can do it. I have to."

"Don't let it become an obsession."

"*Obsession*!" She stared at me. "What would *you* do? What would *you* do if you saw all but one of your family killed right in front of you?" She shook her head. "All I could do was *watch*. I couldn't help them, couldn't run, *couldn't even look*—until one of the raiders held me around my neck and made me watch them kill the men and rape the women, my sisters, my *mother*, and laughed while I cried and screamed and swore I'd castrate every one of them." She shut her eyes a moment, then opened them again. There were no tears now, only a quiet determination. "It made me what I am as much as the Salset made the Sandtiger."

I set the plate down beside me. "I thought you said you'd escaped the raiders."

"No." Her mouth was a flat, grim line.

"Then—" I didn't finish.

"They were going to sell us both, Jamail and I. Everyone else was dead." She hunched a shoulder. Her left one, naked of the sword. "But—I got away. *After* they were done with me. And—I left Jamail behind."

After a moment, I released a long, heavy breath. "Oh, bascha, I'm sorry. I've done you an injustice."

"You didn't take me *or* my mission seriously."

"No."

Del nodded. "I know. Well, it didn't matter. I was just using you to get me across the Punja." She shrugged. "I made a pact with the gods. With my sword. I don't really need anyone else."

"That secret you mentioned once," I said, "is it what you've just told me?"

"Part of it," she agreed. "The other part is—private." And she rose and walked out of the room.

*I faced my opponent across the circle. I saw pale blond hair, tawny-gold suntan, sinews beneath firm flesh. And a sword, in supple hands.*

"Good," observed the familiar voice, and I snapped out of the momentary daydream.

I scowled. Alric faced me across the haphazard circle he'd drawn in the dust of the alley behind his house. The curved Vashni sword was in his hands, but he had dropped the posture of preparedness. "What's good?" I asked.

"You," he answered. "You heal quickly." He shrugged. "No more need for this."

We had practiced for three days. My shoulder hurt like hoolies, but a sword-dancer learns to ignore pain and, eventually, overcome it entirely. Often, you don't get a chance to heal properly. You fight, you heal, you fight again. Whenever it's necessary.

Alric flicked a tuft of spore from his wickedly-curved blade. One bare foot obliterated a portion of the circle; finished with practice, there was no more need for circles drawn in dust.

I glanced over at the girls. They sat quietly against the shaded wall, eyes wide and mouths covered with small fists. Alric had given them permission to watch, but only if they kept silent in the watching. They had. At two and three, they behaved themselves better than most adults.

"We're finished," he told them, giving them their release; both girls got up and headed for the front of the adobe house at a run.

I bent and scooped up my discarded harness, sliding Singlestroke into the sheath. Sand gritted against the soles of my bare feet. Bending over hurt, but not as much as participating in a dance, practice or no.

I hooked the harness over my arms. Did up the buckles. "Why a Vashni sword?" I nodded at Alric's blade. "Why not a Northern sword—one like Del's?"

"Like Del's?" Alric's pale brows jerked up beneath ragged bangs. "I *never* had a sword like Del's."

I frowned, haphazardly erasing the circle with one sweeping foot. "You're a Northerner. And a sword-dancer—more or less."

Unoffended by my gibe, Alric nodded. "Sword-dancer, Northerner, yes. But not of Del's caliber."

"A woman—?"

"Oh, it's true *that's* unusual," he agreed, going over to the bota he'd left sitting in the shade of a buff-colored wall. "But then *Del's* unusual to begin with." He unplugged the bota, sucked down a couple of swallows, then held it out in silent invitation.

I quit erasing the circle and went over to accept the bota. We sat down and leaned companionably against the wall, which was faintly warm even thought it lay deep in shade. In the South, shade is not necessarily cool.

I sucked down my own share of aqivi. "No. I'd never say Del was anything *but* unusual. But that doesn't tell me why you use a Vashni sword."

Alric shrugged. "A fight," he said. "Me against a Vashni. Nasty fellow, too. He managed to break my Northern sword." He raised a silence hand as I opened my mouth to protest. "No—it wasn't a sword like hers. It was—just a sword. And it broke. About the time I was looking up the curving edge of the Vashni's blade, I decided I didn't need *my* sword to kill him. So I grabbed his right out of his hands . . . and killed him with it." He smiled as he looked fondly at the shining blade. The hilt was made of a human thighbone. "I kept it for my own."

"Del calls hers a *jivatma*—a blooding-blade—" Alric nodded. "What's that mean?"

He shrugged and drank more aqivi as I handed him the bota. "What it sounds like. A blade made specifically for drawing blood. For killing. Oh, I know—you can say *any* sword suits that purpose—but in the North, it's different. At least—it is if you're a sword-dancer." He gave me back the bota. "The rituals are different in the North, Tiger. That's why you and I aren't a good match—our styles differ too much. And I imagine even Del and I would have trouble performing the proper rituals."

"Why?"

"Because her style and mine would be similar. *Too* similar, to offer a superior match. Blade patterns, maneuvers, footwork—" he shrugged "—even though we learned from different *kaidin*, all Northerners know many of the same tricks and rituals within the circle. And so it would be an impossible dance."

"But not if the dance were to the death."

Alric looked at me. "Even if I were an enemy, I'd never dance with her."

My brows ran up into my hair. "A woman—?"

"Doesn't matter." He frowned thoughtfully, watching his right foot as he scuffed it in the dirt. "In the South, sword-dancing is made up of levels. A student works his way through the levels as far as he can. You, I've heard, are seventh-level." As I nodded, he went on. "Here, I'd be considered third-level. In the North I'm better than that, but the comparisons don't really apply. It's like comparing a man and a woman—you just can't." Blue eyes flicked up to meet my green ones. "I guess what I'm saying is that the highest level of training in the North has no corresponding level in the South. It isn't a matter of *skill*—at least, not exclusively. It's more a matter of total, absolute dedication and determination, a complete surrendering of your will to the rituals of the dance." He shook his head. "Hard for me to say, Tiger. I guess the best way is just to say that Del—if she's telling me the truth—was *ishtoya* to the *an-kaidin*. And all I can say about that is what I know, which isn't much. I never stood so high." He drank again. "She must be telling the truth. Otherwise she stole that Northern sword . . . and a named blade can't be stolen."

Named blade. There it was again. A deliberate distinction. "*My* sword has a name."

"And a legend." Alric smiled and smacked the bota against my hand. "I know all about Singlestroke. Most sword-dancers do. But—well, it's not the same. A *jivatma* is a little more than that. Only *an-kaidin* bestow them on

205

selected *an-ishtoya*, those students who have proven their worthiness.''

"Why is it *you* don't have one?"

"I don't have one because I never stood high enough in the ritual rankings to be awarded one.'' He said it easily enough, as if the pain of the knowledge had faded years before. Alric, I thought, was content with his lot. "As for what one *is*—it's hard to explain. More than a sword. Less than a person. It doesn't really *live*, although some might say it does.'' He shrugged. "A *jivatma* has particular attributes. Like you or me. In that respect, the sword has a life of its own. But only when matched with the *an-ishtoya* who has earned his—'' he paused significantly a moment "—or *her* right to it, who knows the sword's name, and who knows how to sing the song.'' He shrugged. "*Ishtoya* who achieve the highest ranking from the *an-kaidin* are no longer *ishtoya*. They are *an-ishtoya*. And then *kaidin* themselves, if they choose to be. Or sword-dancers.''

"*Kaidin—an-kaidin*.'' I frowned, mulling over the nuances in the tones. "Del always called her sword-master *kaidin*, without the prefix.''

After a moment, Alric nodded. "The prefix is an honorific. *Kaidin—you* would say shodo—means sword-master. Teacher. Highly skilled, but a teacher. *Kaidin* is someone all *ishtoya* know. But—*an-kaidin* is more. *An-kaidin* is the highest of the high. I think she drops the prefix as a way of trying to deny what has happened.''

I frowned. "What has happened?''

Alric shoved hair out of his face with a forearm. "There is—*was*—only one *an-kaidin* of the old school left in all the North. Newer schools have replaced the old, but many *ishtoya* preferred to follow the old ways instead of the new.''

"Was?'' I asked sharply.

"He was killed a year ago, I heard. In ritual combat against an *an-ishtoya*.''

It happens. Even to the best of us. It isn't always easy to

avoid bloodshed in the circle, even if it's nothing more than an exhibition.

The big Northerner with the curving Vashni sword looked at Singlestroke. "Swords are—*different* here in the South. But in the North, there are swords and swords. A named blade, a *jivatma*, is made of steel that is more than steel. The *an-kaidin* makes them for the special students, the *an-ishtoya* who will someday take the *an-kaidin's* place. Being *ishtoya* only, I never had the chance to learn more about the blooding-blades. But—it is precisely that: a sword quenched in blood. And the first blood is always carefully selected, because the sword assumes all the skill of the life that is taken."

*Selected.* I looked at him sharply. "Then—you're saying it wasn't an accident that killed the *an-kaidin*. That someone desired to assume the skills of the *an-kaidin*."

Alric's face was taut. "I heard it was purposely done."

I thought of the Northern sword. I recalled the alien shapes in the metal; the sensation of ice and death. As if the sword lived. As if the sword knew me. As if it meant to kill *me* as it had killed the *an-kaidin*.

Alric fingered the hilt of his Vashni sword. I wondered, absently, if *it* had a name. "Killing an *an-kaidin*, as you might imagine, is punishable by execution," he said quietly. "Blood-guilt isn't a thing anyone carries lightly."

"No," I agreed.

He met my eyes squarely. "In the North, there is a thing called blood-debt. The debt is owed to the kin of a man—or woman—whose death was undeserved. One person, or two, or even more than twenty, may swear to collect the debt."

I nodded after a moment, thinking about the man who followed Del. Sworn to collect the blood-debt? "*How* is the debt collected?"

"In the circle," Alric answered. "The dance is to the death."

I nodded again. I wasn't particularly surprised. I didn't

doubt the dance *was* justified by the crime that had been committed. A man killed; a teacher slain by his student. Because the student had needed the skill that was *in* the man, and not merely what he had taught.

I blew breath out of stiff lips. I thought of how desperately Del wanted to avenge the massacre of her kin; the enslavement of her brother; the humiliation she must have suffered at the cruel hands of Southron raiders. It was, I thought, a blood-debt owed to her. One she was more than due, regardless of the cost.

I knew full well Del was capable of doing anything she wanted to do.

Anything at all.

No matter what the cost.

# Eighteen

**A**lric handed me the bota. But before I could unplug it and suck down a swallow, the two little girls came running around the side of the house.

They went straight to Alric, tugged on both arms, and babbled at him in an almost unintelligible mixture of Northern and Southron. I wasn't sure how much of the unintelligibility had to do with their age, how much of it with their bilinguality.

Alric sighed and got up. "We're to go inside. Lena sent them to fetch us both." Then he said something in Northern to the little girls, and both went scurrying off again.

"Well-trained," I remarked.

"For girls." He grinned. "Del would skin me if she heard me say that. Well, she'd have the right. In the North, women know more freedom."

"I noticed." I rounded the corner of the adobe dwelling and ducked inside the door that was decidedly too short for Northerners, or Southroners like me.

And stopped.

Alric's house is small. Two rooms. A bedroom, which I had willingly turned back over to Alric and his family once I was feeling better, and a front room, which doubled as sleeping quarters at night for Del and me. There was no question that with four adults and two children, the house was very crowded.

Except now it claimed one more adult, and the room got smaller still.

Del sat cross-legged on a pelt-rug of curly saffron goathair. She watched Alric and I enter, but said nothing. Locked in silence, she sat with her sword across her thighs.

Unsheathed.

I stepped aside so Alric could slip in. Lena stood in the shadows of the room. Her daughters flanked her, one on each side. No one said a word.

I looked at the stranger. He wore a mouse-gray burnous. The hood was pushed back from his head. Brown-haired, like me. Tall, like me. Very nearly as heavy. Other factors I couldn't determine because of the burnous. But I saw the sword-hilt riding his left shoulder, and I knew the hunter had finally run down his prey.

The stranger smiled. The seam of an old scar diagonally bisected his chin. His face had been lived in. There was gray in his hair. I thought he had a good ten years on me, which put him a couple of years past forty. His eyes were as blue as Del's and Alric's, but mostly he looked like me.

He made me the desert gesture of greeting: spread-fingered hand placed over his heart, brief bow. "She says you are the Sandtiger." A cool, smooth voice, tinged with the Northern accent.

"I am."

"Then I am truly pleased to meet the legend at last."

I listened for the bite of sarcasm, the tracery of scorn. There was none. No impoliteness I could discern. But it didn't make me like him any better.

"His name is Theron." Del, finally. "He has been the shadow who was not a shadow."

Theron nodded a little. "I came down from the North seeking the *an-ishtoya*, but circumstances have conspired to delay me time and time again. Now, at last, they are in my favor."

Beside me, Alric let out a breath. "How many of you are there?"

"Only me." So quietly. So assured. "That is how I requested it."

"*So*," I said sharply. "If Del kills you, no one else will take up the hunt."

"For the space of a year," Theron agreed. "A Northern custom bound by agreements and the rituals of the circle. Since you are a sword-dancer—Southron or no—I assume you understand."

"Explain it to me anyway."

Briefly, Theron's cool smile fell away. But then he took it back. "She owes blood-debt to many people in the North. *Ishtoya, kaidin, an-ishtoya, an-kaidin*. Many desire her death, but only one may claim it in the circle—for the space of a year. When that year is done, another—or more—may seek her out again."

"There is more to it than that," Alric said sharply.

Theron's smile widened. "Yes. In all fairness, Southron, I must also say there is a choice for the *an-ishtoya* to make. Although I have been given permission to challenge her to a dance, I must also offer the *an-ishtoya* the chance to gain full pardon."

"How?" I demanded.

"By going home," Del said. "I can go home and face judgment by all the *kaidin* and *ishtoya*."

"Sounds more sensible than facing him in a circle," I told her flatly.

Del shrugged. "I would almost certainly be judged guilty of premeditated murder. That is blood-guilt; why the debt is owed. Acknowledgment of an undeserved—and unnecessary—death."

"Then you don't deny you killed the *an-kaidin*."

"No," Del said in surprise. "Never. I killed him. In the circle." Her hands tightened on the sword. "It was for the blade, Tiger. To blood my blade. Because I needed more sword-magic than what the *an-kaidin* had taught me."

"Why?" I asked quietly. "Why did you need it *so much*? I've seen you dance, bascha, even if it wasn't for real. I can't believe you lacked so much skill as to need the *an-kaidin's* more.''

She smiled a little. "For that, I thank you. But yes—I needed the *an-kaidin's* skill. I *required* it . . . and so I took it.'' For a moment she looked down at her bared sword, caressing the gleaming metal. "There were more than twenty raiders, Tiger. More than twenty men. Alone, would even *the Sandtiger* approach so many men intending to kill them all?''

"Not alone," I answered. "I'm still alive because only rarely am I a fool, and *never* when it comes to figuring the odds.''

Del nodded. Her face was unmarred by frown or anxiety. Except for the continual movement of fingers against blade, she appeared more than composed enough. "It was owed me, Tiger. The blood-debt of more than twenty men. There was no one to collect it but me. There was no one I *wished* to collect it *for* me. My duty. My desire. My determination.'' The hint of a smile at the corners of her mouth. "I am not so foolish as to claim a woman, alone, could kill more than twenty men. And so I took the *an-kaidin* into my sword, and no longer was I a woman alone.''

I felt the faintest chill. "Figuratively speaking.''

"No," Del said. "That is the quenching, Tiger. A named blade, unquenched, is merely a sword. Better than good. But cold metal, lacking life and spirit and courage. To get it, to bring a *jivatma* to life, it is quenched in the body of a strong man, as strong as you can find. The *an-ishtoya*, to become *kaidin*, seeks out a respected enemy, and sheathes the sword in his soul. The sword assumes the will of the man.'' She shrugged a little. "I had need of much skill and power in order to collect the debt the raiders owed me. And so I took it.'' She didn't look at Theron. She looked at me. "The *an-kaidin* knew. He could have refused to join me in the circle—''

"*No*," Theron said sharply. "He would never have

refused. He was an honorable man. He could not, in all conscience, deny his *an-ishtoya* the chance to prove herself."

Now she looked at him. "Let it be known: the *an-kaidin* joined the *an-ishtoya* in the circle, and the blooding-blade was quenched."

I released a slow breath. "As she says, it's done. And—I think maybe she had reason for what she did."

Theron's face tightened. "It's possible the *kaidin* and *ishtoya* would agree her need justified the death. It's also possible they would unanimously convict her of premeditated murder and order her execution."

"Depriving you of your bounty."

Theron shook his head. "If she chooses to go home for judgment, I will be paid my price. If she is sentenced to death, I will be paid my price." He laughed aloud. "There's no way I can lose."

I had conceived a distinct dislike for Theron. "Unless she chooses the circle."

Theron's smile came back. "I do hope she does."

"He's a sword-dancer," Del said lightly. "He was trained by the *an-kaidin* who trained me. Theron was one of the few *an-ishtoya* who were given a choice upon completion of his schooling: would he be sword-dancer or *an-kaidin*?" Her face was very calm as she looked at me. "Do you understand, Tiger? He was *an-ishtoya*. The best of the best. Only *an-ishtoya* are given the choice between teaching or doing." She sighed a little. "Theron chose to be a sword-dancer instead of *kaidin*, and so the dwindling ranks of the *an-kaidin* were denied the younger, stronger man they needed. A man who could have trained promising *ishtoya* to achieve the highest rank."

"*An-ishtoya*," I said. "The best of the best."

"You have heard," Theron said flatly. "You have heard how it was the old *an-kaidin*—the master who taught *me*!—offered the choice to his female *an-ishtoya*, and how she repudiated him. How she invited him into the circle so she could quench the thirst of her blade before it tasted the blood of another." The grave politeness was banished from his tone. "You have heard *her* choice!"

"This is blood-feud," Del said quietly. "Sword-dancer against sword-dancer. *An-ishtoya* against *an-ishtoya*." She smiled. "And, as Theron would also have it, man against woman. So he can prove he is superior."

Theron said something in Northern. The tone was almost a singsong, and it didn't take much for me to recognize a formal challenge. I've given and received my own share over the years.

When he was done, Del nodded once. Said something quietly, also in Northern. And then she got up and walked out of the shadowed house into the light of the day.

Theron turned to follow. But when he reached me, he smiled. "You are welcome to watch, sword-dancer. There should always be a witness to the collection of a blood-debt."

I waited until he was gone from the house. I looked at Alric. "I don't think I much like that son of a Salset goat."

Solemn-faced, Alric nodded. He said something to Lena and the girls—requesting they remain inside—and followed me outside.


The circle Alric and I had used was nearly obliterated. Here and there I saw a trace of the curving line, but we'd obscured much of it with bare and sandaled feet. Now it begged to be drawn again.

I looked at Theron. Quietly he stripped himself of sandals, belt, harness. Of everything save his dhoti. In his hands he held his naked sword, and I saw the alien runes.

For a brief moment we faced one another: Northerner to Southron. Judging. It wasn't our dance, but we judged. Because he knew as well as I did that if he overcame Del, the next opponent in the circle would be a sword-dancer called the Sandtiger.

Deftly, Del stripped out of her burnous. Unlaced sandals

and set them aside. Unbuckled harness and put it with the sandals. Tunicked, with the *jivatma* in her hands, she turned to look at Theron. "I would ask the Sandtiger to draw the circle."

Theron didn't smile. "Agreed: he will draw the circle. But he may not act as arbiter. The Sandtiger would hardly be impartial to the woman in whom he sheathes his *other* sword."

I thought Del would immediately deny it. But she let him think what he would.

It was *me* who wanted to speak; to split open his Northern face.

"I will be arbiter." Alric, next to me. Like me, he looked at Theron.

The older man dipped his head in a gesture of acceptance. "It might be as well. As a Northerner, you will have some better idea of the rituals required." Another subtle gibe at me. Or was it aimed at Del? Hard to tell, though it was possible Theron intended to put her in poor temper.

But I had never seen Del angry, not *really* angry, and I doubted this would do it.

"Tiger," she said. "It would please me if you set the circle in the sand."

For a dance, the ground was treacherous. For a practice circle, it had done well enough because we had no better. The alley between this row of dwellings and that row of dwellings was not particularly wide, although there was more room at the junction of this alley and another running at a right angle from it. The ground was hardpacked, yet veiled in a layer of sand and soft dirt. Alric and I had spent much of our time unintentionally sliding around the circle, trying to keep our feet beneath our bodies. For practice it was all well and good. For a genuine sword-dance, the footing would be deadly.

Del and Theron waited. I saw by the grim set to Alric's mouth he knew as well as I did the implications of a genuine dance conducted here. But the thing was settled. Del and Theron had settled it.

I unsheathed Singlestroke and began to draw the circle.

When it was done, I put my sword away and looked at both of the dancers. "Prepare."

Theron and Del stepped into the circle, placed swords in the precise center, and stepped outside again.

I looked at the weapons on the ground. Del's I knew; at least, as much as I *could* know. Theron's was strange to me. Cold, alien steel, steel that was not steel, as Alric had described it. Del's was the now-familiar salmon-silver. Theron's was palest purple.

They faced one another across the circle. To me, preparation meant positioning oneself outside the circle. Taking up a posture that lends itself to speed, strength, strategy. A moment for introspection and self-evaluation, before the mind tells the muscles what to do. And it was what I expected out of them.

I had, however, reckoned without the Northern rituals. I'd forgotten just how different all the similarities could be. Del and Theron stood quietly on either side of the circle, and they sang.

Softly. So softly I could hardly hear it.

Confidence. Serenity. Exultation, exhortation. All of these, and more.

Deathsong? No. A lifesong. The promise of victory.

Alric took his place. As arbiter, it was his word that claimed the dance was won or lost. Even if it was obvious one of the dancers was dead, the ritual required a declaration.

I moved away. My task was done. Theron was right; there was no way I could possibly be impartial. But not because Del and I had shared a bed.

Because I *wanted* to.

But also because I'd come to know the woman as more than just a woman.

I smiled a little. Wryly. Shook my head. Alric frowned

across the circle at me, not understanding, but I didn't bother to explain. Such things are just too personal.

"Dance," Alric said. It was all either of them required.

Together they reached their swords. I saw Del's hands flash down, flash up; saw Theron's flash down, flash up.

And then I stopped looking at their hands. I stopped listening to their songs. Because the swords had come alive.

Del had told me, once, a named blade *wasn't* alive. But she'd *also* said, neither was it dead. And as I watched, astounded, I perceived the paradox in the explanation. The paradox in the swords themselves.

Salmon-silver, flashing in the sunlight. And Theron's: pale purple. And yet, they changed. The colors shifted, running from hilt to tip, until I saw rainbows in the sunlight. Not the sort that comes after a rainstorm, but rainbows of darkness and light. Pale-rose, raisin-purple, a tint of madder-violet. All the colors of the night. All the colors of a sunset, but showing their darker side. No pastels. No water-washed tints. Lurid luminescence. Raw color stripped down to nakedness.

Both blades were a blur. From wrists too subtle for me to follow sprang patterns I'd never seen. And I *could* see them, clearly, because each blade as it moved traced the pattern in the air. It etched a ribbon of purest color, a streak of livid light, like the afterglow of a torch carried away too quickly.

As if the blades severed the air itself like a knife will cut into flesh.

They danced. How they danced. Spinning, gliding, feinting, sliding, ripping apart the day to leave eerie incandescence in its place: cobalt-blue, livid purple; viridescent, lurid rose.

When I could, I stopped watching the swords. Instead I watched the dancers, to learn what I could learn. To soak up the gift they offered: the gift of the Northern style.

It was, as I have said, far different from my own. With

my height, strength and reach, my best strategy is endurance. I can swing steel with the best of them. I can hack and slash and sweep, thrust and counter and riposte. I wear down my opponents. I can stand toe to toe and hew them down, blocking and stopping their blows. Or I can dance with the fastest man because, for all my size, I am quick. Just not as quick as Del.

Theron, nearly my physical duplicate, might have done better to mimic my style. But he hadn't been trained that way. Like Del, he employed the subtle strength in wrists and forearms, using quick, slashing patterns. Much like a stiletto against an ax, if you were to compare his style to mine. He might have stood there and banged on her sword, but it wasn't Theron's way. And I could tell it wouldn't beat her.

Quite frankly, I'd done the lady a disservice. In all my arrogance and pride in my own reputation (warranted, of course), I'd neglected to acknowledge her own tremendous ability. I'd scoffed, supremely confident a woman could never face a man in the circle and win. Not even against a less than competent dancer. But I'd been too quick to underestimate her talent. Now I saw it plainly, and realized my mistake.

So did Theron. I could see it in his eyes. The grudge-match now was more than a simple determination of guilt or innocence. It had gone past collection of a blood-debt. It had slipped under the guard of his masculine pride and pricked him in the gut, just as her sword tip pricked him in the knuckles.

Del was better than good. Del was better than Theron.

Alien steel clashed, twisted, screeched. Blade on blade in the cacophony of the dance. Slide, slide, step. The belling of the steel. The hiss of bare feet against the grit of sand on top of hardpack.

A latticework of ribbons glowing in the sunlight. Pattern here, pattern there; a tracery of flame. Salmon-silver, palest-purple, and all the colors in between.

Sweat ran down their bodies. It lent a sheen to the pale apricot of Del's tanned skin. Bare arms, bare legs, bared face with white-blonde hair tied back. I saw grim determination in her face. Total loss of awareness except for the dance she danced against a good opponent.

Quite clearly, Theron fought to kill. In the circle, death is not mandatory. Victory is the thing. If a man is overcome and yields at the asking, a winner is declared. Often enough, the dance is little more than an exhibition, or a testing of sheer skill. I've danced for the joy of it before, against good and bad opponents. I've danced to kill as well, though the deaths have never pleased me. What pleases me is surviving.

Del, I thought, would survive. Theron, I thought, might not.

A breeze kicked up. It ruffled the thin layer of saffron sand. Increased to a wind. Lifted the sand and blew it into my eyes. Impatiently, I brushed the grit away.

But the wind remained. Intensified. Ran around the circle like a child's spinning toy. And then I saw how it centered itself as a whirlwind inside the circle: a dust-demon licking at feet. Licking, licking, growing, until even Theron and Del fell away from one another because the demon made them do it.

Spinning, spinning, spinning, so fast the eye couldn't follow. *Mind* couldn't, no matter how hard I stared. And then the dust exploded in a shower of grit and film, and in the dust-demon's place was a man.

Sort of. Not really a—*man*. Rather, a being. Small. Neither ugly nor attractive. Just—a sort of formless shape with the barest suggestion of human features. It hung in the air between Del and Theron, floating in the circle.

"I am Afreet," it announced. "My master wants a sword."

Four of us merely gaped.

"I am Afreet," it repeated, a trifle impatiently. "My master wants a sword."

"You said that already." The thing didn't seem particularly dangerous, just a trifle odd. So I decided conversation wouldn't do us any harm.

Tiny features solidified in a tiny misshapen face. It frowned. It stared, much as we did.

I saw hands form. Feet. Ears appeared, and a nose. But the thing was naked. Quite clearly, the thing was male. And abruptly, I knew what it was.

"*An* afreet," I said. "That isn't a proper name, it's a description of what it *is*."

"Then what *is* it?" Del asked in some distaste.

"I am Afreet," the afreet announced. "My master wants a sword."

Simultaneously, Theron and Del each took a single step back from the tiny floating being. I almost expected them to put their swords behind their backs, as if to hide them from view.

Apparently the afteet did, too. It—*he*—laughed.

And if you've ever heard an afreet laugh, you don't much like the sound.

"I am Afreet," it began. "My master—"

"We know, we know," I interrupted. "Change your tune, little—"—pause—"—*man*. Who is your master, and why does he want a sword?"

"My master is Lahamu, and Lahamu desires a sword of power."

"So he sent you out to get one." I sighed. "Little afreet, you don't frighten me. You're only a manifestation of his power, not a measure of it. Go home. Go back to Lahamu. Tell him he can get his sword another way."

"Tiger," Del said uneasily. "*You're* not the one standing so close to him."

"He can't hurt you," I told her. "Oh, I suppose he could kick sand in your face or pull your hair, but that's about the extent of it. He's just an afreet. A busybody. Not a genuine demon."

"But this Lahamu *is*?" she demanded. "Not so wise to treat his servant badly."

"Lahamu isn't a demon." Alric, from the other side of the circle. "He's a tanzeer. Rusali is his domain."

"A tanzeer with an *afreet*?" That sounded odd even to me. "How'd *that* come about?"

"Lahamu dabbles in magic." Alric shrugged. "He's not the brightest man in the South, Tiger. He inherited the title, which means he doesn't necessarily deserve it." Alric eyed the afreet. "I've heard some odd stories about him, but I don't think I'll repeat them where little ears can hear them. Let's just say he's not known for his—judgment."

"Ah." I scowled at the little afreet. "That means he's after a *magical* sword."

The afreet laughed again. "A magical Northern sword, with magical properties. Power. *Better* than Southron swords only good in the hands of a dancer, or so my master says."

I nodded. "Lahamu fancies himself a sword-dancer *too*, does he?"

"Told you." That from Alric. "Maybe he wants to steal a little of your glory, Tiger."

The afreet glared at him. "Lahamu is *many* things."

This time *I* laughed. "Sorry, little afreet. No time for this right now. We're a bit busy at the moment."

The tiny face glared. "My master wants a sword. My master will *get* a sword."

"How?" I asked gently. "Does he want you to steal one?"

"Steal the dancer, steal the sword." An afreetish grin showed pointed teeth. "But not the woman; *the man*."

Theron never had a chance. I saw his blade whip up as if to halve the afreet, but the whirlwind swallowed him whole. And with him his Northern sword.

A thin veil of dust settled back to the ground. Alric and I blinked at one another across the circle. It was empty except for Del, who glared at me. "I thought you said that little—thing—couldn't *do* anything."

"Guess I was wrong."

"Tell him to bring Theron back! Tell him I wasn't finished with him." Del frowned. "Besides, if Lahamu wanted a Northern sword so much, why take only one when he could have had two?"

"I *think* I know the answer, but I don't think you'll like it much."

Her glance was level. "Why not?"

"Because, being Southron, Lahamu probably doesn't think much of women." I shrugged. "Theron had more status."

Del scowled. Then she swore. Softly, beneath her breath.

"Does it matter?" I asked, exasperated. "At least Theron's out of your hair. You should be grateful to Lahamu for sending out the afreet."

"Grateful? For stealing my fight?" She scowled at me. "*I* wanted to take Theron—*I* wanted to beat him—"

"Beat him? Or kill him?"

Her chin rose. "You think I'm not capable of either?"

"I think you're capable of both."

Del stared at me a long moment. I saw the subtleties of changing expressions in her face. But then she turned away to step outside the circle, and I knew the dance was finished.

But only the one against Theron.

# Nineteen

Alric bought two horses and gear with the money I gave him, and three days later Del and I took our leave. I thanked the big Northerner and his wife for their hospitality, apologized for putting them out of their bedroom, hugged each of the little girls, and left it at that.

Del's farewell was a little more involved than mine, at least when it came to the girls. She picked each one up, whispered something in her ear, hugged her, kissed her, then set her down again. It was an odd dichotomy, I thought: woman with child; woman with sword.

I mounted my blue roan gelding and waited for Del to climb aboard the gray mare Alric had purchased. The mare was little, almost dainty-looking, and yet I took note of the deceptively wide, deep chest and long shoulders that marked endurance and good wind. My own blue roan was larger and rangier, almost clumsy-looking with his jug-head, gaunt flanks and big hips, but nothing really set him apart from other horses, at least in class distinctions. (If anything, he came out of a *lower* class entirely). Another horse had gnawed on his slate-gray tail, leaving it short and very ragged; not much of a flyswatter, now.

I glanced at Alric and gave him a grimace that was half-scowl, half amusement. He knew what I meant. I'd given him enough money for excellent mounts, but he'd purposely chosen horses of unexceptional quality. The better to blend in with other people in Julah.

Sighing, I recalled the bay stud. It would take me years to find another horse like him.

The respite (if you could call it that) in Rusali had made the Punja pale in our minds. Out upon the sands again we quickly remembered the harsh reality; how lucky we were that the Salset had found us while we were still alive. Del pulled up her apricot hood and hunched her shoulders against the heat of the sun; I rubbed at my sore shoulder and wondered how soon it would be before I could use it without pain. A right-handed sword-dancer can't afford to be disabled very long, or he loses more than just a sword-dance.

"How far to Julah?" Del asked.

"Not far. Two or three days."

She twisted in the blanketed saddle. "That close?"

I stood up in the stirrups a moment, trying to urge the roan out of a jagged, rambling trot into a more comfortable long-walk. At this rate, he'd rattle my mouth completely clean of teeth. "As I recall, Rusali is a bit northwest of Julah. Of course it all depends on the mood of the Punja, but we should be within a couple of days' ride." I gritted my teeth and stood up again, removing my backside from the pounding of the shallow saddle. "Fool horse—"

Del slowed her gray mare. No longer competing, my roan dropped into a more comfortable walk beside her. "Better?" Del asked calmly.

"I'm trading in this sandtiger-bait as soon as we get to Julah." I saw the dark-tipped ears twitch toward me. "Yes, *you*." I looked at Del. "Well, have you decided what your plans are once we reach our destination?"

"You asked me that once before."

"And you never really told me."

"No," she agreed, "and I don't know as if I feel like telling you now, anymore than I did *then*."

"Because you don't know."

She slanted me a gloomy scowl. "I suppose *you* have a plan."

"Matter of fact . . ." I grinned.

Del sighed and tucked a wisp of sunbleached hair behind her right ear. The silver hilt of her Northern sword—her *jivatma*—shone in the sunlight. "I should have known . . . all right—what is it?"

"I'm going to become a slave trader," I explained. "One who just happens to have a gorgeous Northern bascha in his possession." I nodded. "This trader is no dummy. He realizes full well what a big market there is for Northern boys and girls. And—since it isn't always easy to steal them—he's decided to breed them."

"*Breed* them!"

"Yes. So, since he's got a prime breeder on his hands, he needs to match her with a Northern male."

Pale brows knitted over her nose. "Tiger—"

"He can't be too old, because *she's* not," I pointed out. "He should be young and strong and virile and as good-looking as she is. That way the children are more likely to be attractive. What I *need* is a duplicate of her, except a male." I waited expectantly.

Del stared at me. "You intend to use me as bait, to flush my brother into the open."

"Bang on the head, bascha. I'll offer a deal to the man who has him: pick of the litter, so to speak. He can have the first child of the mating in addition to my gold, so he can start his own kennel of Northern slaves."

Del stared down at her braided gentian reins. Fingers picked at the cotton.

"Del—?"

"It might work." Her tone was subdued.

"Of course it will work . . . so long as you go along with my suggestions."

"Which are?" A pair of direct blue eyes fastened themselves on my face.

I took a careful, delaying breath. But there wasn't anything for it but honesty and baldness. "You'll have to be my slave. A genuine slave. That means wearing the collar and serving me as a docile slave, submissive and silent."

After a moment, her mouth twisted. "I don't think I'd be very good at that."

"Probably not," I agreed drily, "but it's the only chance we have. You willing to *take* that chance?"

She looked away from me, pushing rigid fingers through the dark-gray stubble of the mare's roached mane. The apricot hood spilled from Del's head and lay tumbled against her shoulders. The once butter-yellow tint of her hair had been almost completely swallowed by the platinum-white of sunbleaching, but it was still glossy as cornsilk in its single braid.

"Del?"

She lookled back at me steadily, taking fingers from the shaven mane. "What would happen if we simply went in looking for a Northern boy of fifteen?"

I shook my head. "For one thing, they'd want to know why I wanted to buy him specifically. For another, if they found out about *you*, they'd make me an offer. If they learned you're a free Northern woman, they'd simply *steal* you." I didn't smile; it wasn't amusing. "But—if you're a slave already, they'll simply try to talk me into selling you. And I, naturally, will refuse every offer."

"You like money," she pointed out. "You like money a *lot*."

"But I wouldn't *dream* of selling you," I retorted. "At least, not until you've paid me in the manner to which we've agreed."

"You don't get *that* until we find my brother."

"And we won't be able to *do* that unless we give this a try."

Del sighed, teeth gritted so hard the muscles in her jaw stood up. "You'd take my knife away from me, then . . . and my sword."

I thought about that sword in my hands again. I thought

about what Alric had told me about quenching its thirst in the blood of an enemy.

Or the blood of an honored *an-kaidin*.

"Yes," I told her. "Slaves don't generally carry knives and swords."

"And you'll put a collar around my neck."

"It's customary."

She swore. At least, I *think* she swore. I needed Alric to translate. "All right," she agreed at last. "But—I think I'm going to regret this."

"Not with *me* as your owner."

"That's *why*."

The first blacksmith we found in the outskirts of Julah was more than happy to make a collar for Del. I already had her sword—harnessed and sheathed—strapped to my saddle and her knife stuck in my belt; she resembled a rather recalcitrant slave as she sat on the sand and waited to have her neck put into iron.

I watched the blacksmith at his anvil, hammering the circlet into shape with speed and skill. He'd taken one look at Del and said he'd waste no time: a bascha like her would surely be worth considerable money: I didn't want to risk losing her. Del, only half-understanding his rough dialect and vulgar Southron slang, glared at him balefully as I told him to hurry it up.

His teeth were stained yellow from beza nut. He spat out a stream of acrid juice and saliva. "Why'nt you collar her before?"

"I bought her off a man who believed slaves had a right to dignity."

He snorted, spat again; hit the beetle he'd been aiming for. "Stupid," he told me. "No slave's got a right to dignity." He hammered a bit more. "Better have a chain, too; from the looks've *her*, I'd say she'd try'n hightail it out've here first chance."

"Fine." My teeth were tightly shut.

"Then tell her to get her rump over here."

I gestured. Del came, slowly. The blacksmith took a good, long look at her and said something that would have earned him her knife in his gut, if she'd understood him. But the tone got through to her. She went red, then white, and her eyes turned dark with anger.

There was nothing I could do. Slaves are less than nothing in the South, and therefore open to insults of all kinds. Del would be a target for nearly any manner of abuse; so long as the blacksmith didn't actually hurt her, there was little I could do.

"You saying that for *her* benefit, or mine?" I asked lightly.

He glanced at me, dull red seeping into his broad, forge-flushed face. "She don't speak Southron?"

"Some. Not the filth you're spewing."

He got ugly. So did I. He reevaluated my size, weapons and the sandtiger claws hanging around my neck.

"Tell her to kneel." He spat again. The dead beetle was flipped over onto its back, legs splayed.

I put my hand on Del's right shoulder and pressed. She knelt after a momentary hesitation.

"Hair." He spat.

Del knelt in the sand, apricot burnous billowing in the wind of the bellows. Her head was bowed submissively, but I could tell from the tension in her body she didn't like the posture one bit. Well, neither did I.

After a moment I swallowed, knelt on one knee and lifted the braid out of the way, sliding callused fingers over smooth skin. I could feel her trembling. Her eyes lifted briefly to mine, and I saw bleakness and fear and darkness in them.

It came to me to wonder, more strongly than ever before, just what the raiders had done to her.

The blacksmith slipped around her neck the hinged iron collar with its length of chain. The lock was fitted through loops, then closed. He handed the key to me.

Del: collared and chained like a dog. At least with the Salset, I hadn't known *that* humiliation.

"Better be careful," observed the blacksmith. "She finds out you care that much, she'll stick a knife in you first chance she gets."

I forgot Del was on a short chain. I stood up so fast I jerked her up with me. "How much?" I asked, when I could speak clearly again.

He named his price. Inflated, but I was too anxious to leave his forge to haggle. I paid him and turned immediately toward the horses, hardly noticing that Del trailed after me like a dog on a rope. I was angry, angry and sickened, because I'd been a slave and here I was making *her* behave like one, when she was the freest thing I'd ever seen.

"I can't mount," Del said quietly, as I put my foot in the roan's stirrup.

I turned back, frowning, and realized belatedly I'd removed from her even the capacity to make the simplest movements. But, under the eyes of the watchful blacksmith, I couldn't give her her own chain. So I mounted my horse more carefully, led Del—on foot— over to the mare, and watched her climb up. Her face was pale and tight and strained, and I had the feeling mine was, too.

"Ought to make her walk," the blacksmith said. "She'll get uppity, otherwise."

Del said nothing. Neither did I. I just kept my hand away from Singlestroke with all the resolution in my body, and clicked my tongue at the roan.

Because of the chain, Del and I had to stay close. Because of the chain, I was so angry I saw red. I'd locked myself into the role of a slave trader as securely as I'd locked Del into iron; I couldn't give her her freedom on the streets of Julah if we were to pull off our subterfuge. Thoughtlessly, I'd declared this was what we would do; now we did it, and I think it made both of us sick.

I sucked in a deep breath. "I'm sorry, bascha."

She didn't answer.

I looked at her in profile. "Del—"

"Is this how you like your women?" No bitterness, none at all; somehow, it made the question worse. As if she believed I did.

"I'd trade places with you if I could." And knew I meant it.

Del smiled a little. "Wouldn't work, Tiger. Besides— haven't you been here already?"

"In a manner of speaking," I agreed grimly, and that ended the conversation.

Julah is a rich city. It skirts the Punja on one side and flirts with the Southron Mountains on the other. It celebrates the wealth of the tanzeers who own the gold mines in the mountains and the slavers who speculate in human flesh instead of ore. Nearness to the mountains means Julah has plenty of water, but for anyone bound north across the Punja, it is the last bastion of safety and comfort. It seemed hard to believe Del and I had come so far.

We found Omar's house easily enough, once pointed in the right direction. It was painted a pale orchid-blue, tiled in yellow-ocher, shrouded by palms and foliage that shielded it from the street, sun and prying eyes. The turbaned gateman took one look at Del, knew what business I had with Omar, and let us through. One servant took our horses and another escorted us into the house, leading us into a cool, private foyer. I sat down; when Del started to, I told her no.

Omar was incredibly polite. Instead of making us wait (we didn't have an appointment), he came in almost at once. He waited until a third servant had served gritty effang tea, then seated himself upon a saffron cushion.

Like his brother Osmoon, he was chubby. Black-eyed. But his teeth were his, lacking the flashiness of Osmoon's gold dentures. He wore a pale-pink turban and darker robes, with pearls strung around his neck. His fingers were ringed. The slave trade in Julah appeared to be more profitable than the desert business his brother ran.

"Osmoon wishes you well." I sipped effang and completed the welcoming rituals, which eat up a lot of time even as they betray a visitor's true feelings. But I'm on to them, and know how to speak blandly about meaningless topics all day long.

Omar knew it. He gave me welcome, then waved a hand to dismiss the rituals. "Your business?"

"Yours," I said smoothly. "I am told you know if there are Northern males to be had."

His face betrayed nothing but polite interest. "Who is asking?"

I considered lying. False names have their uses, just like false trades. But too many people know the Sandtiger; Omar might not know me on sight, but my reputation does generally precede me. That's what reputations are for. "I'm known as the Sandtiger. Sword-dancer. And sometime slave trader."

His black brows moved as he plucked a pale-green grape from a bowl set upon the low laquered table between us. "I know of a man called the Sandtiger. Like you, he is scarred and wears the claws. He is truly a friend of my brother. But he has never, to my knowledge, traded in slaves before."

"No," I agreed, "but after a while one grows tired of seeing the wealth of others engaged in business similar to your own. *My* poor wealth is won only by force of arms."

Omar had studiously avoided looking at Del. As a slave, she had no stake in our discussion. But now he let his eyes drift to her, and over her apricot-shrouded form. "You wish to sell?"

"I wish to *buy*." I said it very distinctly. "A Northern male to put with my Northern female."

His black eyes jerked back to me. "You intend to *breed* them?"

"Provided I find the proper mate for her."

He spat out grape pips. "How much are you willing to spend?"

"As much as I have to. But I will also give the first child to the trader who sells me the right boy." Actually, we didn't have much money left from Sabo's reward. I had thoughts of finding her brother, haggling over the price, withdrawing to consider it. Then I'd turn Del loose, rearm her, and we'd settle on a plan then.

"I'll buy *her*," Omar said, "but I can sell you no Northern boys. I have none."

"None?"

"None." He clamped fleshy lips together.

"Who does?"

No answer.

I sighed. "Look, I'll find what I want *with* your help or without it. If someone's got a monopoly on Northerners here in Julah, you don't stand to lose anything by telling me anyway."

Omar prevaricated a while, not wishing to lose a potential customer, but in the end he agreed there was a monopoly and told me who had it. "Aladar. But he is the tanzeer; you must see his agent if you wish to buy or sell."

"Who's his agent?"

Omar nodded. "I'll tell you, of course, friend of my brother . . . for a price worthy of the Sandtiger."

Sometimes reputations can hurt business dealings. But in the end, I got the name I wanted and he got his price.

"Honat," Omar said.

"Where?"

"At Aladar's palace, of course."

So Del and I went to Aladar's palace. Of course.

# Twenty

**❧⟨⟩❧**

**A**ladar's palace was quite impressive, even coming in the back entrance as we did. The adobe walls were lime-washed white. Elegant tiled archways were patterned with repeating mosaic designs in tangerine, pale-lime, canary-yellow. Even in the stableyard, cream- and copper-colored gravel crunched beneath our sandaled feet. Palm and citrus trees gave the impression of cool spaciousness.

And all of it, I thought, had been paid for by Aladar's slave trade.

I thought briefly about leaving Del with the horses, for fear Honat the agent might take a liking to her and complicate matters considerably. Then I decided she'd be safer with me, in the long run, because it would be a lot easier for them to snatch her *without* me than if she sat—or stood—right next to me.

Honat was an oily little man with a surprisingly deep voice. His fingers were very short and his palms quite wide, reminding me of a toad. His eyes were toadlike, too (peat-green and bulging), which didn't make me feel any better.

He wore a pale-green turban fastened with a glittering emerald. Rather ostentatious, I thought, for a tanzeer's agent. His robes were gold tissue and he wore little gold slippers on his fat, splayed feet. I towered over him; so did Del, but that didn't seem to bother him in the least. He

**233**

JENNIFER ROBERSON

picked thoughtfully at his receding chin a moment (staring at her from baleful toadlike eyes), then gestured for me to sit down on a fat crimson cushion. I did so, doling out enough chain so Del—standing—wouldn't choke.

Honat looked at her again. "The woman may sit."

Well, progress. But she had to sit on the woven rugs because there were no more cushions, which weren't for slaves anyway. By this time Del was getting good at keeping her head bowed submissively. I had no idea what thoughts were running through her mind, but at least Honat didn't either.

He asked my business and I went through the whole story again, making certain he understood I had no intentions of selling, only buying. When I discussed the breeding program, his eyes lighted. I wasn't sure if the response was good or bad.

Honat glanced sharply at Del again, commanded her to lift her head; after I repeated the order in Southron she could understand, she did so.

The agent smiled his oily little smile. "Children from this woman would be beautiful indeed. I see why you wish a match with her."

"Do you have one?"

He waved a hand, curiously naked of rings or ornamentation. "We have several. It's only a matter of selecting the most appropriate one."

True. I didn't know Jamail at all on sight and couldn't look to Del for direction, because a slave has no say over the purchase of a fellow slave. But Del would *have* to see him, because I wouldn't be able to recognize him otherwise. Del's description of him wouldn't do me much good. After five years, Jamail most likely no longer resembled the ten-year-old Del remembered.

"I'm looking for a young one," I explained. "Perhaps fifteen, sixteen . . . no older. Young enough to make certain he has many years left to him, for—as you know—a male will have more time in which to breed than a female.

234

Even *this* one will use up nearly a year carrying but a single child.''

Honat, still staring at Del, nodded understanding. "We have two young Northern boys. I can't say precisely how old they are—they were *acquired* as children, you understand, and sometimes children aren't certain of their ages.'' Blandly, he waited for my answer.

"I'd like to see them." No more would he get from me.

"All in good time," Honat promised smoothly. "First I must discuss this with my master. It is his decision to buy or sell." Toad-eyes flicked in Del's direction again. "I think it likely he would be more interested in acquiring *this* one, rather than selling another.''

"*This* one is not for sale." Equally bland. "I paid a fortune for her. I expect to earn an even greater one when I sell her children.''

Honat studied me. His face was perfectly blank, although in his eyes I saw the merest trace of distaste. "You are cold, Sandtiger. Even *I* don't speak so blithely of selling children in front of the woman who will bear them.''

Inwardly I cursed myself. Was I being *too* cold, *too* unfeeling for a slave trader? I'd believed them less than human. (Or was I simply careless because I knew none of the story was true?)

I shrugged off-handedly. "The Sandtiger's work has taught him to be cold. Hasn't Honat's?''

His eyes narrowed a bit. "Is she virgin?''

I scowled. "We are not discussing this woman, Honat. And if you persist in it, I'll take my business elsewhere.'' I made as if to rise, certain the agent would talk me into staying.

He did. He didn't want to lose the potential profit, for as Aladar's agent he was entitled to a commission on the sale of any property.

Honat smiled. "If you will excuse me, Sandtiger, I will see if my master is willing to have the slaves shown to you." He rose, balancing carefully on his wide toad feet. "Please refresh yourself. There is cooled wine." A naked hand fluttered in the direction of the decanter sitting on the table. He left.

I looked at Del. "Well? Think he went for it?"

"Two Northern boys," she said grimly. "But neither of them may be Jamail."

"I'll take you with me to make sure of a proper match." I poured a cup of wine and held it out to her. "Here. This nonsense has gone on long enough. I don't *care* if Honat comes back and discovers me treating you like a person instead of a thing."

She smiled a little and thanked me, accepting the wine in hands showing the white knuckles of tension. I realized she was deeply apprehensive, for herself *and* her brother. Here within the palace she was a slave. She would be treated as one. No one would listen to her claim that she was a free woman, and if she came face to face with Jamail, he might give away the game. And it would be all over for all of us.

Del gave me back the emptied wine cup. And Honat came into the room, followed by two blond boys. I sat there staring at them both as Honat sat down on the cushion opposite my own. Then I looked at Del.

Color had spilled out of her face. Her breath was ragged and harsh as she stared at the two boys; I saw her teeth close over her bottom lip. She was angered by what she saw, and sickened, but I saw no recognition in her eyes. Only disappointment.

Honat smiled. "Both of these slaves are young and strong and—as you undoubtedly see—whole. Fit for breeding."

Both were naked. They stood before Del and me silently, staring over our heads with frozen faces, frozen eyes, avoiding my own as if not seeing me would keep me from seeing them, thereby diminishing their humiliation. My hand on Del's chain clenched so hard it hurt; I longed to shout at the boys that I *wasn't* a slaver, that I had come hoping to free one of them. I knew the overwhelming temptation to free them both, regardless of their identity. Simply to let them be the men they were originally intended to be.

I felt Del's eyes on me and looked at her slowly, seeing understanding and empathy in her face. Before she had only sympathized with my past. Now she understood it fully.

More than anything I wanted to find her brother for her.

"Well?" Honat asked, and I realized I'd have to continue the farce.

"I don't know," I said. "They look young."

"You said you *wanted* them young." Honat frowned. "They will grow. They're Northern. Northerners grow tall and heavy, like yourself." Peat-green eyes briefly assessed my own height and weight; the conditioning sword-dancing brought. "More wine?"

"No," I answered absently, setting Del's cup on the table. I got up and dropped her chain, walking up to the boys. I had to make it look good. So I walked around them slowly, consideringly, not touching them as one would a horse because I couldn't bring myself to, but I did everything else I could think of. "How do I know either of them is potent?" I demanded stiffly. Slavery can castrate a man even without the blade. I'd known it myself, before Sula gave me back my manhood.

"Both of them have gotten palace slave girls with child."

"Uh huh." I rested hands on hips. "How do I know it was *these* two?"

Honat smiled. "You are a shrewd man, Sandtiger. I can nearly believe you were born to the trade."

I suppose he meant it as a compliment. It made me feel sick, even as I smiled back at him. "I won't be conned by any man, Honat. Not even the tanzeer's agent."

He spread his wide, naked hands. "I'm an honest man. If I were not, word would soon get out and no one would deal with me. My master would dismiss me. I assure you, both of these boys are ideal for your purposes. Which one do you want?''

''Neither,'' I said shortly. ''I'll keep looking.''

Honat's dark brows shot up into a forehead furrowed by surprise. ''But we are the only ones who deal specifically in Northerners, my master and I. You must do your business with us.''

''I do business with whomever I choose.''

Honat stared at me. I got the impression he was judging me, waiting for something. Then he smiled and clapped his hands, dismissing the boys. They turned and filed out of the room. ''Of course you may deal with whomever you choose,'' Honat agreed readily, as if placating a stubborn child. He picked up the heavy decanter as I sat down again. ''Did you like the wine? It is from my master's own vines.''

''I didn't have any wine,'' I told him irritably. ''I prefer aqivi.''

''*Ah*.'' It was a blurt of discovery, and then Honat threw the decanter at me while he shouted for assistance.

By the time I was on my feet with Singlestroke free of his sheath, the room was filled with burly palace guards. They were neither eunuchs nor young boys, and each had a sword in his hands.

The wine dripped from my face and burnous. I'd knocked the decanter out of the way, but it had cost me valuable time. Fast as I am, Honat had used the delaying tactic to get out of my reach. ''Honest man, are you?'' I snarled.

''Honat does what I tell him to.'' The quiet, calm voice issued from the wall. ''It's what I pay him for.'' From a secret door stepped the man who could only be Aladar.

He was a tanzeer, all right; he wore the rich silks and jewels that branded him a desert prince. His pale-brown face was smooth and youthful, framed in a carefully trimmed black beard and moustache. He was a trifle hawk-nosed, and it gave him the look of a predator. Mahogany eyes were very, very cunning. Also genuinely amused.

"The Sandtiger, is it?" One hand stroked his beard, which glistened with scented oil. Aladar was an attractive man, if you like them smooth as honey. "I've always wondered what his growl would sound like."

"Come a little closer. You'll be able to hear his growl *and* feel his claws."

Aladar laughed. His voice was a warm, clear baritone. "I don't think so. I'm many things, but not stupid. I'll keep my distance, thank you, until the Sandtiger is safely netted and declawed." His eyes were on Singlestroke. "I am grateful you have made an offering of yourself. It saves me some little trouble."

"*Me*?" I scowled at him. "I'm offering you nothing, slaver."

"Well, then I'm *taking*." Aladar seemed untroubled by the change of phraseology. "You'll serve my purposes very well, I think. As for the woman—" he looked at Del a moment "—you said you wouldn't sell her, so the only way to get her is to steal her from you. But then—slaves can't own property, can they? Certainly not other slaves."

Not counting Aladar and Honat (neither of whom resembled the fighting type), there were six men. Not bad odds, when you consider I had Del beside me. Her neck was in iron, but not her hands.

"Do you wonder why I want you?" Aladar stroked his beard again. Gems glittered on his fingers, reflecting in his eyes. "I'm a very rich man who intends to become richer. I own gold mines and slaves, and I deal in both regularly. Both are equally important to me. How else does one find labor to work those mines?" He smiled. "With those arms and shoulders, friend sword-dancer, you could do the work of three men."

I felt my mouth go dry. The *thought* of going back into slavery scared me so much I felt the blade of panic cut through my concentration. But something else made me more frightened.

"She's not a slave," I told him clearly. "She's a free Northern woman."

Aladar's brows rose up to his bronze-colored turban with its winking garnet eye. "Then why is she collared, and why do you come to me as a slave trader?"

I wet my lips. "Too long a story. But you're making a mistake if you think you can take her for yourself, because she isn't a slave."

"She is now." He smiled. "So are you."

I pulled Del's knife out of my belt and tossed it to her. Then I invited Aladar's men to take us both.

"Both?" Aladar inquired. "Look at the woman again, sword-dancer . . . she drank the wine meant for you."

I looked. Del wavered on her feet. The knife fell out of useless hands. "Tiger—"

She was unconscious before she hit the ground. I caught her in one arm, easing her down. Then I spun around, letting Singlestroke tickle the throat of the nearest man.

"Surely you can't take all *six*," Aladar remarked.

"Call in a few more," I suggested. "Might as well make it a real challenge."

Aladar tapped one fingernail, long and buffed, against a tooth. "I *have* always desired to see your sword-dance."

"Pick up a sword yourself," I invited. "Dance with me, Aladar."

"Oh, I'm afraid not." He sounded sincerely regretful. "I have other matters to attend to, and I dislike the sight of my own blood." He signaled dismissal to Honat. "It will be a sorry thing to see the Sandtiger's teeth and claws pulled, but I can't tolerate a slave who spends valuable time thinking of rebellion. But you mustn't worry. I'll be watching from my secret closet, which is where I watch all of Honat's transactions."

He was gone. So was Honat. And I was alone with an unconscious Del and six armed, fanatically loyal men.

240

"Come on." I said it with a bravado I didn't entirely feel. "Dance with the Sandtiger."

At first, they did. One by one. It was a contest of quickness and strength, skill and strategy, and each of Aladar's men fought fairly. Then, as two of them went down beneath Singlestroke, they realized I was killing them. Not just testing them. *Killing* them. And it made them angry. I heard Aladar's outraged shout from somewhere deep in the walls, and then the remaining four were on me.

I moved immediately against the wall so no one could come at my back. It left me open on three sides, but Singlestroke and I are very fast; I slashed through the fence of steel that came at me again and again. I nicked a couple of arms and moved on, reaching for others. The problem was, they weren't out to kill *me*. All they wanted was to wear me down.

It's very frustrating when you want to kill a few enemies, and all *they* want to do is capture you.

My shoulder ached. Still I kept Singlestroke flying, slashing out to catch blades, arms, and ribs, but the four men concentrated on me en masse, which made it hard to focus on one enemy when I had three others to worry about. I wanted to swear at them all, but you don't waste your breath on such things when your life (or your freedom) is at stake.

The wall scraped against my back. I felt a tapestry behind me, flapping against my waist. Then the tapestry was whipped aside and an arm came out of the wall to encircle my throat.

Aladar. Aladar in his infernal secret closet.

One-handed, I kept Singlestroke in the fray. With the other hand I reached for the remaining knife tucked in my belt. Aladar's arm was locked tight around my throat; his men fell back. Why should they fight when he'd do it for them?

A red mist rose up before my eyes, distorting my vision.

I saw four pairs of watching eyes and, beyond them, Del's
slack body on the rugs. I jerked the knife free and tried to
stab it behind my back, but one of Aladar's men woke up
to the threat to his master and sliced me across the knuckles with his sword.

The knife clattered to the floor. So did Singlestroke. I
reached behind me, trying to hook both hands around
Aladar's head. All I got was an armful of turban, which
came off and tumbled to the floor in tangled strips of rich
cloth.

Unfortunately, Aladar's arm did not fall with it.

One of his men got bored. Maybe he saw his master
wasn't making as much progress as he hoped. Whatever
the reason, he doubled up a big fist and slammed it
beneath my ribs, which effectively expelled what little
breath I had left.

After that it didn't take long for Aladar to choke me
down, and as I faded into darkness I heard him cursing.

"Double-weight!" he gasped. "I don't want any chance
of him getting loose on the way to the mine."

And that, as they say, was that.

# Twenty-One

**D**ouble-weight meant chains around my neck, waist, wrists, ankles. It meant iron so heavy it dragged with every step, but the steps didn't last long because the guards threw me into a wagon and headed it toward the mountains.

I lay sprawled in the wagon (or as sprawled as you can get while wearing iron). It rattled against the floorboards as the wagon trundled across the ruts in the road. I was bruised, cut, battered and aching, and my throat hurt like hoolies.

But mostly I was scared.

People have called me a brave man. A fearless man. The man who will face anything and everything without flinching or blinking an eye. (None of it is true, of course, but you can't muck around with a legend when that legend is what gets you work.) So I'd gone on about my business without much bothering to acknowledge that yes, even the Sandtiger can be frightened, and now—as I faced slavery once again—I realized I'd been a bit seduced by my own reputation. I *knew* I wasn't any braver than any other man. You sort of come face to face with your own shortcomings when the thing you dread most becomes your immediate future.

I had been stripped of everything but suede dhoti and sandtiger claws. That meant no burnous, no belt, no sandals, no harness. Certainly no Singlestroke, but that didn't

243

surprise me. What did surprise me was being allowed to keep the claws.

Unless, of course, it was some bizarre form of retribution on Aladar's part. How better to get under the Sandtiger's hide than by announcing his identity to the slaves he would work with day in and day out?

Possibly. Aladar struck me as the type of man to enjoy inflicting psychological torture as well as physical hardship. He might be intending to use me as a form of control, saying, in effect: *The Sandtiger is a strong, brave, independent man. See how he is caught? See how he is humbled? See how he does what he is told?*

Hoolies.

I dragged myself up, hearing the cacophony of iron links and cuffs, and knelt on the floor of the wagon. I was escorted by a full contingent of palace guards: twenty men. A compliment, in a way; twenty men for one, and a man who was so heavily chained he could hardly breathe, let alone move.

Of course, it was also practical. Aladar probably *knew* I had every intention of getting free. He probably knew I intended to make my way back to the palace to find and free Del. *Undoubtedly* he knew I wanted to open him up from guts to gullet with any weapon I could find.

I'd do it, too. Once I got free.

I planned my escape all the way to the mine. It took my mind off the journey. It took my mind off imagining what it would be like to be a chula again.

Only when I got to the mine, I realized Aladar didn't really have anything to worry about. I'd be lucky if I *survived*.

The guards took me into the tunnels. They led me deep into the guts of the mountain: twisting, turning, ascending, descending, turning, turning, *turning* . . . until I lost all track of direction and knew myself truly lost.

The tunnels were filled with men; a gut stuffed to bursting on the helplessness and futility of men who were no longer men, but effluvia. *Chula*. Arms and legs. Each man wore iron as I did, but the waist chain was about ten feet long and locked to yet another chain. This one ran along the wall, bolted into bedrock at every other man. The men were stationed some fifteen feet apart. It left each of them with a limited area in which to work. In which to live. I could tell, from the stench of the tunnel, that no one was ever unlocked from the wall. Not even to relieve himself.

In the harsh, stark torchlight, I saw the dead man. He lay on the rock floor: a limp, sprawled body devoid of life. He stank, as dead men do. And I was his replacement.

The body was unlocked. I heard the iron dropping away, ringing against bedrock. Then a guard prodded me in one kidney, and I took a single step forward.

Then backward. Rigidly. Spasmodically. I *could not* make myself take up the dead man's place.

In the end, the guards did it for me. I felt the tug of iron at neck, wrists, waist, ankles as they locked me to the wall and made certain the links were strong. I heard the metallic clangor. I heard the voice of one guard; bored, he droned the information. No inflection. No nuances. Just—noise.

I was to hammer at the wall with mallet and chisel, breaking away chunks of the reef to free the ore, which was hauled out of the mine in wooden wagons. Any man discovered trying to chisel himself free of the chains or the bolts free of the wall would be taken outside, flogged, and left to hang on the post for three days. Without food and water.

If I worked well, the guard droned on, I'd be fed twice a day: morning and night. I was to sleep on the tunnel floor at my station. Water was brought around three times a day, no more, no less. I was expected to work from dawn until dusk, with breaks at morning and evening meals.

This, he said, was my life. For the *rest* of my life. He

dropped the mallet and chisel at my feet and walked away with the other guards, taking the light with him.

I stood facing the wall. Everything was black, black and livid purple; torch brackets were infrequently set into the walls and only half of them were lighted. My eyes would adjust, I knew, because the body makes shift where it can . . . but I wasn't sure I *wanted* to see what I was doing.

I felt the sweat break out on my skin. My flesh rose up on my bones as shudder after shudder wracked me. My belly tied itself into knots until I thought my bowels would burst. Iron rattled. I couldn't stop it from rattling. I couldn't stop myself from shaking.

The stink of the tunnel engulfed me: Urine. Defecation. Fear. Helplessness. Death. The knowledge of futility.

I closed my eyes and set my forehead against the ribs of the wall, digging fingers into the stone. I was in darkness of mind, of body, of spirit. All I could see was madness. It filled up all my senses until I was small again, so small, *so small.*

Even among the Salset I hadn't felt so helpless, so frightened, *so small.*

I forced myself to look at the others. They squatted, all hunched against the wall, staring at me blankly; chained I was, as they were chained, and equally hopeless. I looked at their broken, callused hands; their overdeveloped shoulders; their empty, staring eyes, and realized they had been here months. Maybe years.

Not one of them seemed to have the slightest trace of sanity left. And I realized, staring at them even as they stared at me, that I looked into my own face.

The sun went down and sucked more light out of the tunnel, leaving me in the mosaic of patchwork darkness: madder-violet, gentian-blue, raisin-black. And a splash of brilliant fuchsia whenever I closed my eyes. The evening meal had been served before my arrival; now the men slept. I heard their snores, their groans, their cries, their yips. Heard the continuous rattle of iron.

Heard the wheeze of my own breath as it rasped in and out of a throat constricted by a symphony of fear.

My appetite, after disappearing, eventually returned. It increased with the heavy work of breaking free the reef and ore and loading it into carts pulled by slaves chained to them, but the food ration didn't. I went to sleep hungry and empty and woke up an hour or two later with cramping belly, cramping muscles. When morning came I was dulled from a sleep that didn't refresh me. The water was tepid and foul and often caused dysentery, but I drank it because there was nothing else. I slept in the dirt of the tunnel floor, accustomed to restricted movements and the necessity of relieving myself in my own corner, like a wounded animal. I knew myself degraded, humiliated, sickened; I knew myself a chula. And the knowledge swept away the years I'd spent as a free sword-dancer.

The nightmares came again. This time there was no Sula to make them go away. This time I lived in the lowest level of hoolies. Dwelling on vanished days of transitory freedom was to dwell on madness, and so I didn't think of them at all.

*The circle was drawn in the sand. The swords lay in the center. A two-handed Southron sword, with gold hilt and blued-steel blade. A two-handed Northern sword: silver-hilted, rune-bladed, singing its siren song of ice and death.*

*A woman, standing near the circle. Waiting. White hair shining. Blue eyes calm. Gilded limbs relaxed. Waiting.*

*A man: sunbronzed, dark-haired, green-eyed. Tall. Powerfully built. Except that even as he stood there, waiting to start the dance, his body changed. Lost weight. Substance. Strength. It melted off him until he was a skeleton with a bit of brown hide stretched over the bones.*

*He put out a hand toward the woman. The woman who sang his deathsong.*

\*     \*     \*

Day became night, night became day.

—*daynightdaynightdaynight*—

—until there was no day or night or even *daynight*—just a man in a mine and the mine in the mind of the man—

He squatted. Spine against wall. Hardened rump barely brushing the floor. Forearms across knees. Hands dangling. Forehead against forearms.

Until a foot rattled his iron, and eventually he looked up.

The tanzeer was richly dressed in cloth-of-gold and crimson embroidery. He was a clean man, well-groomed; he was a man who took pride in appearances. In his right hand he carried a slim ivory wand, an ornamental baton, carved and knurled. A nacreous pearly-white.

A brief gesture with the wand. The guard hooked a foot into iron chain and rattled it, until the chained man looked up.

A second brief gesture with the wand. A torch was brought closer. Sulfurous yellow light spilled out of the flame to illuminate the face of the man looking at the tanzeer; the tanzeer saw a beast, not a man. A filthy, befouled, stinking beast, clad in a ragged suede dhoti. Worn down to nothing but skin and ropy sinew, stretched over a frame that might once have claimed a powerful, impressive grace. The face was mostly hidden in dusty hair and tangled, matted beard. But out of the face peered a pair of green eyes, squinting against the blinding torch-light.

"Stand him up," the tanzeer ordered, and the guard jerked his head in such a way as the man knew well.

Rising, the chained man was tall, much taller than the tanzeer. But he didn't stand in the attitude of a tall man comfortable with his height. He stood with shoulders hunched, as if it was difficult to bear their weight.

The tanzeer frowned. "It *is* the sword-dancer, isn't it?" he asked the guard, who shrugged and said as far as *he*

248

knew, it was the same man who had been brought in three months before.

The tanzeer hooked the tip of his wand under the clotted cord around the chained man's neck. He rattled the clots and saw that yes, indeed, the clots—beneath their dirt— were really claws.

Satisified, he let the cord drop back against the man's throat and nodded. "Take him off the wall. Double-weight him and put him in the wagon It's time I hosted him in the palace once again."

Before the woman, unguarded, the tanzeer showed off the man he had brought from the mine. He told the woman what had happened to the man in the mine; he watched her face, her eyes, her posture. He saw what he had always seen: dignity, strength, quiet pride and absolute insularity. In three months, he had not broken her.

But he had broken the man, and he thought it might be enough to break the woman.

He turned from her and faced the man who stank of his own excrescence. "To your knees," and pointed to the floor with his ivory baton.

Slowly the man got down on knees that had been bruised so often they were permanently discolored. Blue-black, against faded copper skin mottled with dirt and chisel cuts; pocked with bits of ore and reef trapped beneath the top layer of his skin. The chains rang against one another and the tessellated floor, spilling around his knees like the entrails of an iron serpent.

The tanzeer looked at the woman. "He will do whatever told. *Whatever* he is told."

The woman looked straight back at the tanzeer. Her disbelief was blatant.

The tanzeer gestured with his wand. "Down," he said. "Face down."

The kneeling man, once young, moved as an old man

moves. Bent forward. Placed palms flat against the patterned stone. Sinews stood up beneath encrusted flesh.

He prostrated himself on the floor.

The tanzeer extended one slippered foot. "Kiss it. Kiss it—chula."

And at last, the woman broke. With an inarticulate cry of rage she sprang at the tanzeer like a female sandtiger, one hand clawing for his face. The other one came down on his ornamental knife and jerked it free—

—jerking it as the man on the floor tore himself from the stone and twisted loops of iron chain around the tanzeer's throat.

Lips drew back from his teeth. But instead of growling he spoke one word. A husky, broken word: "*Keys.*"

"Where?" the woman demanded of the tanzeer. And when he told her she dug them out of the jewelled pouch hanging from his jewelled belt.

She ignored the iron collar around her own throat. Instead, unlocked the cuffs from his ankles, waist, neck—and finally as he twisted the loops more tightly around the tanzeer's throat, she unlocked the cuffs from his wrists.

He shed them all. Sloughed off the serpent's coils as if he sloughed his skin. And all the iron rang down on the floor and cracked the careful patterns.

With the iron he shed his captivity, as much as he could, and she saw in the beast's place a trace of the man she had known. Only a trace, but a trace was better than nothing. Tentatively, she smiled. "Tiger?"

I shoved Aladar up against the nearest wall and took the knife from Del as she offered it. Placed the tip against his flat, tissue-clad belly and bared my teeth at him. "One claw left, tanzeer. Care to feel it?"

He stared back at me, saffron-colored from shock, but he didn't give in. He had too much pride for it.

I flicked a glance at Del. I didn't have much voice left—three months of silence, except for occasional outcries in my sleep, had leached me of the facility—but she seemed to comprehend my abbreviated speech well enough. "Swords and knives. Clothes. Anything. I'll wait."

She ran, leaving me with Aladar.

I was shaking. Reaction had set in. I could almost hear my chains rattling, except I didn't wear them anymore. But I heard them. I hear them still.

I sucked in a deep breath. Bared my teeth again at Aladar. "Ten-year-old boy, five years ago. Northerner. Omar's slaveblock. Jamail. Looks like her." It was all I could manage. I didn't dare let him see how shaky I was; it wouldn't be difficult for him to break free. The mine had stolen strength, flexibility, speed. All I had left was hatred.

A wild, killing rage.

"Do you expect me to know what happens to every slave in Julah?" he demanded.

He had a point. But so did I, and it was pressing against his gut. "What happened to *this* one?"

"He was a *chula*!" Aladar hissed. "I buy them, I sell them . . . I can't keep track of every one!"

The little knife wasn't worth much as a real weapon, but its steel was very sharp. It sliced through the cloth easily enough; I had the feeling it would slice through flesh equally so. "I'm going to cut you, tanzeer, and spill your guts out onto the floor like ropes, so you can trip over them."

Apparently he believed me. Just as well; I meant it. "I had such a boy," he admitted. "I let him go three years ago."

"*Where*?"

"Vashni." Clearly, Aladar knew what he was saying. His pallor deepened. "I gave him as a gift to the chief."

Hoolies. "You have trade with the Vashni?" No one else did. I wondered if he lied.

Aladar swallowed heavily. "I needed it. With this particular clan. I needed access to the mountains, to the mine, for the gold. With—with the Vashni settled there, I stood no chance. So—I sent all manner of things, including chula. One of them was a Northern boy. He was twelve.''

The age fit. ''Where?'' I asked grimly.

Aladar's brown eyes were black with fear and hatred. ''Just ride due south, into the foothills. The Vashni find you even when you don't want them to.''

That was undoubtedly true. ''The boy's name?''

''I don't know!'' Aladar shouted. ''Do you expect me to know the name of a *chula*?''

''Tiger,'' Del said.

I turned my head and saw she wore her tunic again, complete with sword harness. The silver hilt stood up above her left shoulder. She carried a black burnous, sandals and Singlestroke, along with knife and harness. A white burnous was draped over her other arm.

She dropped everything into a pile as she reached up to draw her sword. ''Get dressed,'' she said calmly. ''I'll watch Aladar.''

I stepped away from him. Del saw my face as I turned my back on the tanzeer; something in hers told me I wasn't maintaining as well as I'd hoped. The ornamental knife was slippery in my hand. From sweat. The sweat of tension and emotion.

I let Del go past me to Aladar. Carefully, I bent and picked up the black burnous, concentrating on cutting a slit in the shoulder seam for Singlestroke's hilt. My hands shook. The seam split. The tip of the knife nicked a finger. I didn't feel it. My hands were too callused.

I shrugged into my harness, dismayed to discover I didn't need to undo the buckles. No. I needed to punch new holes. To make the harness smaller. But that would have to wait.

The sandals were hard to lace up. Eventually, I knotted them. Pulled the burnous over my head, glad to cover most of my stinking, scarred hide. Felt a wave of weakness break over my head and threaten to suck me down.

I turned. Del watched me. I felt sluggish heat rise into

252

my face. Sweat stung my armpits. Singlestroke was in my hands, but I didn't raise him. I didn't sheathe him. I looked at Del, and I saw her turn back to Aladar and spit him on her rune-worked blade.

"*No*—" But the shout was little more than a tearing in my throat. "By hoolies, woman, *that death was mine!*"

Del didn't answer.

"Bascha—*mine*—"

Still she didn't answer.

My mouth opened. Closed. I said nothing. I watched as she pulled the blade free. The body, sagging against the wall, slowly slid toward the floor. It bled gently through cloth-of-gold and crimson embroidery.

Del turned, and at last she answered me. "That was for you." The soft voice was incredibly intimate. "For what he did to you."

She was unreadable. I saw the stark harshness of the bones beneath pale flesh and realized she'd lost her tan. She was a Northern bascha again, as I'd seen her originally.

And an incredibly dangerous woman.

There wasn't much room in my throat for my voice. "Del—I do *my own* killing."

She looked directly back at me. "Not this time, Tiger. No."

Something jumped deep in my chest. A cramp. Something spasmodic. "Is that how you killed the *an-kaidin*? Is that how you blooded that blade?"

I saw her twitch of shock. Her face was paler still; had I shocked her that much with my question? Del was aware I knew what had happened to her sword-master, and how. Just not all the reasons for it.

Or was it the *tone* of my accusation that had drawn the reaction from her?

"This was for *you*," she said at last.

"Was it?" I croaked. "Or was it for Del?"

She looked down at her sword. Blood ran from the

blade. It filled up the runes, then dripped raggedly from the steel to puddle on the tessellated floor.

Her mouth twitched a moment, but it wasn't an expression of humor. It was Del dealing with an emotion I couldn't name. "For us both." But she said it so quietly I wasn't certain what words were said.

Three months apart. We owed each other nothing. Not now. The thing had gone past employer and employee. Del and I were free to go our separate ways.

"Jamail is with the Vashni," I told her. "A mountain clan."

"I heard him."

"You're going?"

Her jaw was a blade beneath taut flesh. "I'm going."

After a moment, I nodded. I was incapable of anything else.

Del picked up the white burnous. She slid the sword home in the sheath behind her shoulder—she'd clean it later, I knew—and went out of the room.

But not before she relieved Aladar's body of his jewelled pouch.

I love a practical woman.

# Twenty-Two

**D**el bought our way into a disreputable inn on the disreputable side of Julah. We made an odd pair; I wasn't much surprised at the odd looks we got as we climbed the narrow adobe staircase to the second floor and the tiny room Del had rented for us. She ordered a bath with lots of hot water, and when the serving girl muttered about the extra work, Del cracked her across the face with the flat of her hand. With the mark still blazing red on the girl's tawny skin, Del promised her gold if she hurried. The girl hurried.

I sat on the edge of the threadbare, rumpled cot. I stared blankly at Del, recalling how easily she had slipped the sword blade into Aladar's belly. For me, she had said. But I've long been accustomed to doing my own killing when it needed doing; I couldn't imagine why she would do it for me. Or what it was in me that had triggered her lethal response.

No. More likely it had been for her brother and for the treatment she had known at Aladar's hands.

"You'll feel better when you're clean again," Del said.

The burnous covered most of me. But I could see my sandaled feet, callused hands. Finger- and toenails were split, broken, missing, peeled back, blackened. Nicks and ingrained ore dust discolored faded copper flesh. Across the back of my left hand was a jagged scar, healed over: a chisel had slipped once, in the shaking hands of a dying man chained next to me.

I turned my hands over and looked at the palms. Once they had been callused from years of sword-dancing. It had only been months since they had known the seductive flesh of Singlestroke's hilt, and yet I knew it was too long.

The door crashed open. Del swung around, hands on sword hilt; she didn't unsheathe the Northern blade because it was the serving girl and a fat man. He rolled a wooden cask into the room, dumped it on end, left. The girl began lugging buckets of hot water in one by one, pouring them into the cask.

Del waited until the cask was filled. Then she gestured dismissal to the girl, who took one hard look at me and did as Del suggested. She left. And after a moment, so did Del.

I picked at the knots in my laces. Untied them, stripped off the leather. Dropped burnous and dhoti. Lastly, shed harness and sword. And climbed into the hot water, not even caring that all the cuts and nicks and scrapes clamored protest at the heat.

I slid down into the cask until the water lapped at my chest. Carefully, I leaned my skull against the edge of the cask, giving myself over to the heat. I didn't even bother with the soap. I just soaked. And then I slept.

—*the rattle of iron . . . the chink of mallet against chisel, chisel against stone . . . the yips and cries of sleeping men . . . the sobs of dying men*—

I woke up with a jerk. Disoriented, I was aware of flaxen light in the room, slanting through the slatted window . . . a *room*, not a tunnel! No more torchlight. No more darkness. No more *iron*.

A hand, against my back. Scrubbing soap into the flesh, until I was coated with yellow-brown lather. Del's hand pressed down on my head as I began to rise. "No. I'll do it. Be easy."

But I couldn't. I sat stiffly in the cask as she scrubbed,

working the brown soap into the filthy skin. Her fingers were strong, very strong; she kneaded at the tension knotting shoulders, neck, spine.

"Be easy," she said softly.

But I couldn't. "What did that bastard do to you?"

I could feel her shrug. "It doesn't matter. He's dead."

"Bascha." I reached and caught one of her hands. "Tell me."

"Will you tell *me*?"

At once I was back in the mine, swallowed up by darkness and despair. I felt the emptiness teasing the edges of my mind. "*No*." It was all I could do to form the word, to expel a sound from my mouth. I couldn't. I couldn't tell her.

"Shave?" she asked. "You need a haircut, too."

I nodded. Washed hair and beard. Nodded again.

Considerate of my modesty, Del turned away while I heaved myself up in the cask, washed the parts of me which Del hadn't, rinsed, and dripped across the floor to the rough sacking on the cot. There was also a fresh dhoti and brown burnous. I dried myself, pulled the dhoti on, told her she could turn around.

She did. I saw momentary pity in her eyes. "You're too thin."

"So are you." I sat down. "Rid me of this rat's-nest, bascha. Make me a man again."

Carefully, she cut my hair. Carefully, she stripped the beard away. I watched her face as she tended mine. The flesh was drawn tight over her bones. Aladar had kept her indoors for three months; the honey-tan had faded. Except for the sun-frost in her hair, she looked so very much like the Northern woman I'd met in the little cantina in the nameless town on the edge of the Punja.

Except I knew what she was, now. Not a witch. Not a sorceress, though some might name her that because of the *jivatma* and all its power. No. Del was just a woman bent on doing whatever it was she had to do. No matter what the odds.

Finally she smiled. I felt gentle fingers briefly touch the claw marks on my face. "Sandtiger." It was all she said. All she needed to say.

"Hungry?" When she nodded, I pulled on the burnous and Singlestroke, and we went down to the common room.

The food was spicy and tangy; not the best, not the worst. Certainly better than what I'd known in the mine. And I learned I couldn't eat much more than I'd eaten for the last three months. My belly rebelled. And so I turned to aqivi instead.

Finally, Del reached out and put a hand over the rim of my cup. "No more." Gently said, but firmly.

"I'll drink what I want."

"Tiger—" She hesitated. "Too much will make you sick."

"It'll make me *drunk*," I corrected. "Right about now, drunk is precisely what I'd like to be."

Her eyes were very direct. "Why?"

I thought she probably knew why. But I said it anyway. "It'll help me forget."

"You can't forget that, Tiger. No more than you could forget your days with the Salset." She shook her head a little. "There are things about *my* life I'd like to forget; I can't, so I live with them. I think them through, deal with them, put them in their place. So they don't affect the other things I must do."

"Have you forgotten the blood-guilt, then?" I couldn't help myself; the aqivi made me hostile. I looked at her whitening face. "How did you deal with *that*, bascha?"

"What do you know of blood-guilt, Sandtiger?"

I shrugged beneath brown silk. "A little. I recall how the chula felt when he realized his conjuring—his *wishful thinking*—had made a dream come true, at the cost of innocent lives." I sighed. "And another story about an *ishtoya* who killed an *an-kaidin*. Because of a blooding-blade." I looked at the hilt standing up behind her shoulder. "It had to be quenched in the blood of a skillful man, so the *ishtoya* could seek revenge."

"There are needs in this world that supersede the importance of other things." Flat, unwavering tone.

"Selfish." I swallowed more liquor. "I saw what you did to Aladar, and I know you're capable of killing for the sake of revenge. Of *need*." I paused. "Obsession, bascha. Wouldn't you agree?"

Del smiled a little. "Maybe." And the word had an edge, like the blade of her Northern sword.

I put down my brimming cup. "I'm going to bed."

Del let me go. She didn't say a word.

*A shadowed figure approached from the end of the tunnel. The light was stark behind it, throwing it into sharp relief: a silhouette wihtout features. Without shape. Simply a form in a black burnous. And in its hands was a sword, a Northern sword, silver-hilted and worked with alien runes.*

*The figure approached the first slave slowly. He was chained five men down from me. The sword flashed briefly in the muted light. I saw two hands lift it, rest the tip against the man's upstanding ribs, push. The blade slid in silently, killing without a sound. The man sagged against his chains. Only the rattling of the iron told me he was dead.*

*Withdrawn. Blood shone on the blade, but in the strange light from beyond the tunnel it shone black, not red.*

*The figure came closer. The next man died, silently as the first. The next. Blood dripped from the blade. I saw, as the figure approached, that it was hooded, and the black burnous wasn't black at all, but white.*

*Two more men died and the figure stood before me: Del. I looked into her hooded face and saw blue, blue eyes, pale, fair skin, and a mouth. A mouth filled with blood as if she had drunk that which spilled from each man she had killed.*

"Bascha," I whispered.

*She lifted the sword and placed the tip against my chest. Her eyes did not waver from my face.*

*The Northern sword pierced my flesh and sank into my heart. Soundlessly, but for the rattle of the chains, I sank against the wall.*

*I died.*

I woke up with a hand on my shoulder. I thrust myself into a sitting position, reaching for Singlestroke; realized it was Del. Realized I had, in my drunken stupor, gone to sleep on the floor, as if I were still in the mine. And I realized it was my own fear I smelled, filling up the darkness.

I heard my breath rasping raggedly in the silence of the room, and I couldn't stop the sound.

"Tiger." Del knelt at my side. "You were dreaming."

I shoved an arm across my face and knew I'd been doing more than that. I'd been crying. The realization, and the instant humiliation, was horrible.

"No," she said softly, and I knew she'd seen it.

I was shaking. I couldn't help it. I was cold and scared and sick on too much aqivi; lost on the borderland of illusion and reality. Aqivi rolled in my belly, threatening to spew out of my mouth; it didn't only because I put my head down on my upthrust knees. Trembling, I swore softly, repeatedly, until Del's arms slid around my neck from behind and hugged me like a child.

"It's all right," she whispered into the shadows. *"It's all right."*

I threw off her arms and lurched to my feet, staring at her. The candle was gone but the moonlight crept between the slats covering the window. It slanted across her pale face and striped it: dark—light—dark—light. Her eyes were hidden in shadow.

"It was *you*." The shaking renewed itself. "You."

She knelt on the floor and stared up at me. "You dreamed about me?"

I tried to speak evenly. "One by one, you killed them. With your sword. You spitted them. And then you came to me." I saw the hooded face before me. "Hoolies, woman, *you stuck that sword into me as easily as you stuck it into Aladar!*"

Silence. The echoes of my accusation died away.

"I saw it." Her voice was little more than a whisper, but I detected the faintest trace of despair. "I saw it. In that moment, when I turned away from Aladar, I saw the hatred in your eyes. For *me*."

"No." It was expelled all at once. "No, Del. I hated *me*. Myself. Because I've done it so often, and with less compunction—less *reason*—than you did." I began to move, unable to stand still. I paced. Like a caged cat. "I saw myself when I watched you kill Aladar. And it's never easy to look at yourself and acknowledge, at long last, exactly what you are."

"Sword-dancer," she said. "Both of us. We are neither of us better or worse than the other. We are what we have made of ourselves, because we had reason. Justification. Because of obsession." She smiled a little. "Chula: freed by his own courage. Free to take up a sword. Woman: freed by rape and murder. Free to take up a sword."

"Del—"

"You said once I wasn't cold enough. That I lacked the edge." She shook her head. The braid moved against her right shoulder. "You were wrong. I *am* cold, Tiger; too cold. My edge is honed too sharp." She didn't smile. "I've killed more men than I can count, and I will go on killing them when I have to—because of murdered kin . . . a stolen brother . . . violated virginity." The moonlight set her pale hair shining. "Your dream was right, Tiger. I would kill a hundred Aladars . . . and never look back while the bodies fall."

I looked at her. I looked at the proud sword-dancer who knelt on the hard wooden floor of a dingy Southron inn and knew I looked at someone worth all the sacrifice in the world because she had made and accepted her own.

"What have you done?" I asked hoarsely. "What have you done to yourself?"

Del looked up at me. "If I were a man, would you ask that?"

I stared at her. "What?"

"If I were a man, would you ask that?"

But she already knew the answer.

# Twenty-Three

**D**el and I did not leave Julah immediately. For two reasons, actually: Aladar's murderer was sought by palace guards, and I wasn't in any shape to leave as yet. Three months in the mines had taken their toll. I needed food, rest, exercise. Mostly I needed time.

But time was a commodity we didn't have. Now that we were so close to Jamail (both Del and I were pretty sure Aladar had told us the truth about giving Jamail as a gift), she was understandably anxious to track down the Vashni. But she waited. With more patience than I've ever seen in anyone, let alone myself.

We didn't speak again about past experiences or reasons for what we had become. We spoke instead about plans for shaking Jamail loose from the Vashni. I'd never had much experience with the tribe, but I'd learned some over the years. Unlike the Hanjii, they weren't overtly hostile to strangers. But they were dangerous. And so we had to plan accordingly.

"No more slave and slave trader scam," I told Del on the third day of our freedom. "It got us into too much trouble the last time. If this Vashni chieftain has acquired a taste for Northern slaves, we don't want to risk losing you as well."

"I thought you might eventually come to that conclusion." Del's head was bent as she wiped the blade of her sword with soft chamois. "Do you have another idea?"

I squatted on the floor, hunched against the wall. The posture had become habitual, though now there were no chains. "Not really. Maybe it would be the best if we just rode in and checked out the lay of the land."

"We'll have to have something the chieftain wants," Del reminded me. "Otherwise, what would tempt him to give up Jamail?"

I scratched at the scars on my face. "We've still got most of the money that was in Aladar's pouch. And the pouch itself, which is worth a small fortune because of all the gems." Absently, I shrugged my left shoulder. "When it comes right down to it, he may want to *reward* us for ridding him of Aladar. Seems to me it cancels the trade alliance."

The Northern blade shone. Del glanced over at me. Unbound, her hair was like platinum silk in the saffron sunlight. "I hired you to guide me across the Punja, to Julah. I didn't hire you to risk your life for my brother."

"In other words, you don't think I'm ready for sword-work—if it comes to that."

"Are you?" she asked calmly.

We both knew the answer. Three days out of the mine; three months in. "I said I'd go."

"Then we'll go." She put the tip of the sword against the lip of the leather sheath and slid the blade home. A sibilant song: steel against fleece-lined leather.

In the morning, we went.

We rode into the foothills of the Southron Mountains on yet another pair of horses. Del's was a white gelding generously speckled with black from nose to rump. He had odd, watchful eyes, almost human, and a frazzled motley mane and tail. My own mount was also a gelding, but less colorful than Del's; he was a plain, unremarkable brown horse. Not bay, not like my old stud; he lacked black points, black mane and tail. Just—brown. Like his personality.

We rode out of sand into the saltpan hardpack of the border between desert and foothills. With each step the earth changed, chameleonlike; first sand, then hummocky patches of dry, wispy grass, then footing akin to something more like a natural topsoil.

I watched Del's gelding. He had a funny way of stepping out. He appeared almost to *mince*, womanlike; I'd have mentioned it to Del, except I couldn't think of any time at all when *she* had minced.

At any rate, the speckled gelding was full of *something*. He minced, sashayed, whiffled through flaring nostrils, slanting my gelding coy glances out of eerily human eyes.

"I think I know why he was gelded," I said finally. "As a stallion, I think he'd be a washout."

Del's brows shot up. "Why? He's a perfectly good horse. A little skittish, maybe—but there's nothing wrong with him."

"*It*," I reminded her. "There isn't any *him* left in him. But I'm willing to bet there wasn't any *him* in him when he was *whole*."

Del chose not to answer my charge. Well, he—*it*—was her horse. Maybe she felt some loyalty.

We left behind the saltpan, the dry, hummocky grass, the webbing of healthier growth. Horse shoes clinked against slate-colored shale, gray-green granite. We climbed, though the elevation was debatable; the Southron Mountains, even at their summit, are not tremendously tall. From the sloping shoulders, spotted with scrubby trees and catclawed brush, steel-blue shalefalls dribbled toward the desert.

Del was shaking her head. "Not like the North. Not like the North at all."

I leaned forward, half-standing in my stirrups as the brown gelding negotiated a jagged shale escarpment. "No snow."

"Not just that." Del tapped her speckled horse with

sandaled heels, urging him to follow me. "The trees, the rocks, the soil . . . even the *smell* is different."

"Should be," I agreed, "seeing as it's Vashni you're smelling, not mountains."

I stopped my horse. The warrior sat on his own sorrel mount about twenty paces away. Around his bare brown neck hung an ivory necklace of human finger bones.

Del stopped next to me. "So it is."

We waited. So did the warrior.

He was young. Probably about seventeen. But the first thing a Vashni male knows in this life is a sword; a Vashni woman, giving birth, cuts the cord with her husband's sword. And then the male child is circumcised with it.

No, you don't underestimate a Vashni warrior. Not even the young ones.

This one was mostly naked, clad only in leather kilt and belt. Even his feet were bare. His bronzed flesh was oiled to a feral sleekness. He wore his black hair long, longer than Del's; like her, he braided it. But the single braid was wrapped in furred hide. From his ears depended earrings of carved bone. What part of the human body *they* came from, I couldn't say.

He made certain he had our full attention. Then he turned and headed south. Across his back, naked except for the thin harness, was strapped a traditional Vashni sword. Unsheathed, the wickedly curved blade gleamed. The hilt was a human thighbone.

"Come on," I told Del. "I think we're expected."

The young warrior led us into the Vashni encampment: a clustering of striped hyorts staked out almost cheek-by-jowl against the sloping mountainsides. We rode through a tribal reception party: two parallel lines of Vashni, winding like a serpent through the encampment. Warriors, women, children. All were silent. All watched. And all wore as finery the bone remains of men, women, children.

"They're *worse* than the Hanjii," Del breathed to me.

"Not really. The Vashni don't believe in live sacrifice,

like the Hanjii. The trophies you see are honorable ones, won in honorable battle.'' I paused. "Taken from *dead* people.''

Our guide escorted us to the largest hyort, dropped off his horse and gestured us to dismount as well. Then he signaled me forward. But as Del stepped forward also, he shook his head sharply.

I looked at Del and saw the conflict in her face. She wanted so much to argue with the warrior; she knew better, and didn't. Instead, she moved back to her speckled horse. But not before I saw the desperation in her eyes.

"Do you speak Vashni?" she asked.

"A couple of words. But they speak Desert. Most people in the South do. Bascha—" I didn't touch her, though I wanted to. "—Del, I'll be careful what I say. I know what this means to you.''

She let out a ragged breath. "I know. I—know. But—" She shook her head. "I guess I'm just afraid he won't be here after all. That he'll have been traded or sold off to someone else, and we'll have to search some more.''

There was nothing more I could say. So I left her with the horses, as most would do with a woman. I turned my back on her and stepped inside the chieftain's hyort, and I came face to face with her brother.

I stopped short. The flap fell down behind my back; Del would not be able to see in. She wouldn't be able to see her brother as I saw him: braided, like a Vashni. Kilted, like a Vashni. Mostly naked, like a Vashni. But blond. Blue-eyed. Fair-skinned. Like Del. And lacking sword and fingerbone necklet.

Which meant he wasn't—quite—a Vashni.

He was nearly Del's height. But not quite. He was nearly Del's weight. But not quite. And never would be. Because I knew, looking at him, that his physical growth had been impaired by castration.

I've seen it before. It's in the eyes, if nowhere else. Not all of them grow fat, like Sabo. Not all of them grow effeminate. Not all of them look that much different from a normal male.

Except in the eyes. Except in the odd, almost eerie physical immaturity. A permanent immaturity.

In no way did I betray I knew who he was. In no way did I betray I knew *what* he was. I simply stood there silently, waiting, and trying to deal, in my own way, with the horror and shock and grief.

For Del's sake, because she would need me to be strong.

Jamail stepped aside; I saw the old man seated on a rug on the floor of the hyort. The chieftain of all the fierce Vashni: white-haired, wrinkled, palsied. And half-blind; his right eye was filmed completely over. His left showed signs of the same disability, although not as advanced. And yet he sat rigidly upright on his rug and waited for Jamail to return to his side.

When the boy did, the old man took hold of a soft, fair-skinned arm and did not let it go again.

Hoolies. How in the name of valhail do I deal with *this*?

But I knew. And when the old chieftain asked me my business with the Vashni, no doubt expecting a wish for trade expressed, I told him. Everything. And I told him the absolute truth.

When I was done, I looked at Jamail. He looked back out of Del's blue eyes. Not once had he said a word or made a sound of disbelief, grief, relief. Another man might have said the boy was afraid to indicate his feelings, out of fear for retribution. But I knew better. I saw how the old man clung to his Northern eunuch; how the old man depended on his Northern eunuch, and knew the Vashni chieftain would never hurt him. He wouldn't so much as speak a harsh word to him.

But he spoke to me. In Desert, the old man gave me Jamail's side of the story; as much as he knew of it. It was true Aladar had offered a Northern slave-boy as part of a trade treaty. It was true Jamail had been accepted as chattel. But it was not true he had remained such. It was not true he had been treated as chula. It was not true the Vashni had castrated him. It was not true the Vashni had cut out his tongue.

And so I knew why Jamail said nothing. Mute, he couldn't. Castrated, he might not want to.

"Aladar," I said only.

The old man nodded once. I saw the trembling in his chin. The tears forming in his failing eyes. The brittle strength in his palsied hands as he held Jamail's arm. His mouth twitched as he formed the words of his question: "Will the Northern woman want a man who is not a man?"

I looked at Jamail. Trapped forever in physical immaturity, he looked more like Del than he should. But I knew better than to think for one moment that what her brother had suffered would alter her intentions.

Still, I couldn't speak for her. "I think the woman will have to say."

After a moment, the old man nodded again. He gestured permission; I rose, gathered what courage I could muster, and went out to tell Jamail's sister.

Del listened in rigid silence. She said nothing when I finished speaking. She went in.

It wasn't my place to follow. But Del didn't speak Desert, and Jamail couldn't translate her words to the chieftain. So I ducked back into the hyort.

Jamail was crying. So was Del. So was the old man. But all of them did it in silence.

Del didn't look at me. "Ask the chieftain if he will let Jamail go."

I asked. The old man, crying, said yes.

She swallowed. "Ask Jamail if he will come."

I asked. Jamail, at length, nodded. Once. But I saw a fair-skinned hand creep out to touch the old man's liver-spotted one and cling in a dependence all too evident.

Del was dry-eyed now. "Tiger—will you tell the chieftain thank you? Tell him—*sulhaya*."

I told him. And then Jamail, because the chieftain told him to, got up to go out of the tent with his sister.

Del stopped him with a hand pressed lightly against his chest. She spoke in soft Northern, with tears in her eyes, and when she was done speaking, she hugged the brother she had sought for five long years and gave up her claim on him.

After a moment, I followed her out of the tent.

# Twenty-Four

Stark-faced, Del had said nothing on the journey from the foothills to the oasis on the border of the Punja. And now, as she sat in the muted shade of six palms with her back against the cistern's rock wall, I saw the beginnings of shocked comprehension coming into her eyes.

A goal achieved often brings no joy. Only a fleeting sense of satisfaction in the knowledge that the thing is done, but also the first taste of anti-climax. In this case, that taste was fouled by the additional knowledge that what she had done was for nothing.

Well, not entirely for *nothing*. But it seemed that way to her.

"They were kind to him," I told her. "For two years he lived in hoolies with Aladar. The Vashni gave him welcome. They gave him dignity."

"I'm *empty*," was all she said.

I heard the anguish in her tone as I sat down next to her. She'd built a little fire near one of the palms as the sun went down, using the kindling we carried in our pouches as well as a couple of dead palm fronds. We'd sat on spread rugs, chewed dinner, drunk wine, thought silent, private thoughts, and watched the sun go down across the desert. Now, except for the wind-whipped fire and snorts from hobbled horses, there was no noise at all.

Del turned her face to me and I saw the pain in every line. "Why am I so *empty*?"

"Because what you wanted most has been taken from you by circumstances you can't begin to change." I smiled a little. "There's no circle for this, bascha. No dance. No *kaidin* or *an-kaidin* to show you how to overcome it with skill and training. Not even a magicked sword can help, Northern- or Southron-forged. "

"It hurts," she said. "It hurts *so much*."

"For a long time to come."

We sat shoulder to shoulder against the cistern wall. I could feel the warmth of her skin through the thin silk of my burnous; the thin silk of her own. Neither of us were in harness, having shed our swords not long after dismounting. But both weapons lay in easy reach; neither of us is a fool.

I thought of how maybe once I might have asserted a certain degree of somewhat forceful masculine interest in the woman at my side. How maybe once I might have pressed physical attentions when she wasn't desirous of them, knowing so many women wanted to be teased and hugged and kissed into capitulation. But Del was not most women. Del was Del, sword-dancer first, and I respected her for that.

But not to the extent that I could ignore the fact I wanted her more than ever.

It became apparent her thoughts were much the same as mine. I saw the softening of her mouth; a slight smile widening slowly. Her glance was sidelong. Eloquent in its directness. "There was a deal, sword-dancer," she said. "A bargain we struck, because you wouldn't enter the circle with me otherwise. Payment for a sword-dancer's services, because I had no other coin."

I shrugged my left shoulder, naked of Singlestroke's weight. "We split Aladar's purse. Payment enough, bascha."

"Is that a *no*?" she asked in astonishment. Amusement,

as well; she was not affronted by the idea I might not want her after all. But neither did she seem particularly relieved. "After waiting so patiently?"

I smiled. "Patience is as it must be, or some such thing. No, bascha, it isn't exactly a *no*. Just—an equivocal yes." I reached out and tucked a sunbleached strand of hair behind her ear. "I don't want you on the basis of a bargain. I don't want you if you feel it's obligatory. Or even a form of thanks." The calluses on my fingers caught and snagged the silk of her burnous. "Neither do I want it if you're simply feeling lonely and unfulfilled because your search is at an end."

"No?" Pale brows rose a little. "Not the Sandtiger *Elamain* knew, is it?"

I laughed out loud. "No, thank valhail. No."

Del's fingers—callused as my own—were cool on my silk-clad arm. "That's not why, Tiger. But if we *each* of us took, gave, shared—on an equal basis . . . regardless of the reasons?"

"Equal basis?" In the South, a man in bed with a woman knows so little of equality, being taught from childhood he is unquestionably superior.

Unless, of course, he grows up a chula.

Del laughed softly. "Think of it as a sword-dance."

I thought at once of my dreams. Del and I, in a circle. Facing one another. The image made me smile. The circle she offered now had nothing to do with dreams. At least, not *those* dreams; another sort entirely.

"Freely offered, freely taken." I thought it over. "Interesting idea, bascha."

"Not so different from Elamain." Del didn't smile, but I saw the twitch at the corner of her mouth.

"*You're on.*" I rolled on one shoulder and caught her in my arms—

—Just as the stranger's voice came out of the deepening twilight—

—but not a stranger's at all.

**273**

The voice was clearly Theron's, challenging Del to a dance.

*Theron's* voice?

Del and I were on our feet instantly, swords bared. In the light of a full moon I saw the man approaching from the other side of the cistern. He walked. But beyond him, in the distance, stood a horse. A very familiar horse.

*My stud—*

I broke off the thought at once. Theron had purposely—and cleverly—dismounted, approaching on foot so our own mounts would not give warning.

And in our mutual lust (or love—call it what you will), we hadn't heard him. We hadn't heard him at all.

He wore the mouse-gray burnous. The hood was pushed back from his head. Still brown-haired, like me, with a trace of gray. Still tall, like me. But heavier now, because the mine had stripped too much weight from me.

Theron looked at Del. "We have a dance to finish."

"*Wait* a minute," I said "The afreet *took* you."

"But I'm here now, and this is none of your concern, Southron."

"I think maybe it *is*," I declared. "How did you get away? What exactly are you doing here?"

"It should be obvious. There is a bit of business remaining between the woman and me." He looked straight at Del, ignoring me entirely "I came here to finish a dance."

"Maybe you did." Butting in had never bothered me in the least. "But before you two continue your unfinished business, I want some answers."

Theron didn't smile. "As for the afreet, he lacks a master. As Rusali lacks a tanzeer."

Well, I wasn't really surprised. Alric had said Lahamu wasn't terribly bright. And Theron was clearly a dangerous man to cross.

I looked at the dangerous man. Quietly he stripped himself of sandals, burnous, harness. Of everything save his dhoti. In his hands he held his naked sword, and I saw again the alien runes, iridescent against the steel of palest-purple that wasn't—really—steel.

Again, we faced one another. Again, I saw the man who wanted to kill her, and I thought of killing him myself.

But it was Del's dance. Not mine.

Del stripped out of burnous, sandals, harness. Set them aside. With the naked sword in her hands, she turned to look at me. "Tiger," she said calmly.

I walked away from the rugs and the cistern, closer to the fire. I set Singlestroke's tip into the sand and began to draw the circle. There was moonlight, more than enough to see by. There was firelight. More than enough to die by.

The circle was drawn. Singlestroke was sheathed. I indicated they were to place their swords in the center of the circle. Silently, they did so, and stepped outside again.

They faced one another across the circle. In the argent moonlight it was a shallow ring of darkness; a thin black line in the ash-gray sand. But the line wavered. It moved on the sand like a sidewinding serpent. Because, though it had no beginning and lacked an end, the wind-whipped flames of the freshening fire lent the line a measure of life. An aspect of independence.

"Prepare."

I heard the soft songs begin. I looked at the swords in the center of the circle. Both silver-hilted. Both rune-bladed. Both alien to my eyes.

Slowly I walked to the cistern wall. I sat down. The stone was hard against my buttocks. But not as hard as the word I spoke.

"*Dance*," I said; that only.

They met in the center, snatching up swords, circling in the perpetual dance of death and life. I saw how Theron measured her more closely now, as if he recalled all too well how very good she was. No more male supremacy; he took her seriously.

Barefoot, they slipped through soft sand made softer by

fire-cast shadows. The curving line of the circle wavered in the light. Such a thin, blade-thin line. For *me* to say if a dancer stepped outside the circle.

I saw the flash of silver as both swords met and sang. And all the colors poured out, shredding the darkness into a lace of luminescence. Ripples, curves, spirals, angles sharp as the edge of a knife, slicing across the shadows. I began to see the patterns clearly, as if Del and Theron wove of a purpose. A dip here, curlicue there, the whip-stitch of a sudden feint.

Thrust, counter, thrust. Parry and riposte. The darkness was filled with light; my ears knew deafness from the crash of ensorcelled steel.

Thighs bunched, sinews rolled. Wrists held firm as they unleashed lurid luminescence. Del's face was stark in the wavering light, planed down in concentration. But I saw Theron begin to smile.

The shift was so subtle I nearly missed it altogether. I was aware mostly that the sound changed, the clash and hiss of rune-worked blades. Then I saw how the patterns began to change as well; how the intricate latticework became a slash here, slash there, bold and aggressive, until the slashes began to resemble my own.

Theron stood in the center of the circle and rained Northern steel on Northern steel, but the style was distinctly Southron.

No longer did I sit atop the cistern wall. I was at the edge of the circle, frowning at the man who began to dance against Del in a style she didn't, *couldn't* know.

But neither, I thought, could Theron. Or he would have used it in the first dance *before* the afreet arrived.

He broke her pattern. Once. Twice. A third and final time. He knocked the sword from her hands.

"*Del*—" But she didn't need my warning. She leaped up and over his blade, then dropped and rolled. Her hands were bare of blade, but she avoided his as well.

More closely, I watched him. I saw the light in his blue

eyes and the satisfaction in the curving lines of his mouth. He was not a man who fought fairly, was Theron; not now. Maybe once. Maybe when he had faced her before. But now there was an *edge* to the look of the man. As if he had somehow acquired a style he had lacked before.

"*Del*—" This time I didn't wait. Not even for Theron. I simply dived over the curving line, caught Del in my arms and carried her out of the circle.

The *jivatma* lay outside as well. Del, cursing me angrily, pressed herself into an upright postion. "*What are you doing, you fool—?*"

"Saving your life," I said grimly, pressing her down again. "If you'll give me a chance, I can explain."

"Explain *what*?—how you lost this dance for me?" Del was vividly, impressively angry. And even as she struggled to shout curses into my face, she lost her Southron entirely.

Theron walked across the circle. With the song silenced, the sword was quiescent in his hand. The darkness was dark again, except for the argent moon.

"Forfeit," he said, "or yield. That is the only choice I will give you."

"Neither," Del answered. "This sword-dance isn't finished."

"You have left the circle."

Even in the South, the custom is the same. Out of the circle: out of the dance. She had no choice but to yield or forfeit.

"Not my choosing!" she cried. "*You* saw what he did!"

"He forfeited the dance *for* you." Theron smiled. "What's done is done, *ishtoya*." He paused. "Pardon. Your rank is *an-ishtoya*."

"I'm a sword-dancer," she threw back. "No rank. Just the dance." She struggled briefly. "Tiger—let me *up*—"

"No." I pinned her down again. "Couldn't you sense the change? Couldn't you feel the difference?" I looked over my shoulder at Theron. "He isn't the man you faced in the circle in Rusali. He's someone else entirely."

"Not quite," Theron said. He stood near the perimeter of the circle. The silver hilt of his blooding-blade was grasped lightly in his hand. "I'm the same man, Sandtiger. Only the *sword* is different."

Del frowned. "It's the same sword. It's *your* sword."

"What did you do?" I asked sharply. "What *exactly* did you do to Lahamu?"

"I killed him." Theron shrugged. "The tanzeer was foolish enough to take up my *jivatma*. Even you must know that isn't a thing for anyone but me to do. But I was wise enough to let him do it." He smiled as he looked at Del. "A lesson from you, *an-ishtoya*. When you are in need of a special skill, you acquire it however you may."

"You requenched." Del stiffened into absolute rigidity in my arms. "You *requenched your jivatma*—"

"*You* summon up the wind and storm and ice with that one of yours," Theron told her. "*You* suck down all the power of a banshee-storm with that sword! I know *that* much—so does every student who has learned the history of the *jivatmas*—even if I don't know the proper name for that butcher's blade." He bared white teeth in a smile of feral intensity. "And how do you defeat Delilah's famous Northern *jivatma*? With heat. With fire. With all the power of the *South*, invested in this blade."

"Theron—requenching is *forbidden*—" But her protest wasn't heeded. I wasn't sure he *heard* it.

One big hand caressed the glowing runes. "You felt it, didn't you? A weakness. A warmth. A sapping of your strength. Otherwise, I'd never have ripped that hilt from your hands." He smiled. "I know it, *an-ishtoya*. So do you. But it's important for me to win. I'll use what methods I can. So—yes, I requenched. I used the forbidden spell."

Del's lips were pressed flat, pale against her face. "The *an-kaidin* would be dishonored by his *an-ishtoya*."

"That I don't doubt," Theron agreed. "But the *an-kaidin* is also dead."

Del wasn't making an effort to go anywhere now. So I let go and sat up slowly, brushing sand from my hands. "If requenching means what I think it does, you've gained more than Southron heat. You've also gained the Southron style." And he was big enough to do damage.

"Yes," Theron agreed. "The tanzeer was hardly as good as you are—perhaps third level, instead of seventh—but he knew the rituals. Matched with my natural skill, the style isn't hard to use effectively."

"Probably not," I agreed. "Of course, against *another* Southron sword-dancer, the odds are decidedly different." I shed harness, burnous and sandals and dropped them all to the sand. "My turn, bascha."

"It's *my fight*—" she said. "Tiger—you can't—you're not fit for the circle yet."

She was right. But the choice had been taken from us. "You need to go home," I told her flatly. "You can't enter the circle again—you're too honorable to cheat. But I can. I can take your place."

"Is this to pay me back for killing Aladar?"

I laughed. "Not even close. I just want to *beat* this son of a Salset goat." I grinned at her. "Go home. Face your accusers. You have a chance with them. More than you have with Theron, who intends to cut you to pieces." I shook my head. "Del—he's countermanded the rituals of the dance. He's sought means he shouldn't have. There isn't a choice with him." I took Singlestroke into the circle.

Theron barely raised his brows. "And does the woman forfeit? Does the woman yield?"

"The *an-ishtoya* bows to necessity," I answered. "Will you accept a seventh-level *ishtoya* in her place?"

The sword-dancer smiled. "But who will arbitrate? Who will start the dance?"

I walked past him and placed Singlestroke in the center

of the circle. "In the South, we do a lot of things on our own."

He accepted the challenge calmly. Stepping to the center, he set the requenched sword next to Singlestroke. Both weapons were of a like size. Probably of a like weight. Theron and I were evenly matched in height and reach, but now I lacked the weight. Maybe the speed and power. Because most of what skill I claimed had been left in Aladar's mine.

"Tell me something before we begin?" I asked.

Theron, frowning, nodded.

"Where'd you get that stud?"

It was obviously not the question he expected. He scowled at me blackly a moment, then sighed a little and shrugged; tolerance is not his virtue. "Found him in the desert, at an oasis. He was standing over a Hanjii warrior. A very *dead* Hanjii warrior."

I smiled. I suggested we begin.

Theron sang. I just danced.

Noise: the clangor of blade against blade; the sloughing of feet in sand; the inhalations of harsh, hurried breaths; grunts and half-curses expelled against our wills. The screeching hiss of Southron steel against an alien blade forged in the North and quenched in the blood of an enemy . . . requenched in the flesh and blood of a Southron tanzeer.

Color: from Theron's blade, not mine, pouring out of the black night sky filled up with the light of the moon, the stars, the fire, and all transfixed upon the Northern blade as it slashed out of the shadows to blind me with its light, that all-encompassing Northern light.

So much noise . . . So much color . . .

So much—

—*fire* . . .

So much—

—*heat* . . .

280

So much—

—*light*—

But all I knew was pain.

"Tiger—*no*—"

In shock, I came back to myself. I saw the lurid lights before me, with Theron in their midst. And felt the unsettling lack of balance in my sword.

Singlestroke.

I glanced down. Saw the broken blade. Heard the shriek of Theron's sword as it slashed down through the darkness and lit up the sky beyond.

"Tiger—*no*—"

Del's voice. I threw myself aside. Felt the icy blast of the winter wind; the scorch of a Punja summer. Heard Theron's contented laugh.

"*No sword*, Theron!" Del's voice shouted. "You dishonor your *an-kaidin*!"

The lights died. The winter/summer went away. I found myself kneeling in the sand with a broken sword in my hand, while Theron scowled down at me.

*Singlestroke.*

Blankly, I looked at the broken blade. A blemish? No. Blued-steel, shodo-blessed, doesn't ever break. Not of normal means.

I looked at the requenched weapon Theron held in his hand. At the alien shapes in the hilt; the alien runes in the blade. And I hated that sword. Hated the power that made it more than just a sword. Singlestroke's destruction.

Bewitched. Ensorcelled. Magicked. Cheater's blade; no better.

*Singlestroke.*

"Yield," he said, "or forfeit. For the woman and yourself."

"No." In my anger, in my shock, one word was all I could manage. But I thought it might be enough.

Theron sighed. "You have no sword. Do you mean to fight with your hands?"

"No." From Del this time, as she came up to the edge
of the circle.

"Bascha." But she had the sword in her hand—

—and she put it into mine.

"Take her," she said softly, so only I could hear. "Use
her. Her name is Boreal."

Theron shouted something. Something about breaking
oaths. Something to do with the sword. The name of the
sword, divulged. But by then it didn't matter. By then the
sword was mine.

Boreal: *cold winter wind*, screaming out of the Northern
Mountains. Cold banshee-storm blast, freezing flesh to the
ice-cold hilt. And yet I gloried in the ice. I gloried in the
wind. I gloried in the pain. Because I needed it all to win.

Boreal: *a sword*. A sword of alien metal. The North
personified. Empowered by all the strength of Del herself.
And the skill of a dead *an-kaidin*.

The Northern sword-dancer didn't stand a chance against
the Southron one.

How we danced, Theron and I. How we did our best to
carve the guts from one another; to cut the heart from one
another. No finesse. No intricate, glowing patterns. No
delicate tracery. Simple power, unleashed within the circle. An elemental fury.

Cut, slash, hack. Catch a blade and try to break it. Thrust,
engage, riposte. Try to scythe the head from shoulders.

The requenched sword made him good. The requenched
sword made him better. But no better than Del's made me.

—*fire*—

—*light*—

—*pain*—

And a wailing winter wind . . .

"Tiger?"

I woke up: silence. Opened my eyes: morning. Prepared
myself for pain: nothing happened. "Del?"

No immediate answer. I was flat on my back; rolled over onto my belly. I lay sprawled within the circle. I vaguely recalled collapsing after sheathing Del's sword in Theron's belly.

I turned to look over my shoulder. Yes—still dead. Had to be, with all his blood and guts spilled into the sand.

I turned back. "Del?"

I saw her then. She knelt outside the circle, still not profaning it with her presence. For her, regardless of what had happened, the rituals were still in force.

*Hoolies.* Got up slowly. Felt earth and sky trade places a moment. Waited. Scrubbed a hand across gritty, burning eyes. "That's some sword, bascha." Anything else would be overkill.

"Can I have her back?"

I glanced behind me and saw the sword lying in the circle. I wasn't sure she'd let me touch her.

Del smiled. "She won't bite, Tiger. Not anymore. You know her name."

I retrieved the sword and gave her to Del outside of the circle. "That's the key, then? Her name?"

"Part of it. Not all. The rest is—personal." Pale brows knitted. "I can't say. You're Southron, not Northern—I don't have the language. And it takes years to comprehend. An *an-kaidin* to teach you the rituals involved."

"You're an *an-kaidin*."

"No." She looked past me to Theron's body. "No more than *he* was. *An-kaidins* never kill."

I looked back at the body. "Do you bury your dead, up north?"

"Yes."

So I buried him under a palm, beneath the Southron sun.

From atop her speckled horse, Del looked down on me. "It's a sword," she said, "that's all. Theron's dead. No one but Theron knew the blade's true name, so it will never be to you what it was to him. But—it's still a sword. A *sword* sword—nothing magical. Not a *jivatma*. But it'll work.''

"I know it'll work." The hilt was a hilt in my hand. No eerie, discomfiting cold. Nothing but alien shapes. Runes unknown to me. And if Del knew, she wasn't saying. "But—it's not Singlestroke."

"No," she agreed. "I'm sorry, Tiger. I know what he was to you."

I sighed, feeling the now-familiar pinch of sorrow in my gut. *No more Singlestroke*— "Yes, well, the aqivi's spilled. Nothing I can do."

"No." She glanced northward a moment. "Now that I've decided, I guess I should get started. It's a long ride across the Punja."

"You remember all the markers, like I told you?"

"Yes."

I nodded. Turned to the stud and swung up into the shallow, blanketed saddle after I sheathed my Northern sword. Waited for him to settle. "Go on, Del. You're not getting any younger."

"No." She smiled a little. "But I'm not so very old."

No. She certainly wasn't. Too young for the South. Too young for a man like the Sandtiger.

On the other hand . . . "My offer stands," I said. "You've got a whole year before they can send anyone else out after you. And it's pretty obvious you'd beat any sword-dancer in the circle." I grinned, knowing she expected me to add *except for the Sandtiger*. "It's freedom, Del, for a while. Ride with me, and we'll hire *both* swords out."

"No." The sun was bright on her white-blonde hair. "Better to have it settled for once and for all. If there's a way the blood-debt can be pardoned . . . ." She frowned a little. "I make no apologies. Even to those who grieve for the death I gave the *an-kaidin*. But—I'd sooner be free to face them all, to know the final decision—instead of for-ever running.''

I smiled. "Good. No sense in running when you can walk.'' I *suggested* the stud turn his head in the direction of Rusali; for a change, he acquiesced. "I'll tell Alric what you're doing. I think he'd like to know.''

Del nodded. "Goodbye, Tiger. *Sulhaya*.''

"No thanks necessary.'' I reached out and slapped her horse on his speckled rump. "Go home, Del. No sense wasting time.''

She clapped heels to the gelding and went away from me at a run.

I reined in the stud as he crowhopped, complaining about the gelding's departure. He wanted to run as well; to catch up and forge ahead. To compete. To prove he was unquestionably the *best*.

I grinned. "A lot like me, old son.'' I patted his heavy bay neck. "Glad to have me back?''

Horselike, he didn't answer. And so I reined him in—ignoring his disgruntled protests—and turned him toward the east.

But I didn't let him run. It's hard to think when a horse like the stud is going on, because you never know when he'll take a notion to drop a shoulder, duck his head and catapult you from the saddle. It's not particularly enjoy-able. And one day it might even prove fatal.

So I made him walk, to preserve my life and because I could ruminate a little, turning things over inside my head.

—*can't go to Julah. Not with Aladar dead. So I'll bypass it entirely and head for Rusali another way*—

Pulled up. Held the stud in check, even though he stomped and sidled, snorting his displeasure, indicating he wished I'd make up my mind.

I ignored him and stared fixedly after Del. Glared.

In the distance, I could see the veil of saffron-colored

dust raised by the northbound horse. Could see the white blot of her silken burnous—

"Ah, hoolies, horse, we've got nothing better to do—"

—so I turned the stud loose and went north.

**DAW**

# Jennifer Roberson

### THE NOVELS OF TIGER AND DEL

Tiger and Del, he a Sword-Dancer of the South, she of the North, each a master of secret sword-magic. Together, they would challenge wizards' spells and other deadly traps on a perilous quest of honor.

☐ SWORD-DANCER                        (UE2376—$4.50)
☐ SWORD-SINGER                         (UE2295—$4.50)
☐ SWORD-MAKER                          (UE2379—$4.95)
☐ SWORD-BREAKER *(Available July '91)*   (UE2476—$4.99)

### CHRONICLES OF THE CHEYSULI

This superb fantasy series about a race of warriors gifted with the ability to assume animal shapes at will presents the Cheysuli, fated to answer the call of magic in their blood, fulfilling an ancient prophecy which could spell salvation or ruin.

☐ SHAPECHANGERS: BOOK 1            (UE2140—$3.99)
☐ THE SONG OF HOMANA: BOOK 2     (UE2317—$3.95)
☐ LEGACY OF THE SWORD: BOOK 3     (UE2316—$3.95)
☐ TRACK OF THE WHITE WOLF: BOOK 4 (UE2193—$3.50)
☐ A PRIDE OF PRINCES: BOOK 5       (UE2261—$3.95)
☐ DAUGHTER OF THE LION: BOOK 6    (UE2324—$3.95)
☐ FLIGHT OF THE RAVEN: BOOK 7     (UE2422—$4.95)